Toxic VENGEANCE

VENGEANCE SERIES

KAYLEA CROSS

TOXIC VENGEANCE

Copyright © 2020 Kaylea Cross

* * * * *

Cover Art: Sweet 'N Spicy Designs
Developmental edits: Deborah Nemeth
Line Edits: Joan Nichols
Digital Formatting: LK Campbell

* * * * *

ISBN: 9781710352801

DEDICATION

For Big Weasel. Love you to infinity. Thanks for the plot bunny on this one.

Mom xo

Author's Note

When first brainstorming ideas about my Valkyrie characters, I came up with a list of specialties for them. One of them was toxins, and I thought Eden's personality fit that expertise perfectly. Get ready for more thrills and action with this badass cast of female characters!

Up next—Marcus and Kiyomi's story to cap off the series.

Happy reading,
Kaylea

Prologue

Eden finished writing the note on the hotel stationery, then hesitated, her gaze straying across the room to the king-size bed. The man in it was sprawled on his stomach in the rumpled bedding, his dark head turned toward her, his expression peaceful in sleep.

The room service cart from last night sat against the wall near him, filled with their empty plates and glasses from the late dinner they'd shared. As her eyes caught on the tumbler that had held his scotch on the rocks, she pushed aside the unwelcome stab of guilt. This wasn't the first time she'd snuck out on a man in the middle of the night.

But it *was* the first time ever that she didn't want to go.

She should be halfway to Amsterdam by now. She should just get up and walk out the door without making this any harder. But she couldn't.

Needing to touch him one last time, instead she crossed to the bed and sat on the edge of it near his hip, unworried about waking him. The dosage she'd given him would keep him under for the next hour at least. Then he'd wake alone and wonder what the hell had happened to her.

Until he saw the note.

At least she wouldn't be here to see his reaction. Imagining it was hard enough.

Shoving down the emotions welling up inside her, she reached out to brush a lock of dark hair away from his forehead. The deeply buried part of her that she'd been trained to ignore wished he would open those storm-gray eyes and give her that sleepy smile she loved.

From out of nowhere a bolt of pain tore through her chest, taking her off guard and stealing her breath. Blinking against the unfamiliar sting of tears, she snatched her hand back.

Just get it over with. You know you have to.

Pushing to her feet, she expelled a shaky breath. This whole affair had been a mistake. She should never have let things go this far, or for this long. But she'd always done what she was ordered to. What she'd been trained to do, even if she hadn't liked it. Just this once, she'd wanted something for herself. Something no one could take away from her.

Steeling herself, she bent to kiss his bristly cheek. "I'm sorry," she whispered, then straightened and set the note on the table beside the flower arrangement she'd made. A pink camellia floating in a glass, surrounded by a ring of dead leaves. He wouldn't understand the symbolism of it. That was okay. It was enough that she did.

Guilt pricked her with sharp needles as she headed for the door, but she kept walking. This was the only way. She wasn't free to do what she wanted. Wasn't free to offer her heart to anyone, and if she'd stayed with him any longer, she was afraid she might have been tempted to do just that.

At the door she made the mistake of pausing. Losing the battle with herself, she looked back at him one last time.

He was safe here, but everything about this still felt wrong. The lying. Drugging him. Sneaking out on him. She wanted to stay, no matter how dangerous it was for both of them. Wanted to slide back under the covers beside him, wake him up with soft kisses and caresses to lose herself in the magic they had together.

It wasn't real. He doesn't even know who or what you are.

Abruptly she turned away, her right hand automatically going to the grip of her pistol hidden in her waistband as she hit a mental switch and forced herself back into operator mode. She'd been lucky to have this stolen time with him. Now she had to put it all behind her and face the hard, dangerous reality waiting outside this door.

The hurt would fade in time eventually, she told herself as she strode down the hall.

It had to.

Chapter One

Nine months later
Sevastopol, Crimea

Serving platter in hand, Eden paused by the kitchen doorway to survey the elegant dining room beyond the threshold. The place was unbelievable.

Over the course of her career she'd conducted all kinds of missions in various places, but none of them as over-the-top as this. It was ostentatious. The cutlery was gold plated, and the enormous crystal chandeliers hanging over the thirty-foot-long mahogany table each cost as much as a high-end luxury sports car.

At the middle of the table, a peacock preening in the midst of the dinner guests, sat the man she was here for.

Target acquired.

Notorious Turkish arms dealer Serkan Terzi. He was the guest of honor tonight, wined and dined in the utmost luxury by a Russian admirer he sometimes did business with. Mostly he dealt in weapons and drugs, but sometimes people—vulnerable women and girls.

She had crossed paths with him before, when he'd

been on the perimeter of her radar during previous ops. Through her handler, the U.S. government had sent Eden to eliminate various targets, men who posed a risk to national security. But never Terzi himself.

Since he bought U.S. weapons and materiel, and the government wanted the business bad enough to overlook him, he'd been left alone. Even though he sold those same weapons to criminal groups and terrorist organizations in Syria because it fed his bank account, posing a direct risk to American interests and personnel there. Because money meant everything to those in power.

But the rules were about to change.

The Valkyrie Program had been scrapped, and the handler she'd kept infrequent contact with since had gone silent several weeks ago. Eden wasn't sure if Chris was dead or not. Either way, she was on her own now. And that meant she no longer had to stay within the parameters imposed on her for so long. It was incredibly freeing to do things her way.

Terzi had been allowed to live for far too long already, by too many powerful people willing to overlook his evil deeds. Eden was here to change that. Not only was he a threat to global security, but recent intel she'd gathered confirmed he was a direct threat to her and her kind. Several months ago he'd been involved in the death of at least one Valkyrie. Rumor was he was currently on the hunt for others, to reap the bounty being offered by a wealthy source Eden hadn't been able to locate yet.

For her the stakes had never been higher. Coming here was a huge risk considering he and his people might have information on her, but she had to take him out before he got any closer to her and the others. Wherever they were.

"Sonya, are you finished serving the prawns?" a woman asked in clipped Russian.

Staying in character, she turned to the head of the catering company hired for this event and put on a smile. "Yes, I was just headed back into the kitchen to get the next platter."

The woman gave her a stern look and strode off to check on another server. Eden bustled back into the kitchen to get another silver tray of hors d'oeuvres. She'd set up a fake ID for this background weeks ago before applying to the catering company, because the host was every bit as cagey as Terzi, and had his security vet each catering employee's credentials before granting them access to the estate. Luckily her credentials were impeccable, thanks to prior help from her former handler.

For all his brash arrogance and illusions of being untouchable, Terzi had proved frustratingly difficult to isolate. She'd been trying to get to him for almost three months now, and tonight was the best shot she was going to have.

Out in the dining room she circulated among the guests, keeping careful watch of who was here and where everyone was positioned. Her light-brown complexion and eyes made her stand out somewhat amongst the crowd, so she needed to otherwise make herself as unnoticeable as possible in her black uniform. Terzi was still at the table, now sipping on a flute of champagne, all smug and feeling invincible.

Eden would make sure he found out otherwise tonight.

His chief bodyguard was positioned in the far corner of the room, keeping watch. Two weapons were hidden in shoulder holsters beneath his custom-tailored suit jacket, and another in an ankle holster made visible by the slight bulge every time he took a step. The host's security was more discreet, stationed throughout the house and dressed in formal wear. Eden had memorized their placements earlier, as well as their schedule during previous recon of the estate over the past two days.

She wasn't worried about the tight security. She'd killed in front of an audience before and no one had ever been the wiser. All she had to do was deliver the fatal dose and disappear before they sealed off the mansion to question the staff. Once she did that her ID would be burned, but it didn't matter.

She had several points going in her favor tonight. The number of guests and staff would make it easier for her to slip out unnoticed in the ensuing chaos. And Terzi had a fondness for marzipan she was about to exploit to the fullest.

She stayed as invisible as possible throughout the first three courses. After the main meal was served, while everyone relaxed around the table with another round of drinks, she got busy in the kitchen gathering the tools of her trade.

When she got the cue from the head of the catering company, she picked up the tray and followed another server bearing a tray of cocktails into the dining room. Several others were already there pouring tea and coffee for the guests, along with serving different kinds of dessert.

Eden kept her expression neutral as the server with the cocktails moved around the table and stopped at Terzi. He smiled up at her, taking the Amaretto Sour and saluting his host.

Eden waited until he'd taken a large sip before offering the guest beside him an exquisite, handmade marzipan fruit from the plate she carried. Terzi's gaze cut to the pretty little morsels, a smile spreading across his face.

Certain of her mark, Eden lifted the tray to avoid another server passing by and quickly placed the laced marzipans in her clenched fist on the plate. Deftly turning it as she positioned herself beside Terzi again, satisfaction punched through her as he took four of them.

The dosage was tricky. He needed to eat at least two of them for it to be fatal, and she didn't want to make it too obvious that it was poison. Better if it seemed like food poisoning at first, or a reaction to his blood pressure and heartburn meds. The cocktail would help. It was fortunate that Terzi had a weakness for almond-flavored things, disguising the scent of the cyanide.

Lifting the tray as she moved to the next guest, she "accidentally" knocked the final laced marzipan off the tray. As soon as it hit the floor another server swooped in to pluck it up and discard it, allowing Eden to move to the next guest without fear of poisoning them.

A few minutes later as she made her way to the other side of the table, she cast a surreptitious glance at Terzi out of the corner of her eye. He'd only eaten one marzipan and already looked ill.

He was sweating lightly, frowned as he put one hand on his protruding stomach. Dabbing at his face with his linen napkin, he reached for his Amaretto Sour and took another gulp. Then he picked up a second marzipan, paused to examine it, and popped it into his mouth.

Excellent.

She was headed through the kitchen doorway when she heard the first indication of alarm. At a sharp gasp and a cry, Eden ducked around the doorway into the kitchen.

Hidden from view, she glanced back in time to see Terzi lurch from his chair. He made it two steps before doubling over and vomiting all over the priceless Persian rug beneath the dining table. People gasped and shoved from their seats as security moved in.

Time to go.

A thud sounded somewhere behind her as Terzi hit the floor in the other room. She pushed her way through the flurry of people moving around the busy kitchen. She didn't have to see Terzi to know what was happening. He'd be convulsing now, helpless as his body struggled for oxygen it could no longer absorb, foaming at the mouth even.

Good. Bastard deserved to die in terror.

Three more servers were bringing fruit trays down the hallway when she got there. Security agents rushed past them, faces grim.

Eden gave them blank looks and moved out of their way, staying in the periphery. As soon as they were past her, she rushed down the hall, heading for the powder room she planned to escape from.

Ten feet from her goal a man stepped out of the doorway and stopped, blocking her way. Strong hands shot out to wrap around her upper arms.

She wrenched free and reached for the weapon at the back of her pants, then froze when she looked up into his face. Shock blasted through her as she stared up into a pair of stormy gray eyes she never thought she'd see again.

WHAT THE *HELL*?

For a moment Zack was too stunned to speak. He'd convinced himself it was his mind playing tricks on him again when he'd spotted her going into the kitchen earlier. Had convinced himself that it couldn't be her. Because he'd been imagining seeing her everywhere for months and never found her—in hotels, train stations, airports…in his dreams.

Yet here she was. Nina. Standing right in front of him after all this time.

"What are you doing here?" he blurted, concerned and still struggling to process everything. Finding her here and now was way too damn suspicious under the circumstances. One of his teammates had just informed him that Terzi had been poisoned at the dinner table.

Her expression closed up, and she looked at him like he was a stranger. "You need to get out of my way," she said in a clipped voice, those unforgettable honey-brown eyes filled with resolve. That look said either he moved, or she'd make him.

Before he could respond, more shouts came from the kitchen. Someone yelling for security to lock down the place. He had no doubt they wanted Nina. And that if they caught her, they would kill her.

He focused back on her, the hard set of her features, and made a snap decision. It meant breaking his cover, but he was willing to pay the consequence to get Nina out of here. "If you want to live, come with me now." Grabbing her arm, he turned them and began leading her down the hall.

She was stiff at first, so stiff he tightened his grip, then she relented, jaw tense.

He dragged her through one of the side doorways just as more security agents rushed in through another. Zack glanced around the brick courtyard. They were already locking the estate down. His car was parked out on the road but they'd already closed the main gate.

He released her arm but snagged her hand to make it look like they were a couple, and held on tight in case she had other ideas. Once they were clear, he was going to get some answers. "We're gonna have to scale the wall."

She didn't say a word, just hurried toward it with him. Twenty feet from the eight-foot-high structure, she broke free of his grip with a practiced move that took him off guard, and ran toward it. He watched, stunned, as she jumped up to catch the top, then nimbly swung over it and dropped down on the other side like a pro. Zack quickly followed suit, half-expecting to have to chase after her when he landed.

But she was standing there scanning the road instead. "We're clear, but we need to hurry."

The contrast between this tough, capable woman and the one he'd thought he'd been falling in love with was jarring. Just who the hell was she, really? Not the flight attendant she'd pretended to be when they'd met in St. Petersburg all those months ago, that much was clear.

And he was really, *really* concerned that she might be a whole lot worse.

"This way." He grabbed her arm again, his mind still reeling, and hurried them to his car. Cops had been stationed near the mansion for extra security. They were just coming down the road as he pulled away from the curb and got them away from the estate. But he wanted answers, and he couldn't hold back for another second.

"Who are you?" he demanded, a sinking feeling taking hold in his gut.

The night they'd met in St. Petersburg he'd been posing as an American businessman trying to get in with an arms dealer. He'd seen her sitting at the hotel bar in that tight skirt suit uniform, and her welcoming smile had made his brain short-circuit. Her cover story had checked out, and he'd been so sure the attraction was mutual that he'd invited her to be his date to an event with the arms dealer the following night.

Throughout all their time together she'd never done or said anything to make him suspicious that she wasn't who she claimed to be. Not once, for that entire three-day weekend they'd been glued to each other, and then every time they'd met afterward over the next seven weeks.

Until he'd woken alone in that Moscow hotel the last time and found the note she'd left, leaving him bewildered and crushed. Now it all made a horrible kind of sense, and he was a fucking idiot for ever falling for her ruse.

"My name's Eden," she said quietly.

He shot her a sideways glance as he sped down the darkened street. She looked the same as Nina had, but there was a hard edge to her now that hadn't been there before. He had no idea if she was telling the truth or not, but he'd be a fucking idiot to trust one word that came out of her mouth. A mouth he'd known intimately not too long ago, and still dreamed about it moving over his skin.

"Did you kill Terzi?" He couldn't believe he was asking that, but it was impossible to ignore the evidence before him. Because this was the *second* time the man he'd been trying to gain the trust of had died of probable poisoning while she was around.

She didn't respond. And that was all the answer he needed.

Goddammit. He bit down hard to stifle the expletive that threatened to burst out of his mouth. She'd used him to get an intro to her previous target. Had made him think she felt something for him. But he'd been a means to an end, nothing more, and now she'd just fucked-up a five-month-long sting to nail Terzi and his inner circle.

But then why spend all that time with him after the job was done in St. Petersburg? Why pretend she'd felt something for him for so long? Unless she'd been hoping to kill someone else he was connected to, and when she decided he was no longer of use, she'd ghosted on him.

"Who are you, really?" he ground out, pissed off at himself as much as her.

Her gaze was fixed on the side mirror as he drove. "Just drop me off at the next street."

"No way. I have to take you in." His CIA contacts would want to question her—right after he did.

She snorted. "That's not happening."

Anger punched through him, surprising him with its force. "Oh, it's happening." He turned right at the next light and sped through the light traffic. He wanted to get her some place safe so they could talk in private, find out what the hell was going on and who she was working for. "In the meantime, you need to explain what—"

He broke off at the sound of the door opening, gaped in astonishment as Nina/Eden dove out onto the road and rolled away from the car.

"Jesus Christ!" He hammered the brake, wrenched his gaze up to the rearview mirror as "Eden" rolled to a stop on the pavement behind him, then popped up like a seasoned stuntwoman and darted for the sidewalk.

Zack threw the car into park and jumped out to chase her. He bounded over a hedge and tore after her, his shoes pounding against the pavement. Just as he rounded the corner he caught a flash of her as she veered from the sidewalk back toward the road, then lost sight of her in the traffic waiting at the light.

Cursing under his breath, he searched frantically left and right as traffic passed by. Where the hell was she? She couldn't have gone far.

He glanced back at his vehicle—

Just in time to see her hop into it and drive away.

Swearing, Zack whipped around and raced after her, urgency screaming through him. He couldn't lose her. Not after all this time, not after what she'd done. But his efforts were useless. Within seconds she'd blown past him and had vanished from sight.

"You gotta be *shitting* me," he muttered, pulling out his cell phone to report it, even as he knew it was a waste of time. By the time anyone located his car, she would be long gone.

Who the hell was she? Who had sent her after Terzi tonight?

Whatever the answers, there would be hell to pay for what she'd done tonight. Zack had to find her and bring her in before she got herself killed.

Chapter Two

Eden didn't stop her rental car until she reached her destination—a mid-sized town six hours away in mainland Ukraine. She found a nondescript hotel and paid for a room in cash, interacting with the innkeeper as little as possible before hobbling up the stairs to her room.

In the bathroom she gingerly peeled her jacket and pants off, exposing the raw, scraped mess of her knees and elbows that had gotten stuck to her clothes. Jumping out of that car had been her only shot at escape. She'd rolled to minimize the brunt of the impact, but at that speed, she'd lost some skin.

She winced as she stepped under the spray of the shower and the water hit her abrasions. Blood dripped down her skin, forming pinkish rivulets as the water swirled down the drain. The pain centered her, drove away some of the numbness she'd been encased in since running into Zack Maguire seven hours ago. He'd gone by the name Zack Mitchell back when they'd first met, but she'd already known who he really was.

Of all the things that could have happened tonight,

running into him in that hallway was the last thing she'd expected.

She'd only gone with him in the first place because it helped her get out of the estate faster. He was a contract officer for the CIA, and must have been there tonight on some sort of operation. Maybe involving Terzi, but maybe not, as there were plenty of other potential targets in attendance. Sticking around any longer would have been disastrous for her.

Seeing him again had shaken her to the core. She'd spent the better part of a year doing her best to forget him and move on, but that had been futile. He was even more gorgeous than she remembered, and she remembered plenty because she still thought about him every day. Wondered where he was, what he was doing. Whether he'd tried to look for her after she'd left. She wasn't sure if it would be better or worse if he had.

Eden knew exactly when things had shifted between them. The night before the op to kill her target in St. Petersburg. She and Zack had gone to dinner together again. Up in her hotel room later, rather than moving straight to sex as they had been, he'd led her out onto the balcony instead. Gazing out at the lights of the city below them, he'd wrapped his arms around her from behind and held her in total silence, just absorbing each other's presence. When he'd finally spoken, he'd asked her about meaningful things like her hopes and dreams while wrapping his jacket more tightly around her and angling his body to shield her from the cold breeze.

That was the moment he'd ceased being just an asset and became something far more important. Something that had made her question everything.

He was a liability to her now, and her for him. She'd risked too much by continuing their relationship for as long as she had, and had wound up almost paying the ultimate price for it when she'd left him that morning. That was all the reinforcement she'd needed to cut ties with him forever.

An empty ache filled her chest as she got out of the shower, dried off then dressed her wounds with antibiotic ointment and bandages. No one had ever gotten to her like he had. She'd never let anyone in that far before. She'd shown him parts of herself that she normally kept hidden—even if she'd lied about who and what she was. He still knew her better than anyone else ever had.

With Terzi dead, she had to go to ground. The pressure was higher than ever before. Invisible enemies were closing in, and she still hadn't received word from her handler, though Eden had reached out again days ago asking for help. Now Zack would be searching for her too, along with whomever he answered to within the CIA.

At least with Terzi gone, it would disrupt that organization for a while. It would also disrupt the shipments of weapons and women sold off to fund more arms deals and criminal or terrorist activity all over the globe.

Dressed in shorts and a loose-fitting top to give her bandaged knees and elbows some breathing room, she carefully stretched out onto her back on the bed, every bump and bruise protesting. Using a secure phone she checked her messages.

Zero.

Worry ground in the pit of her stomach. It wasn't like Chris to go this long without responding.

She turned on the TV to see if the story about Terzi had hit the media yet. A local news station was talking about his death. It was already being reported as a murder.

She'd leave before dawn and get out of the country using a disguise and a fake ID. But this time…she was concerned. She'd never felt so isolated and alone as she did right now.

It made her think of the woman she'd been in contact with a few times several months ago regarding a shipment of women being transported from North Africa by Syrian crime boss Fayez Rahman. Eden was almost certain the woman had been another Valkyrie.

Could it have been Kiyomi? She'd wondered about that all this time, and had been tempted to ask. They hadn't been roommates when they were in the Valkyrie Program, but they had been trained in several areas together. Had spent countless hours studying and sparring together. But Kiyomi had been the femme fatale of the Valkyrie world, and chances were good she'd died long ago.

Picking up her phone, Eden accessed some old emails she'd saved in a protected account, and reread the ones from the suspected Valkyrie. Eden didn't have proof to back up her theory, it was more of a gut feeling. And right now, it was her best chance of getting help, because she needed to drop off the grid immediately.

After debating it for another few minutes, she decided it wouldn't hurt to reach out and see if the woman was even still active on that email account. If she was and things felt right, Eden might consider asking for assistance.

She had no idea if she'd get any, but now more than ever she was desperate to find and connect with the sisters she'd lost so long ago. They were the only ones who would understand her. The only ones she could trust to help, rather than hunt her down.

The time had come. If she wanted to stay alive, she couldn't operate alone anymore.

****

Sunlight gleamed on the surface of the water above her, beckoning to her with its warmth.

Kiyomi pushed hard off the bottom of the pool and propelled herself toward the surface, giving her tired arms and legs a break. She'd been doing laps several mornings a week for more than a month now, to help rebuild the muscle tone she'd lost during her recovery.

Swimming was far more enjoyable than running, and she liked the peace and quiet of being beneath the water, of shutting out the world for a little while. Her body had healed since her rescue in Syria. The twice-weekly remote therapy sessions and meditation were slowly helping the rest of her heal too.

Breaking the surface for a breath, she swept the water out of her eyes with one hand and turned onto her side to swim for the stairs, only to stop when she saw the man standing motionless at the edge of the pool. Marcus Laidlaw, master of this beautiful estate.

He wore swim trunks and a T-shirt he'd been in the act of pulling off, but quickly yanked it back down to cover his chest. "Sorry. Didn't know you were here," he said quietly. She loved his Yorkshire accent. He sounded just like Sean Bean, only deeper. Darker.

Damn. She'd come here early specifically to be gone before he showed up so as not to interrupt his morning swim, but he must have changed up his routine for some reason. She frowned at him, not liking that he felt the need to cover up in front of her. As if he was embarrassed by his scars, or maybe afraid of disgusting her.

"Don't do that," she admonished, treading water.

He frowned a bit. "Do what?"

"You know what." She nodded at his shirt, now covering the burn scars he'd suffered from an explosion while on a combat mission in Syria a couple years ago during a mission gone awry with the SAS. They marked the left side of his chest, shoulder, neck and face, and around his left eye. His short, dark beard covered most of the damage on his face, except for the spots where hair no longer grew on his cheek and jaw.

But those marks weren't even close to the worst

things he'd survived.

His features were tense, his expression broadcasting his discomfort. "Habit," he muttered, and broke eye contact.

"They don't bother me. And you've already seen mine."

That deep brown gaze swung back to hers. Held. And in that moment, she knew they were both thinking about the day she'd arrived here months ago, after fellow Valkyrie Amber and her boyfriend Jesse had pulled Kiyomi out of that prison in Damascus.

Without them, Kiyomi would have been subjected to a living hell, and she bore the marks on her back to prove it. Lash marks that had cut deep into her flesh between her shoulder blades. Marcus had seen them as Amber and her sister Megan had tended to her wounds when she'd first arrived at Laidlaw Hall.

Kiyomi had a lot in common with her Valkyrie sisters, but she and Marcus shared a connection that none of the others did. Against all odds, they had both survived a brutal captivity. So no, he had nothing to be ashamed or embarrassed about with her.

She cocked a challenging eyebrow at him. "You coming in?"

Marcus held her stare for a long moment, unmoving. It was strange that she still couldn't read him.

Even after living under his roof for this long, even though she was an expert at reading people, he remained a mystery to her. A quiet, intensely private man, he was close with Megan, who had pulled him from a certain slow, agonizing death at his captors' hands. He didn't say much and rarely socialized with any of them except Megan, but there was something about him that drew Kiyomi with a strength she couldn't deny.

He was watchful, almost standing guard on the periphery to ensure she and the others were safe here at his home. After the things she'd done in the name of duty and all she'd endured, feeling safe was foreign and unthinkable. But somehow Marcus gave her that sense of security.

"Well? Are you?" she prompted, a little unnerved by her train of thought.

He cleared his throat. "I was going to sit in the Jacuzzi awhile," he said, nodding to the raised hot tub at the corner of the pool area. "Leg's stiff today."

His left one. Megan had told her his hip and thigh had been shattered when the vehicle he was riding in hit an IED embedded in the road. His captors had subsequently crushed what was left of the joint. After he and Megan were finally extracted, surgeons had done what they could to repair the hip joint and femur, but he would walk with a pronounced limp the rest of his life.

Kiyomi felt a keen empathy for what he'd been through. And she was glad the men responsible for his torture had been sent to hell where they belonged. Most of the people responsible for her suffering had been killed, except the man who still haunted her nightmares. But he would die for what he'd done someday, and by her hand. She'd vowed it to herself.

"Any luck finding your friend?" Marcus asked.

Eden, he meant. "I wouldn't say we're friends." They had been once, however. "I haven't seen or spoken to her since we graduated from the Program. But no. We haven't found her yet."

Kiyomi remembered her vividly. Eden was beautiful, with flawless light brown skin, light brown eyes, and a mass of black curls. For a time the cadre had contemplated making her an intimate assassin, like Kiyomi. Instead they'd moved her into toxins, where she could use her expertise, beauty and body to make kills up close in a different way. "The truth is, I don't have many friends."

Just as he opened his mouth to respond, the bleating of her cell phone dragged her attention away from him.

She got out of the pool, completely unselfconscious of her body and the scars on her back, aware of Marcus's eyes on her as she bent to pick up her phone. She was used to men staring, lusting, spinning sexual fantasies about her. The difference here was, part of her *wanted* Marcus to look, yet she couldn't tell if he was interested or not. That was a first.

"It was Chloe," she said as she turned to face him, the cool air raising goosebumps across her skin and beading her nipples tight. He hadn't moved, and to his credit his gaze remained on her face, rather than her breasts. He quickly offered her his towel.

Interesting. After wrapping it around her body, she called the explosives expert Valkyrie back, her pulse quickening. For Chloe to call this early, it must mean something important had happened.

"Hey, you're up early," Chloe said, sounding like she'd been awake for hours. Or maybe she'd never gone to bed at all last night. You never knew with Chloe, who was addicted to caffeine and junk food. "Where are you?"

"I was just getting my laps in," she answered, watching Marcus. It wasn't a hardship. At forty-four the man was in his prime with a solid, muscular build he worked hard to maintain. "Something up?"

"Yeah. I just got another message from my former contact on the Dubois trafficking thing. Amber's traced its origin to somewhere in the Ukraine."

Amber was their resident hacker. She could do things with electronics and code that would scare the shit out of intelligence agencies all over the world had they known, but these days, she was using her skills for good—to help find the missing Valkyries and give them all a secure future. Before they all went their separate ways, however, they were going to go after the people behind the Program to mete out their own particular brand of Valkyrie justice. It was the only way for her and the others to truly move on and be safe.

"You think it might be Eden," Kiyomi said.

"Maybe. But there's more."

Chloe's uncharacteristically grave tone gave Kiyomi pause. "Tell me."

"Rycroft called a few minutes ago." Alex Rycroft, former NSA superstar and now "retired", was helping their team out with his resources where and when he could. "An American contract officer with the CIA apparently reported a woman matching Eden's description at a big dinner last night on the Crimean Peninsula. The guest of honor was Serkan Terzi."

"And he experienced an unfortunate, lethal bout of food poisoning during or soon after dinner," she guessed.

"Exactly. The contractor had the suspect woman in his car, then she dove out and disappeared."

Goosebumps rippled over Kiyomi's skin, and not because she was standing wet in the cool air. God, she loved hearing stories about how incredible her colleagues were. "Sounds like Eden."

"Good. Problem is, we can't find her now. She's gone to ground. There's a chance she might still be in contact with her former handler in Vermont. Amber found the woman's contact info in Eden's file. Nobody can reach her, either, so Rycroft's going to send Trinity there to check it out in person since she's already Stateside. He wants to know if you're ready to be operational if Trin needs backup, since you knew Eden."

Kiyomi paused. She was ready to be an operator, but not the kind she'd been before. She was never doing that shit again, and Trinity understood that. Of everyone Kiyomi had met here at Laidlaw Hall, she was the closest to Trinity. The elder Valkyrie was several years older than Kiyomi, and they were the same kind. The rarest kind of Valkyrie. Lethal, expert-level seductresses.

Over the past few months Trin had been a huge help

in setting Kiyomi on the path to healing rather than self-destruction, and they talked several times a week. "Of course." She'd lay down her life for Trin—and the others.

"Great, I'll let him know. And just so you're aware, as of right now we're all on standby if we get a lead on Eden."

"Understood." In a way it would be a relief to be involved in some kind of action again, as long as it didn't involve having to seduce anyone.

"Perfect. Okay, that's it. Say hi to Marcus."

"Will do." Kiyomi lowered the phone, met the dark-chocolate gaze of the ruggedly gorgeous man in front of her, and smiled. "Chloe says hi. And I think we may have a promising lead on Eden."

Chapter Three

The woman was a ghost.

Tired and frustrated, Zack set his laptop aside on the hotel bed and swung his legs over the edge of it to rake his hands through his hair. It had been twelve hours since "Eden" had dived out of his car in Sevastopol, and he was no closer to finding out where or who she was. Every avenue he and his contacts explored led to another dead end.

He'd flown here to Kiev last night, positioning himself near major transportation centers so he could go after her as soon as a solid tip came in. Upon arrival he'd spoken to his handler about the Terzi murder, and the potential killer.

This was the first time Zack had been torn about being involved in a manhunt. His duty was to find "Eden" and bring her in for questioning about Terzi's murder before someone else found and killed her. Problem was, this was also the first time it had ever been personal.

He wanted to know who the hell she really was. Maybe it was stupid of him to think it, but he just couldn't accept that everything between them before had been a lie. Even if she'd used him as a means to an end. Even if she'd been that coldly calculated all along. What they'd shared was way too special, too intimate to be completely fake.

You just don't want to believe it was all a lie.

No, he sure as shit didn't. He'd known all along that there was more to her than she'd let on. That she'd held a lot back. But he'd never once suspected that she might be a trained killer. A straight-up assassin.

How the hell had he missed it? That drove him crazy. He'd gone over everything that had transpired between them again and again in his mind, looking for clues, for answers. Trying to see clearly with the benefit of hindsight. It hadn't helped.

His cell phone rang on the nightstand. His CIA handler's number showed on the screen. "Hey," he answered, impatient for a solid lead. "Got something?"

"Maybe," Rod said. "We think she's been trying to reach someone in the intel community."

"Who? What agency?"

"The person she's contacted is retired CIA. Might be a former handler or something, we're still looking into it. Our tech people traced the origin of a recent email from our female suspect to the former officer from mainland Ukraine about five hours ago."

His pulse picked up. "Where in the Ukraine?"

"Near Odesa."

Dammit. He was way too far away to get to her before she left. "Nothing else?"

"Afraid not. Except…"

"Except what?"

"Anything else you want to tell us about your previous interaction with her?"

"No." He kept his voice even and his tone calm, made sure he didn't blurt it out or sound defensive. Until a few hours ago, he hadn't realized what she was. Back when he'd initially reported Eden to the Agency, he'd thought she was simply a flight attendant.

The cover she'd used had checked out, with him as well as the CIA. As a contract officer he hadn't felt the need to disclose that he'd continued to see her in a romantic capacity after that initial weekend together. He hadn't been obliged to disclose anything else about their involvement since he'd been merely doing recon for another job at that point, and she hadn't been part of it.

Unless she had been, and you were too stupid to realize it.

Shit.

Rod grunted. "You've heard of the Valkyries?"

Zack went completely still. It even seemed like his heart stopped for a moment as cold rippled beneath the surface of his skin.

Oh my God. All of a sudden it all made a terrible kind of sense. Including the brand on her hip that she'd said was a stupid drunk decision back in college. It was far from that—a symbol of what she was.

"Yeah," he finally answered. Elite female assassins trained for a CIA black ops program. It had supposedly been shut down a while back...unless it hadn't. Things weren't black and white in the intelligence world, and government agencies used the gray in between to their advantage, contract officers like him included.

"All indications point to her possibly being one of them. The Agency's trying to locate any of them that might still be alive. So if you hear anything or make contact with her again, you need to let us know asap."

Zack's heart beat faster, a hard, uncomfortable rhythm as the implications hit home. "Understood." He had no illusions. If the CIA saw the remaining Valkyries as potential threats, they would be treated as such and eliminated to sanitize the situation. And if he tried to interfere on "Eden's" behalf, he would be fair game as well.

Either way, they'd be watching him more closely

now.

"Good," Rod said. "Where are you headed next?"

With Terzi's death, his contract for this op was officially over, but he still had to file an official report and they'd no doubt want him to follow up any leads on Eden. "Frankfurt. Flight leaves at 11:00 tomorrow."

"Have a safe trip. I'll be in touch."

Zack leaned back on the pillows he'd stacked against the wide headboard, then pulled up the only picture he'd kept of Eden from a secure file accessed with his laptop. She'd been camera shy, not wanting him to take any photos of her. Now he knew why.

He'd snagged this one candid shot of her when she hadn't been looking after dinner together one night in St. Petersburg. She was standing on his hotel room balcony railing in profile to him with the city lights below illuminating her. She was laughing at something he'd said, he couldn't remember what now.

God, just looking at it was a kick to the gut. She looked so happy. So relaxed and carefree—and insanely sexy.

They'd spent a magical three days together that time, mostly staying in that room because they couldn't keep their hands off each other. The following morning, he'd woken up confused and alone, with nothing but a pounding headache and a few hastily scrawled lines of apology lying on the table.

He set the laptop aside, trying to reconcile the woman he'd thought he'd known with this new evidence. A Valkyrie?

She'd never once done anything to put him in danger, or threaten him in any way. And based on what he knew now, she could have. Easily. Especially since he wouldn't have been ready for it.

It bothered him that the CIA was searching for her and any others, and the extra heat on her was partly his fault for reporting her. His internal radar was pinging, certain she was in danger. He'd heard things, rumors and whispers over the past few months since the Valkyrie Program had been exposed in the media spotlight. The CIA was no doubt scrambling to cover its ass, and that meant trying to erase anything and everything that might implicate the agency in matters it would rather keep secret, by whatever means necessary.

He sat back up, frustration and anger eating at his insides. After searching for her so long and finding nothing under the fake cover she'd fed him, he'd actually found her—by accident—and had been as close to getting answers from her as he'd been since the day she'd walked out on him. And that awful goddamn note. He'd burned it, but the words were carved into his memory forever.

I'm sorry, I had no choice. I wish things could be different. I'll never forget you.

She'd left him a flower, too. A single, bubblegum-pink flower floating in a glass, with a bunch of dead leaves around the base. Whatever that meant.

He'd been gutted, had felt guilty as hell on top of it because he'd wanted more than a few days at a time together, and the whole time he'd lied to her about who he truly was and what he did for a living. Things between them had been so good, she'd mattered to him enough that he'd made up his mind to tell her the truth. He'd meant to tell her that morning, then she was gone.

Except it turned out she'd been lying to him too. Big time. Had he known *anything* real about her?

Zack didn't know, but imagining her being targeted by a CIA hitter chilled his blood. They'd both lied to each other, and no matter what the truth about her was, he *knew* she'd cared about him to some extent. That not everything between them had been a lie, and it wasn't just his bruised—okay, battered—ego talking.

Whatever she'd done, including kill that piece of shit

Terzi, she didn't deserve to die for it. So what the hell was he supposed to do now?

The answer came swift and sure, straight from his gut.

I have to find her.

Find her and learn the truth. All of it. Then warn her. Help her, if she'd let him.

He'd been halfway in love with her when she'd walked out. If any part of their time together had been real for her too, then he was prepared to do whatever it took to protect her. Including putting his loyalty to her above that to the agency he'd served and bled for.

Resolved, Zack got up and began packing his stuff. He needed to head for Odesa immediately and try to pick up her trail, without alerting anyone watching him what was really going on.

She might not want to ever lay eyes on him again, but too bad. He was going to find her. Like it or not, considering the growing threat closing in on her, it looked as if he might be the only thing standing between her and certain death.

****

Glenn Bennett zipped up his jacket to his chin and hunched against the rain as he ran down the front steps of his contact's house to his waiting car. But even with the heater going full blast a minute later, the warmth couldn't chase away the ice that had formed in his bones.

For all the care he'd taken to insulate and protect himself from this threat, it seemed his past sins had finally caught up with him.

Everyone sinned. Everyone had secrets they wanted to take to the grave. But not everyone's sins or secrets put them in their grave before their time.

Ever since the Program had been exposed in the media, he'd put as much distance between it and himself as possible. He'd kept careful watch as the Valkyrie body count climbed. Professionals were out there hunting the survivors right now. So why hadn't there been any more intel about the remaining Valkyries' deaths? Either within the intelligence community, or in the media?

There were only a small number of operatives left unaccounted for. Less than a dozen. Surely with all the intelligence resources being used to track them, they should all have been dealt with by now.

Christ. He'd come to this meeting because of recent chatter he'd heard about another Valkyrie surfacing in the Crimea last night, who was apparently still alive. The contact he'd just met with—an insider from the Valkyrie Program's second phase—had confirmed that this same female operative had been in Sevastopol last night to kill an HVT during a dinner at a private estate.

Eden Foster. Trained to use whatever toxin was available to incapacitate or kill her target, with anything from insect and reptile venom, to deadly plants and synthetic chemicals. She could kill by tainting food and drink, by vaporizing the lethal substance into the air, or even by having the victim ingest it through their skin.

Unease threaded up his spine like the brush of cold fingers. The Valkyrie operatives were without a doubt the most incredible project he'd been involved in in all his time with the CIA. He'd helped spearhead the initiative, and had a hand in creating them. Now those same women posed the single greatest threat to him and the others.

To make matters worse, as of this moment, Eden Foster was once again in the wind. On the loose, and likely being helped by the other Valkyries who were unaccounted for and, he feared, still alive. He wasn't accustomed to feeling fear, but this was unlike any threat he'd ever faced before.

His contact had just confirmed what he'd long suspected, that someone had managed to hack into the
Agency's Top Secret files containing all kinds of damning
information about the Valkyrie Program. Including how
it functioned, the female operatives involved, operations...

And a shitload of incriminating evidence on the people responsible for creating the program in the first place.

No one was sure how much the hacker had gotten,
but anything posed a serious problem because it meant he
and other high-level officials within the CIA—and the il-
legal things they'd done—might be exposed.

There were too many unknowns and coincidences
happening for him to dismiss. All the evidence pointed to
one chilling possibility.

The remaining Valkyries were banding together and
forming a team.

His heart rate quickened at the thought. It would be
a logistical and security disaster for him and the others.
The Valkyries knew too much, could expose all his and
his former colleagues' dirty secrets. The whole purpose of
making the women solo operators, of keeping them all
isolated from one another, was to avoid this very scenario.

He'd warned others involved with the program about
the possibility of this exact scenario happening one day,
and no one had been willing to listen, all convinced that
the women would be dead within five-to-eight years of
being put in the field. They simply hadn't been expected
to survive beyond that.

But he'd been right. His concerns had been founded
all along, and now he had to take immediate and decisive
action to counter this threat before it was too late. Exposing what he'd done would destroy him and his family,
maybe even land him in prison. If the Valkyries had uncovered anything to incriminate him, then it meant he now
had a target on his back.

He pulled over partway home and took out the private, heavily encrypted cell phone he rarely used, glancing in his mirrors every so often in case he was being followed or watched. Going home wasn't safe now. Not with everything he'd learned over the past forty-eight hours.

A lead weight sat heavy and cold in his gut. He hadn't reached out to the Architect in years, had avoided it at all cost, but now it seemed he had no choice. They'd done their best to bury the program after it was shut down due to the media exposure and fallout from the Balducci trial. Just as Glenn had feared, their efforts hadn't been enough.

If the surviving Valkyries were joining forces, then this was a matter of life and death, and personal history with the Architect that he'd rather not deal with didn't mean shit.

He brought up the number, hesitated for just one moment, then called.

"Who is this?" came the curt greeting.

"It's Bennett."

A startled pause answered him. "I thought I told you never to contact me again."

Glenn bit down hard on his back teeth at the dismissal in that arrogant tone. "There are extraordinary circumstances involved." *Or I wouldn't be calling.*

"Such as?" Now the tone was bored.

In as few words as possible he explained what he'd uncovered. The potential disaster and lethal threat facing them all. "I think they're working together." He stiffened, his gaze locking on a car that slowed as it approached, then kept driving. God, now he was jumping at shadows.

The Architect laughed. "You're being paranoid, Glenn, as usual."

No, he fucking wasn't. "And if I'm not?"

"You are. Everything's being taken care of. There's no way anyone can expose us now, so don't worry."

How could he not worry? A single Valkyrie was lethal to her enemies and targets. A group of them working together could do unbelievable damage, and would prove a hundred times harder to locate, let alone kill. "So you're going to just pretend nothing's happening?"

"I'm not pretending anything. It's being taken care of."

"Care to explain?"

"No."

He set his jaw, reining in his temper with effort. He was considered an outsider since his retirement, and the Architect couldn't resist letting him know it. "This is happening, whether you want to believe it or not. It's already in motion, so whatever measures you've taken to try and counter the threat, I promise you it's not enough."

A hard, brittle silence filled the line. Then, "I think I know better than anyone what they're capable of. Now, don't call me again, or—"

Fuming, Glenn hit the button to end the call and immediately set about dismantling the burner phone so he could dispose of it. He wasn't being paranoid. And he didn't give a fuck about whatever the Architect or anybody else had going on behind the scenes to deal with this. Whatever it was, it wasn't enough.

He wiped the back of his hand over his sweaty upper lip, his mind racing furiously as he took his pistol from the center console and ensured he had a round in the chamber. They were all under threat now, whether they wanted to face it or not. If none of the others would help him, then his only option was to take matters into his own hands. Because he was *not* going down with this ship he'd helped create, and he didn't trust the Architect not to come after him now.

Pulling back onto the road he did a U-turn, heading away from his house and coming up with a cover story to tell his wife. He had hunting to do. But first he needed to flush out his prey.

He'd start with Eden's handler, use her to find Eden. Use Eden to find the others. Then they'd all die.

Fishing out another burner phone, he made another call. "It's me," he said when the man answered. "I've got a priority target I need taken care of immediately. Take care of it in the next twenty-four hours and I'll pay double your usual fee."

Chapter Four

Outside Eden's studio apartment window, the New Jersey skyline was just beginning to glow with a faint line of peach along the eastern horizon. She'd been up for hours already, prepping for this last-minute trip.

At the kitchen counter she poured herself another cup of coffee before stopping in front of her laptop. Dawn was coming fast, and she needed to get moving if she was going to make it to the meeting in time.

After weeks of Eden trying to establish contact, Chris had finally responded to her five hours ago and set a meeting up, apologizing for the lapse as she'd been visiting family on the West Coast. Whatever she wanted to say, it must be important, because Chris wanted a face-to-face meeting. But in spite of the tight timeline with the long drive ahead, Eden couldn't make herself leave without doing just a little more checking on Zack first.

He was dangerous to her in so many ways. She'd tried to move on and put him behind her, but failed, and seeing him the other night made that painfully clear. Looking back, Eden wasn't even sure exactly when she'd started getting too attached to him. She'd started out using him as a vehicle to gain entry into the social circle her target was part of.

But after finishing that mission, everything that had come afterward between them had been real. Too real, and since Sevastopol she'd constantly struggled to put him out of her mind long enough to focus on one task to the next.

None of her rigorous training had prepared her for this, because she'd been trained never to let it happen in the first place. She'd broken all her rules for him, had risked too much and was still paying the price. Look at her, sitting here searching for articles about him on her laptop instead of getting in her car for the long drive to Vermont.

Just five more minutes, then I'll go.

She opened an article from an online military newspaper talking about a mission he'd undertaken as a security contractor in Afghanistan four years earlier. It showed a candid picture of him wearing a snug black T-shirt and khaki cargo pants, dark shades covering his eyes. Amidst his short, dark beard, his teeth flashed white as he grinned at a teammate standing off to the side.

Something flipped low in her belly as she remembered that same smile aimed at her, and how it had made her pulse race. That same short beard as it had rubbed against her naked skin, those sexy lips skimming their way down to the throbbing flesh between her thighs.

Shit. I have to stop this. He'd turned her into a junkie, and he was her drug of choice. She craved him, even now. Even in the face of the threat he posed.

Chilled by that sobering thought, she shut the laptop, put it in its hiding spot, then grabbed her small bag and took the stairs down to her car parked in the underground lot beneath the building. She left the city long before rush hour, heading north.

It took just shy of five hours to reach Brattleboro,

Vermont, a small town ten miles north of the Massachusetts border. She arrived at the specified diner almost twenty minutes early, but as soon as she was seated in a booth near the back of the restaurant, bells chimed as the door swung open and Chris walked in.

The fifty-three-year-old retired CIA officer strode in like she owned the place, wearing skin-tight jeans, a black leather jacket, riding boots, carrying a helmet in one hand. Her iron-gray curls were like a helmet of their own, cropped close to her head, and her medium-brown skin was still without a single wrinkle. The no-frills hairstyle suited Chris's anti-bullshit personality perfectly.

"You made good time," she said curtly as she slid into the opposite side of the booth from Eden and removed her sunglasses to expose laser-like amber eyes fringed by dark lashes.

Eden grinned. "You rode your bike here?"

Chris shrugged and turned to flag down the waitress. "It's perfect weather for a ride, I couldn't resist." She pushed both coffee mugs to the end of the table for the waitress to fill, then dismissed her with, "We'll let you know when we're ready to order."

The woman left. Eden shook her head as Chris poured the first of two plastic cup creamers into her coffee. "I ever tell you how much I admire your people skills?"

"You might have mentioned it one time or another." Chris took a big sip of coffee, lowered her mug and reached inside her leather jacket, withdrawing her wallet. "My treat this time," she said, taking out a fifty.

"No argument from me. We eating first?"

Chris raised her eyebrows and gave her a look. "Uh, yeah. At least I'll know you've put something in your stomach today."

"I love how you mother me."

Chris snorted and picked up the menu. "Shut up.

Now figure out what you want to eat. I want to take the scenic route back and I need to be home by dark before all the assholes get on the road with me."

"Okay, then." Damn, she'd missed Chris and her bluntness.

"So," Chris said after they'd ordered, eyeing her critically. "You good?"

"Yeah."

"You look good."

"Thanks." A beat passed, and Chris was still watching her intently. "What?"

"You tell me."

Nope. Not here, with possible eavesdroppers around. "Nothing to tell." She sipped at her coffee and redirected the conversation. "How was your visit with your dad and sister?" Chris had been in Washington State while Eden had been reaching out to her.

Chris grimaced. "Old man needs to just die already."

Eden almost choked on her coffee, her eyes widening. "Wow, that's harsh, even for you."

Chris shrugged. "He's goddamn miserable being confined to a wheelchair with his mind deteriorating. It makes my sister miserable in the process, which by extension also makes me miserable. The ornery bastard just wants to die, and we hope he's quick about it. If we're lucky he'll go in his sleep one night soon."

End of conversation. As soon as the waitress brought their food, Chris waved a fork at Eden and dug into her waffle with berries and whipped cream. "All right, eat up so we can get outta here. We've got business to attend to."

What was so important that Chris had summoned her here at the last moment? Eden had to wolf down her meal to be done by the time Chris flagged their waitress back down and paid the bill.

Sliding her sunglasses back on, Chris raised her eyebrows over the top of the frames. "You done yet?"

"Yep. Right behind you," Eden said around a last giant mouthful of corned beef hash, leaving at least four more on her plate. The pitfall of eating with Chris was that she always left hungry. "Where we off to now?"

"Someplace no one will bother us," Chris said, marching for the door.

Eden followed Chris's bike to a Victorian-era brick house near the historic center of the town. It had a quaint, village-type feel to it, with similar-style Victorian houses and tidy yards. Every street was lined with trees and pretty gardens bursting with fresh green foliage.

They both parked around back in an alley running between the houses. Chris grabbed something from her saddlebags and started up the back steps without looking back. Eden hurried after her, one hand at the small of her back out of habit, ready to grab her weapon from her waistband.

"You can relax," Chris said on her way through the kitchen. "We're safe here."

Eden still locked the door behind her before holstering her weapon and going to what looked like a home office near the front of the house. "Is this a rental?"

"Nope. Belonged to an aunt before she lost her damn mind. Went batshit crazy, wound up in the mental institution across town and died there years ago. This place has been sitting vacant ever since. I come down every now and again for a day or two, make sure it's maintained." Chris planted herself behind the small antique-looking desk and leaned back in the chair to whip off her sunglasses and study Eden, signaling an end to that topic of conversation. "So. You had a close call in Sevastopol."

"Not that close." Pretty damn close.

One perfectly arched eyebrow went up. "No? Your old flame thought it was pretty close."

Eden stilled. "How'd you know about that?" She'd told Chris about Zack when she'd first decided to use him as a means to getting close to her target, but not about their subsequent relationship.

"Because an old source from the Agency told me. Zack Maguire and other Agency assets are looking for you."

That wasn't a surprise after the other night. "Does he know what I am?"

"Not officially, no, at least from what I can tell. But I'm sure he knows by now. He's no dummy."

No, he was the opposite. And that amplified the threat he posed.

Chris pinned her with that coffee-brown stare that dared her to try and bullshit. "Have you made contact with him since?"

"No," she said, insulted that Chris would ask. She was weak when it came to him, but not stupid.

"Are you going to?"

"No."

"But you want to."

Eden paused. She could lie but Chris would know, and what was the point? Her former handler was the closest thing to a friend she had in this world. A kind of older, protective sister. Her shoulders sagged a little. "Yeah."

"Figured as much." Chris shook her head, a frown drawing her eyebrows together. "He's dangerous. One, because he's in your head, and two, because of who he works for."

"You worked for them too until a few months ago," Eden pointed out.

"That's different. I'd take on a grizzly with my bare hands to protect you."

That made Eden smile. "I know. But you wouldn't get the chance, because that bear would take one look at you, say to itself *nope*, and run the other way."

A faint glow of amusement in those intense eyes was her only reaction. "Zack Maguire won't run," she said softly.

"No." And dammit, that was so freaking hot. "But he's only a contract officer. His loyalty is to the mission, not the Agency."

"You willing to bet your life on that?"

Good point. "No." If he knew what she was, then he would know she'd lied to and used him before. A man in his position wouldn't let that go. And he was relentless enough not to stop until he saw her punished for it.

Chris watched her in silence for a long moment. "I know you. I know what you're like when you make up your mind about something. You're gonna do what you're gonna do about Maguire, but promise you'll be careful. Otherwise you'll wind up on my shit list. And no one likes to be on my shit list."

No kidding. "Got it."

"Say you promise."

She didn't dare roll her eyes. "I promise."

Chris's expression softened with real affection, a slight smile tugging at her lips. "I never wanted to be a handler, you know."

Eden cocked her head, surprised. "You never told me that."

A tight shrug. Chris hated talking about herself. "I wanted to be out there in the field, in the middle of the action, not working a desk job. And I most definitely didn't want to be a handler to a female operative half my age who looks like I could pick her up and snap her in half."

"Like to see you try," Eden scoffed.

Chris grinned. "No, you wouldn't."

"Did you handle other Valkyries?"

"Nope. Just you. And you kept me plenty busy." She ran a hand over her short, springy hair, the smile fading and the frown returning. "Look, my hands are tied here because I'm out of the loop now, but I did find out some

41

things you need to be aware of."

"Like what?"

Pulling open a small drawer in the desk, Chris took out a small rectangular gift wrapped in Christmas paper. "Happy birthday."

"My birthday's in August." Or she thought it was. The Agency had lied about a lot of shit, so she wouldn't put it past them to lie about her birthdate too, to throw her off the trail if she ever tried to dig into her past.

Chris waved the present at her. "I know when it is. Close enough."

Eden took it, and immediately knew it was a book. "Is it a romance, I hope? A steamy one." Just because she was perpetually single and killed for a living didn't mean she didn't have a romantic side.

"No, but hopefully it will result in a happy ending all the same. Don't open it until you get home, and keep it safe. I'll contact you in a few days to talk once I'm sure we're still in the clear."

Unease curled inside her. This was the most secretive Chris had ever been in the thirteen years they'd worked together. Something was wrong. "Are you all right?"

"I'm fine. Just be smart about this and keep that secure." She nodded at the book. "It wasn't easy to get my hands on that copy, and let's just say it's one of a kind."

"Kind of like you," Eden said with a smile, trying to lighten the mood because she didn't like the feel of this at all. What had Chris uncovered that had her so concerned? Something to do with Zack? Why not just say it if they were safe here?

"Like both of us. Now, meeting's over. I wanna hit the road." She stood, came around the side of the desk and paused.

Eden rose slowly, her heart beating faster because of the way Chris was looking at her. Fondly. But there was also a hint of worry lurking in her eyes that Eden had never seen from her before. "Hey, are you sure you're all r—"

"Come here, brat."

Caught off guard, Eden stiffened when Chris pulled her into a quick hug. It was over almost as soon as it started, but it was sincere and tight.

Alarm shot through her. In all their time together Chris had never initiated any kind of affection between them, it was always Eden and Chris merely tolerated it. "Chris, no shit, you're scaring me."

"Good. I want you on your toes. Have a safe drive back to Jersey. I'll be in touch." And with that she put on her sunglasses and sauntered out of the room, helmet tucked under one arm.

Alone in the office, Eden glanced down at the book in her hand. Chris had to have hidden something inside it. A clue, or a message of some sort. But why not just tell her up front and explain everything? Was she worried someone had followed them? She'd said it was safe when they'd arrived here.

Eden stepped into the hallway and shrugged into the straps of her backpack just as Chris's bike started up outside. The pitch changed as it began driving away.

Pop, pop.

Eden tensed and reached back to draw her weapon, then two more shots sounded, followed by a loud impact.

No.

She raced for the back door, intent on protecting Chris. She burst out onto the back steps, holding her pistol in a double-handed grip as she scanned for the shooter. Chris's bike was lying on its side just up the alley.

Eden ran down the steps, paused at the end of the short driveway behind a brick light post and whipped her upper body around the corner, weapon up. There was no sign of a shooter.

Chris lay pinned beneath her bike in a crumpled heap

two-hundred-feet away where she'd crashed into a garage three houses down. She wasn't moving. Eden ran for her, heart in her throat as she kept watch for the shooter.

Motion to her left made her pivot and take aim. Bits of brick exploded from the low wall next to her, the bullets missing her by inches. Eden leapt behind it for cover, waited a beat, then popped up to return fire. Another shot slammed into the brick just as a man jumped over a trashcan and ran for a low garden wall beyond it.

Eden fired a heartbeat before he rounded the corner. Her bullet hit him in the back of the shoulder. He grunted and stumbled but stayed on his feet as he disappeared from view a split second later.

She couldn't chase him. She had to help Chris.

Leaping over the wall, she raced for her friend. Blood was already forming a pool beneath her on the pavement.

"Chris," Eden said in an urgent voice as she dragged the bike off the older woman and dropped to her knees beside her. "Chris, can you hear me?" She pulled the helmet off, doing a visual sweep to assess the damage.

It was bad.

Two shots had hit Chris in the left upper chest, but they weren't bleeding. The holes in her belly were, however. Her friend's eyes were barely open, her skin already turning a ghastly grayish tinge from shock and blood loss. She was breathing in shallow, raspy draws, blood bubbling out of the holes in her stomach, coming out her nose and mouth with each breath.

Shit, shit, shit.

Eden ripped open Chris's leather jacket and found a ballistic vest with two holes in it. Damn. Chris had been concerned enough to armor up before coming here, but it hadn't protected her belly, and from the amount of blood spurting from one wound, it had hit a major artery—possibly the aorta.

Eden whipped out her cell phone and called 911 while watching for the shooter, then applied pressure to the wounds with both hands to try and stem the bleeding. Someone moved off to the right. She snatched up her weapon, froze when a dark-haired woman stepped out from behind the next garage, a pistol held at her side.

"Stand down, I'm here to help," the thirty-something woman said in a calm voice as she glanced around. "The shooter's gone." She wore black cargo pants and a long-sleeved shirt over full curves, her grip on the weapon as rock-steady as the deep blue gaze pinning Eden.

"Freeze right there. You've got one second to drop your weapon, or I drop *you*," Eden warned.

Surprising her, the curvy woman calmly holstered her weapon and angled the left side of her body toward Eden. "Like I said, I'm here to help." Moving slowly, palms facing outward, the woman reached down to pull down the waistband of her pants to expose her left hip—

Revealing the Valkyrie tat on the side of it.

Stunned, Eden wrenched her gaze up to the woman's face, fighting to cover her shock. Another Valkyrie? Here? The timing and circumstances were way too suspicious. "Who are you?" She still had one hand on Chris's belly, her palm and fingers sticky with warm blood. Too much blood, pooling around them. Her knees were soaked with it now.

"Trinity Durant." The woman approached them, looking at Chris now. "Is she alive?"

The gurgling sounds had stopped. Eden put two fingers to Chris's carotid pulse. It felt like a giant fist reached up to crush Eden's windpipe. "No." *Oh, God, no, this can't be happening.* She immediately started chest compressions.

Trinity knelt beside her. "You called for an ambulance?"

"Yes." Little good it would do Chris now, but Eden

still didn't stop. "How do you know the shooter's gone?"

"He got into a car and drove south."

Eden kept up with the chest compressions, struggling to fight back the rising tide of emotion and not trusting anything about this situation but unable to ignore the significance of having another Valkyrie standing before her. The woman could easily have shot Eden while she'd been attending to Chris, but hadn't. Maybe she was telling the truth.

After a minute Trinity placed a hand on top of Eden's. "She's gone," she said softly.

Eden threw Trinity's hand off and kept going, choking back the sob that wanted to rip free. Her brain knew Chris was dead. Her heart refused to accept it.

This time Trinity grabbed hold of Eden's hands. Hard. "Stop. We have to go."

Eden went rigid, forced her gaze to Trinity's. "I can't leave her like this."

"You have to. The shooter might come back, and he might not be working alone. We need to go."

She was right. Of course she was right. There would be too many questions, too many possible entanglements. Chris's murder hadn't been random. It had been a targeted hit. Why? Because of Eden? Because of what Chris had given her today?

But the thought of leaving Chris lying here in her own blood without anyone to stay with her ripped her heart out.

"Eden. *Now.*"

The steel in her voice was like a slap. Eden sucked in a painful breath, forced her hands away from Chris's chest, and pushed to her feet.

"Come on," Trinity said quietly, taking Eden's arm and leading her away.

Stay sharp. Stay sharp, Eden repeated to herself as they walked away, watching for any sign of danger. She couldn't think about Chris lying alone back there. Just couldn't.

Trinity took them to a silver minivan parked one block over and put Eden in the front passenger seat, sliding the backpack off and placing it at Eden's feet. "Take these and clean up as best you can," she said, handing Eden a pack of bleach wipes. "Put everything in this plastic bag when you're done."

Eden took them and began wiping Chris's blood from her hands. She had to scrub it from around the edges and beneath her nails. "My car's parked in the driveway."

"I've got someone coming to take care of it."

Eden was too upset to bother asking more.

"I'm sorry for your loss," Trinity said as she steered down the street moments later.

Eden couldn't answer, still trying to take it all in. Goddammit, it hurt. Chris had been caught off guard back there, oblivious of how close the threat was. They'd both been oblivious. If Eden had gone outside with her, maybe she could have prevented this.

Or you might be dead now too. "How did you find me?" she forced out.

"Been looking for you for a while now. Me and the others."

It made no sense. "Others?"

Trinity handed her a cell phone. "Call the number on screen. Kiyomi wants to talk to you."

The name forced the remaining air out of her lungs for a moment. She hadn't heard it in years, and it brought sharp flashes of memory to the front of her mind. A slender Asian girl with liquid brown eyes. Learning to spar together. Learning how to read body language and intent in a target. How to approach them to seem the most non-threatening. Various means of incapacitating or killing them.

With a stiff finger she hit the call button and waited

for the call to connect.

"Hello?"

"It's me," Trinity said from behind the wheel. "Eden's on the line."

"Eden? This is Kiyomi Tanaka. Do you remember me?"

This was surreal. "Yes. How…?"

"Are you all right?"

Physically? "Yes."

"Good. Trinity's going to explain everything once you're secure. You're safe with her."

Eden wasn't about to just accept that. This could still be an elaborate trap. She'd been trained not to lower her guard. To be suspicious of anyone who tried to get close to her. But that tat on Trinity's hip, and being put in contact with Kiyomi directly afterward… What if this was real?

Sirens sounded in the distance. First responders on the way to help Chris. Far too late. She swallowed, not wanting to talk anymore. Not sure what to think, what to believe. "I have to go."

"I understand. I just wanted you to hear a familiar voice. Stay close to Trinity, she'll get you out of there safely. We'll talk soon. Bye." She ended the call.

Eden handed the phone back to Trinity. A fire truck and two police cars roared past them. Eden bit the inside of her lip. Chris had been there for her when no one else had. They'd had good times and bad times, and even after the Program had been shut down, Chris had chosen to stay in contact, risking her safety to help Eden. Today she'd paid the ultimate price for it.

Pain expanded in Eden's chest. She thought of Chris's half-closed eyes staring sightlessly up at the sky.

I'm sorry, Chris. So, so sorry.

"How did you follow me here?" she finally asked Trinity.

"I didn't. I was here for your handler. I wanted to see if she knew where you were."

"Why?"

"We've been tracking you for months, trying to find you." Trinity turned down another side alley, watching around them carefully. "I'm part of a taskforce responsible for locating and bringing in all remaining Valkyries. Kiyomi's one of them. She's back at our headquarters in the UK. We want you to come back there with me."

Was this for real? "For what?"

"For your safety. We're under threat, Eden. Being hunted by people within the Program. So we're recovering all of us still out there, before it's too late, and joining forces. We're going to end the threat, and then we'll all start over without the constant fear of having to look over our shoulders every minute."

Eden stared at her, having a hard time processing everything Trinity had said when her mind was still full of Chris lying dead in the alley a few blocks away. "How many of us are left?"

"Nine, maybe ten. After you, there are only one or two more still alive."

Holy shit. She'd never imagined anything like this happening.

"I know this all comes as a shock, especially after what just happened. But I'm hoping you'll consider it." Trinity glanced across at her. "Did Chris give you anything today? Any important intel?"

"A book." It was in the backpack.

"What's in it?"

"I don't know, she told me not to open it—" She stiffened as Trinity hammered the brakes and brought them to a sudden stop.

Following Trinity's gaze, she spotted the black car in the ditch across the road. Its right tires had slid off the road. Two bullet holes marked the windshield. In the driver's seat, someone was slumped over the steering wheel.

"Shooter's car." Trinity threw the car into park and got out.

Eden was right behind her as they crossed the road, weapons up. Blood spattered the driver's side window and dash. Then Eden got close enough and found herself staring down at Chris's killer. "It's him."

"Yeah." Trinity glanced up and down the road. Finding it deserted for the moment, she pulled on gloves, took out a small device and opened the driver's door to take his fingerprints. Stepping back, she looked around them once more. "His killer's long gone. Let's get out of here."

Jesus. Two hitters, different targets. Somebody had a specific hit list and wanted to keep things quiet. But *who*?

Eden hurried with her back to their car, her mind going a hundred miles an hour. She pulled the book Chris had given her from her bag and tore open the wrapping paper. It was a hardcover copy of a Robert Ludlum novel. Opening it, she found a niche carved into the pages containing a flash drive.

Trinity pulled a U-turn and sped back the way they'd come, reaching for her phone. "Hey," she said to whoever answered. "I've got Eden, but there's a situation. Chris is dead, and so is the hitter who killed her. A few blocks away, double tap to the head. I'm sending his fingerprints to you, and Eden's got a thumb drive we'll need analyzed asap."

Eden listened to every word, her thoughts divided between their security and coping with the guilt of abandoning Chris's body to strangers.

Trinity ended the call. "Do you remember Amber Brown?"

Eden blinked as a vague image came to mind. Thin, oval face. Brown hair, green eyes. Hacker? "The name's familiar."

"She's our resident tech whiz. She's going to analyze everything as soon as she gets it." Trinity glanced over, hit her with that dark blue gaze. "I've got a flight chartered back to the UK. I want you to come with me. Will you?"

Eden was cautious by nature. Except with Zack, and except right now. Because while she rarely made knee-jerk decisions, there wasn't time to sit and debate her options. She wanted answers and justice for Chris. Wanted to find out who had killed her and why, and for a chance to meet the others if what she'd been told was true. Someone was out to kill her. And Zack might be involved somehow.

We're being hunted...

She wanted justice. And revenge.

"Yeah," she answered, resolve hardening like steel inside her. "I'll go with you."

Chapter Five

Eden roused herself from the mental fog she'd been in for the past few hours and focused on the terrain outside the car window as Trinity passed a slow-moving tractor. Rural England wasn't the kind of place Eden had imagined the Valkyrie headquarters would be located. She'd imagined a secret location somewhere smack in the middle of London, or maybe Manchester or Southampton. But the Cotswolds?

She and Trinity hadn't talked much on the flight over, because Trinity had been busy taking call after call from team members here in the UK and some back Stateside. Eden hadn't wanted to talk anyway, beyond ensuring that Trinity had someone she trusted who would contact Chris's family, and that her body would be flown back to Washington State for burial once it was released. Authorities were already at work on the investigation into her murder, while Eden and her newfound teammates would do their own digging.

Eden had stayed in her seat staring out the window at the clouds and ocean passing below them, thinking about Chris and the dangers still facing her and her fellow Valkyries. Emotionally exhausted and tired from the long, draining day, she'd eventually fallen asleep and woken minutes prior to landing at Cotswold Airport.

This whole area was like something out of a Beatrix Potter painting. The two-lane road was bordered by tall hedgerows on both sides. In the gaps between them, rolling hills in various shades of yellow and green stretched out as far as the eye could see, dotted by more hedgerows and trees.

"We'll be there in another fifteen minutes," Trinity told her, pulling back into the left-hand lane after passing the tractor. They were stuck behind a big delivery truck now, going half the speed limit. "I'm starving. Hopefully Mrs. Biddington has a big spread out when we get there."

"Who's that?"

"The cook. She's seventy-three and only works part time—usually a couple mornings a week and Sunday lunch. The rest of the time we all just fend for ourselves."

Eden was hungry, but her rumbling stomach could wait. She wanted to find out what was on that thumb drive so she could target whoever was responsible for Chris's murder. "Will everyone else be at the house when we get there?"

"Yes, for a change. Usually at least a few of us are off doing other things, either in London or outside the UK."

A few minutes later Trinity turned them off the main highway and continued down into a little green valley. "There's Laidlaw Hall," she said, pointing to her right.

Eden followed Trinity's finger and spotted a large mansion off in the distance, like something from Masterpiece Theatre. A big manor house built of honey-colored stone set in pastoral grounds. "That's headquarters?"

"Yep. You'll meet the owner at some point, but he's pretty private and mostly keeps to himself."

"Why did he let you guys set up here?"

"He's a good friend of Megan's—Amber's sister."

Eden whipped her head around to stare at her. "Amber has a sister?"

"Long story, but yes, and they're both Valkyries. Megan's our resident ninja thief."

To Eden's surprise, nerves danced in the pit of her stomach when they reached the massive gate at the end of the long driveway. Much as she'd dreamed of finding her lost Valkyrie sisters someday, she wasn't sure she had the energy for this right now.

"Megan and her boyfriend live in the gatehouse here," Trinity said as they drove through the gate and passed the smaller honey-colored building on the left. "Everyone else is up at the main house."

It took almost a full minute to reach the house from the road. Just as Trinity pulled up front around the circular end of the driveway, the tall front door opened and four women stepped out.

"There's the welcoming committee now," Trinity said with a wry smile. "Come on, let's get the introductions over with, and then get you settled. I know you're tired."

Grieving. She was grieving and angry and emotionally drained.

Eden climbed out of the car, putting aside her grief and unease, hiding everything going on inside her. Chris was gone. This was Eden's new reality and she had to adjust.

A slender Asian woman with long black hair started down the steps, and Eden breathed a sigh of relief when she recognized Kiyomi. "Hey, it's been a long time," Eden said as she approached.

"Sure has." Kiyomi shook Eden's hand, her welcoming smile vanishing a moment later. "I'm sorry to hear about your handler."

"Thank you." Eden didn't want to talk about it, however. She was focused on revenge.

"Glad you're okay, and we're all happy to have you here. You up to meeting the others?"

Looked like they were all waiting for an introduction, so might as well get it over with. "Sure."

Kiyomi led her up the steps, and Eden felt inexplicably nervous. All of these women were Valkyries? It was so hard to wrap her head around that.

Two brunettes with similar features stood side by side next to a blonde. "Do you remember Amber?" Kiyomi asked.

"Vaguely, yes." She gave the darker brunette a smile.

Amber returned it and stepped forward. "I remember you. Well, mostly I remember your back kick. You caught me off guard during a sparring session and knocked me on my ass in front of the instructors," she said with a grin, and shook Eden's hand. "Welcome. This is my sister, Megan. And this is Chloe."

Eden shook hands with the others. "Nice to meet you all." She'd worked alone her entire career, and had only been close with Chris—and then Zack. Meeting Trinity ten hours ago had been a shock. Staying in a fancy country manor headquarters with four other Valkyries was completely surreal.

"Bit of friendly advice—you need to watch out for Chloe," Megan said, her hazel eyes dancing. "She's straight-up crazy."

"Am not," Chloe argued, elbowing Megan in the ribs. Then to Eden, "She's just jealous because my specialty's way cooler than hers."

Eden played along, fascinated and cautious at the same time. "What were you trained in?"

Chloe popped her gum and grinned. "Making things go boom."

"She's good at it, too," Trinity said, "but we like to keep her on a tight leash around here, just in case. Okay, let's get Eden inside and show her to her room. Where does Marcus want her?"

"The amethyst room," Megan answered, then added to Eden, "Hope you like purple." With that she turned and led the way up the steps into the house.

The first thing that hit Eden when she stepped inside was the smell. Clean, but old. Lemon oil or soap, the sweeter underlying scents of old wood and leather. She stopped in the foyer to glance around, unable to keep from gawking. "Holy cow."

"I know, it's pretty amazing," Chloe said, hooking her elbow through Eden's. It was evident right up front that Chloe was the social butterfly of the group, and that boundaries were probably going to be an issue. "The rooms are great, but wait until you see the study and library. And the grounds."

Chloe chattered away to her while Megan led them up the main staircase with its scarlet-patterned runner, down the second-floor hall to another staircase that led to the third floor, and stopped at the second room on the right. "Here we go." She swung the door open, revealing...

Purple. Deep plum carpets and drapes, elegant and expensive-looking patterned wallpaper in a pretty lavender shade, and a four-poster canopy bed that looked at least a couple hundred years old. It was draped in purple tone-on-tone damask satin, with a matching spread and pillowcases.

Eden stared from the doorway, trying to take it all in. "I'm going to be staying...here?"

Chloe clapped her on the back. "You'll get used to it. Your en suite is through there, and your room overlooks the side lawn." She took Eden's bag from her and set it on the small sofa placed against the foot of the outrageously posh bed, then faced her with hands on hips. "Now. You hungry?"

"I...not really."

Shrewd brown eyes measured her. "Too bad, because you need to eat. Come on." She started for the door.

"You'd better offer her real food, Chloe, not just an
energy drink and whatever junk food you've got squir-
reled away," Megan said from the hall where Trinity and
Kiyomi also waited.

Chloe shot her a dirty look. "Who says I hid it? It's
right there in the main pantry so everyone can help them-
selves. Unlike some people, I know how to *share*."

"Whatever, you just know none of us will eat that
crap," Megan said, making the others grin. The banter felt
natural and easy, and Eden couldn't help but smile a little
too, some of the residual tension inside her easing. She'd
never imagined being back with her own kind, but if they
could help her find the person responsible for Chris's
death, then this was where she wanted to be.

"Ignore her," Chloe said, hooking her arm through
Eden's again. "We'll get you something to eat and then
we can talk after. Sorry about your handler, by the way."

"Thank you," Eden murmured.

"For God's sake, Chloe," Trinity said with a roll of
her eyes. "Give her some room to breathe."

Chloe blinked her big brown doe eyes at the elder
Valkyrie. "What, I'm just making her feel welcome."

"Let's maybe give her a little time to adjust to her
new surroundings," Kiyomi suggested gently, and offered
Eden an understanding smile. "Being made part of this all
of a sudden is pretty overwhelming."

Eden was grateful for the understanding. This was a
lot to take in all at once.

"Okay, I'll escort you down and leave you alone
while you eat, and keep things light," Chloe said, unfazed.
She led Eden back down to the main level while the others
followed, chattering away as they walked, telling Eden
about her boyfriend, Heath. The floors here were sand-

colored flagstone, worn shiny and smooth over the centuries by the passing of countless feet.

"We've got a team codename, by the way," Chloe continued on the way down the hall toward the back of the house.

"A codename?"

"Yeah, and it's awesome. Wanna hear it?"

It would be rude to say no, and she got the sense that Chloe would just tell her anyway even if she declined. "Sure."

A smug smile curved Chloe's mouth. "We're the Bitchilantes." She sounded extremely proud of the term, and Eden caught a glimpse of a wild glimmer in Chloe's eyes. It wasn't hard to picture that same gleam being there while Chloe blew up a target. "Okay, here we are. Breakfast room. Take your time, and we'll see you when you're done."

Chloe shut the door, leaving Eden in sudden and welcome silence. She was a little surprised Trinity wasn't with her, since the other Valkyrie said she was hungry on the drive here, though in all honesty Eden was grateful for the break. Chloe seemed nice, but was a little like being near a human tornado.

The large rectangular table was already laid with two place settings. Boiled eggs sat in little glass cups, toast was waiting in actual toast racks, halved and roasted plum tomatoes were set on a platter, along with jam and butter in little silver pots, plus coffee and tea.

Eden sank into a chair, stared at the food a moment and then let her gaze stray out the tall windows at the back of the room into a well-manicured garden. She thought of Chris, probably in a refrigerated drawer in a morgue now, awaiting autopsy, while Eden sat here in the lap of luxury in this luxurious mansion, perfectly safe in the midst of a bunch of strangers.

A lump formed in her throat and tears pricked the

backs of her eyes. She'd lost a friend today. Her only friend, really. Now her Valkyrie sisters, while strangers for the most part, had welcomed her here without question. Deep down, Eden had longed for this kind of acceptance and belonging for most of her life, had always wondered what had become of the other women in the Program.

Chris would be happy for me.

That hurt too. As gruff as Chris had been, she'd cared about Eden. No matter what, Chris would want her to embrace this opportunity. To use the intel on the flash drive and find justice with it—justice for Chris, and for all of them now in the crosshairs of whoever was gunning for them.

A soft tap on the door broke her from her thoughts. Kiyomi stepped inside with a soft smile. "Mind if I join you?"

Eden smiled back, Kiyomi's quiet energy soothing to her jagged nerves. "I'd like that."

Shutting the door, Kiyomi took the seat opposite her and poured herself a cup of tea. "I know it takes some getting used to, being here. When I first came here I felt just like you did—like I'd been ambushed and dropped into the middle of a sorority house."

The description made Eden grin. "Pretty much, yeah."

Kiyomi smiled at her over the rim of her teacup. Everything about her was dainty, almost fragile, and yet Eden could see the steel hidden inside the woman, reflected in her posture and eyes. Without it, Kiyomi wouldn't have made it through what she'd had to do. "I'm really glad you're here. When we initially identified you as one of the other surviving Valkyries, I kept hoping we'd get verification that you were still alive and okay."

Eden wasn't sure how much Kiyomi and the others knew about her past, or current situation with Zack.

Though she didn't much feel like eating she needed fuel, and helped herself to some breakfast. "Who was I talking to via email all those months ago, anyway, do you know? Trinity never said." There were so many things Eden wanted to know and hadn't had the chance to ask yet. Everything had happened so fast; this entire day had been a blur.

"Chloe. Or, should I say—Bam Bam."

The humor in it didn't escape her. "Oh my God, of course. It all makes sense now." Turned out Bam Bam was handy with explosives. Might come in handy when Eden found out who'd ordered Chris's death, but then, Eden wanted whoever it was to suffer. A few bullet holes in painful and not immediately life-threatening places first.

"Chloe and the others saved those women you tipped her off about, you know."

"I heard. Score one for the good guys." It didn't happen often enough.

Kiyomi nodded, her expression turning thoughtful. "It's not easy for most of us to fit into a group like this, but... It's worth it."

Eden nodded, willing to be part of the team as long as they helped her hunt down whoever had targeted Chris. "I'll get there."

"I know you will. We're survivors. Adapting is what we do." She set her teacup down. "After you eat, Trinity wants us all to meet in the library. You'll meet the guys later."

Eden paused in chewing a mouthful of toast. "Guys?" No one had said anything about guys, beyond Chloe talking about her man.

"Amber, Megan, and Chloe's significant others. They're part of the team too. So is the owner of this house. All the guys have elite military backgrounds, and have been thoroughly vetted by Trinity and Alex Rycroft.

You've been told about him, I assume?"

Trinity had mentioned the former NSA agent on the way to the airport in Vermont, and how he was assisting in their efforts. "Yes." But Eden still had a lot to learn about all this—and everyone involved.

As soon as they ate, Kiyomi took her down the hall. The library was a gorgeous, sun-drenched room with wall-to-wall bookshelves stuffed with what had to be over a thousand books. The walls were a pale apple green with cream trim, and the large pieces of furniture were made of tufted velvet and leather. All the other Valkyries were waiting when they entered.

"Doing okay?" Trinity asked, giving Eden a critical once-over.

"So far, so good." As long as she didn't think about Chris.

"I just brought everyone up to speed on this morning's events, and Amber analyzed the contents of the thumb drive during our flight. I also got an update from Rycroft a few minutes ago."

Eden braced herself for bad news.

"Zack Maguire reported you to his superiors the other night," Amber said.

"I know."

"According to Rycroft's team, Maguire worked several ops with the dead hitter in the past," Trinity added.

Eden stared at her as cold seeped through her body. "You're saying Maguire was involved today?" The toast curdled into a gummy ball in her stomach. She'd expected Zack to keep looking for her. But to think that he could have followed her with the intent to kill her, and may have been involved with Chris's death? That was unthinkable.

"No, just noting the connection for now. The team's investigating it." Trinity leaned forward and set her hands on her knees, the others all quiet as she continued. "We need to talk to Maguire. See if he knows anything that might help us figure out why Chris was targeted, and who might be actively hunting us now." Those deep blue eyes drilled into Eden's. "What do you know about him?"

The room went eerily quiet, all eyes fastened on her. They all knew some things about Zack, especially Trinity and Amber. Eden wasn't going to volunteer her past with Zack to them, however, even if they were fellow Valkyries. Not now, maybe never. "He was my way into a circle that included a previous target on an op in St. Petersburg last summer. I don't know what he's involved in at the moment, but he's been a contract officer with the CIA for a few years now. He specializes in gathering intel."

"He's former Army intelligence."

"Yes."

Trinity nodded. "Rycroft's going to contact him personally and set up a meeting. Better if he does it rather than us, given Maguire's ties to the CIA."

Eden's insides clenched at the mere possibility of crossing paths with him ever again. Of confronting him face-to-face now, after everything that had happened. "Does Rycroft think Maguire was directly involved in Chris's death?" *Please, God, say no.*

"It's too early to be sure at this point, but Alex is looking into every possibility." Trinity cocked her head slightly. "You know what our mission here is. You know what the stakes are. So I need to ask you. Do you think Maguire would kill you if he had the chance?"

"No," she answered immediately. "He'd report intel about me to his superiors, and might assist in trying to capture me, but he wouldn't kill me." That wasn't how Zack was wired. At least, she didn't think he was.

"You're sure."

"Ninety-five-percent sure. He had the chance to kill me in Sevastopol and never even drew his weapon." Whether it was because she was a woman or because of their past and that he actually cared about her, she couldn't say. Her gut said it was both.

"Do you trust him?"

"Somewhat." He could be out for revenge now.

"How much?" Chloe pressed.

"Enough not to shoot me dead on sight," Eden answered.

"Think he'd help you if you asked?" Amber said.

"I don't know." Eden wouldn't trust him that much now that he knew the truth.

"All right. Then will you meet with him and find out whatever you can about what's happening to us?"

Seeing Zack again was the last thing she wanted, but saying no wasn't an option. Chris was dead, there was no one left to help her except these smart, deadly and dedicated women. They each bore the Valkyrie mark on their left hip, a badge of solidarity and sisterhood. Eden wasn't going to let them or Chris down.

She sat up straighter, glanced at the others before looking at Trinity once more. "Yes. I'll meet with him whenever Rycroft wants."

Chapter Six

This would either be really good, or really, really bad.

Zack ordered himself a coffee and a breakfast sandwich at the counter before finding a seat in the busy café in the heart of Covent Garden. This area of London was always busy, but on a Saturday it was even more crowded.

His phone buzzed with an incoming call. He expected to see Rod's number on the display, but it was his dad calling instead.

Zack sighed. He loved his dad, but he had the worst damn timing when it came to phone calls. It was three in the morning back home in Indiana, so he must be really worried.

Zack wouldn't normally answer at a time like this, but it had been over a week since they'd last spoken. Zack had texted, but that wouldn't cut it with his father—his old man always wanted to hear Zack's voice as proof that he wasn't dead when he'd been out of touch longer than a couple weeks. "Hey, Dad. I'm just at a meeting right now, so I can't talk." He scanned the café as he spoke, looking for Rycroft or anyone paying too close attention to him.

"Are you okay?" his dad demanded.

"Yeah, I'm fine."

"We haven't heard from you in a long time. Where are you?"

"On a job."

"You still coming back for a visit soon?"

"Everything's on hold at the moment. I'll know more in a few days. Call you later, all right?"

"You actually going to follow through with that promise this time?"

Zack couldn't help but smile a little at the dig. "Yes, promise. Say hi to Paula." His stepmom worried about him, but she was the calmer, more levelheaded one in the marriage.

His dad gave an irritated sigh. "Okay, son. Take care."

"You too." He ended the call and started eating his breakfast.

Why did Rycroft want to meet with him here? Zack had been in Frankfurt when he'd received the call yesterday, so it had been a short flight here. Rycroft was flying in from the U.S. and coming straight to the meeting from the airport.

Based on their short conversation Zack was hoping this had to do with Eden, but even if it didn't, he still would have come. When Alex Rycroft called and asked you for a face-to-face meeting, you showed up.

At this point he needed all the help he could get if he was going to have a prayer of tracking Eden. The woman was like a damn shadow. It bothered him that he hadn't been able to find out anything more about her, though if Rycroft was involved with her somehow, he would only divulge as much intel as he wanted Zack to know. At this point, however, anything was better than nothing.

Eden had made him a desperate man.

He looked up when someone approached his table,

expecting Rycroft, and nearly choked on the sandwich when he found *her* standing there instead.

His heart stopped beating for an instant, then went into double time while the food turned into a hard lump he had to force down his throat.

"Morning," she murmured, pulling out the chair opposite him and sitting.

She looked amazing as usual, but edgy in a pair of snug jeans that molded to her hips and thighs, a turquoise top that hugged her breasts, and a fitted black leather jacket. Her hair was pulled up into a ponytail, little black curls framing her face. She wore no makeup except for a light pink lip-gloss that made it hard to look away from her mouth as he recalled the way those same lips had parted beneath his. How they had made him delirious with pleasure as they wrapped around his cock.

With effort he got the lump of bread, egg and bacon down his throat. "Morning." He glanced around, searching for Rycroft.

"He's not here. It's just us."

Zack eyed her, wary and hopeful and heartsick all at once. It was still hard to believe it had come to this—that they were essentially strangers now, and suspicious of each other. "Did you set this up?"

"No. He did."

He waited a beat, then held out a hand. "Hi. I'm Zack. Nice to meet you finally," he said, all sarcasm.

She shook it, cool and unreadable.

"What's your last name?" he asked.

"Foster."

Strange how that surname hadn't come up once in all the digging he'd done on her. Not that much *had*. The first time he'd heard it was yesterday during the brief conversation with Rycroft. "Is that your real name?"

"Yes."

He didn't know if she was being honest or not, but

that honey-brown gaze was damn near hypnotic. If he wasn't careful she could easily pull him back under her spell. The impact of her mere presence was a jolt to all his senses, and sitting this close had him itching to touch her. Grab her and take her face between his hands, make her tell him the truth. She smelled incredible, a mix of vanilla and musk he wanted to breathe in.

Shit. He was every bit as attracted to her as he had been the first time they'd met. His whole body was amped. "Why are you here?"

"Because we have questions."

"We?"

"Rycroft and I."

Was this a setup? If Rycroft had been here Zack would have been less suspicious.

He leaned back and folded his arms, not giving a shit if it broadcast his defensiveness, though the abrupt shift straight to business was almost a relief rather than talking about their past and her ditching him. "Such as?"

"A good friend of mine was killed yesterday in Vermont."

The pain and anger in her eyes bothered him. He wanted to wipe it away, fix everything and make things the way they had been before. "Sorry to hear that."

Her wary expression didn't change as she pulled out a small photograph from her jacket pocket and slid it facedown across the table. "We found the hitter dead in his car nearby a few minutes later. Apparently he did contract work for the same people as you. You know him?"

He took the photo and flipped it over. Shock punched through him when he saw the face of the dead man slumped behind the wheel, followed immediately by a sharp pain in the center of his chest.

Yeah, Zack knew him.

He turned the picture facedown, stared at the back of it as he absorbed the blow, unable to get the image of

John's bloody face out of his mind. "When was this taken?"

"Yesterday morning."

Why hadn't Zack received word that John had been killed? John's parents had Zack's cell number. God, what an agonizing loss this would be for them. As to who had killed John... The woman across the table was more than capable of it.

He collected himself before looking up at Eden again, fighting back his anger. "Did you do it?"

Surprise and a flash of indignation flared in her eyes, then was gone. "No. But he killed my friend and tried to kill me as well. I wounded him in the back of his right shoulder before he got away."

Her answer seemed honest. She might be a consummate actress, but Zack believed her, and relaxed a little. She'd been defending herself. If she'd killed John, this would have been way harder than it already was.

Eden studied him, cool and remote. A virtual stranger compared to the woman he'd known. "Who is he?"

"A friend of mine."

"How good a friend?"

"Good enough." Enough that this news hurt like a bitch. He and John had worked together off and on for a couple years. He knew John's family. Had spent some time with them, sat at the parents' kitchen table at Thanksgiving.

"Did you send him after me?"

"No," he said, adamant. So who had?

Eden set her jaw, anger now visibly bubbling beneath her calm surface. "Why did he target my friend and me?"

"Who was your friend?"

She was silent a moment. "My former handler."

Zack covered his surprise. John always obeyed the

rules. So if he'd gone after Eden and her handler, it was because he'd been following orders.

A long, taut silence built as he and Eden stared at each other, suspicion and mistrust filling the space between them. And he hated it. Couldn't stand it another moment.

He broke eye contact to glance around the place, assuming they were being watched, but didn't spot anyone who stood out. Decision made, he met her gaze once more. "Can we talk somewhere more private?" There was so much he wanted to say and ask, but not here, not in public and not while her shields were up. She had to be wearing a wire or whatever. He didn't want anyone else overhearing the conversation he had in mind.

Eden debated it for a few seconds, then relented with a nod. "Fine, follow me."

She was up and out of her chair before he could move, left him staring after her as she made her way to the door. He followed, watching for signs of someone tailing him, but this whole area was too crowded so it was hard to know for sure.

She didn't slow or look back, making it clear she wasn't going to wait and didn't want to be close to him. If they were being tailed, he couldn't tell.

He stayed within fifty feet of her as she walked to the tube station, then boarded the same car as her heading east on the Piccadilly Line while she completely ignored him.

Wherever she was taking him, he intended to get some sort of closure. Find out exactly who she was, who she worked for, and then why she'd left him so abruptly.

They'd take care of business first. Then he was getting answers and walking away for good, no matter how much he still wanted her.

****

69

Having Zack so close and yet out of reach was a subtle form of torture.

Eden was hyper aware of everything about him as he followed her into the hotel room twenty minutes after leaving Covent Garden. She was keyed up, on edge about being alone with him. He might still try to capture her and turn her over to the CIA, but it was their history that made Eden so nervous now.

As a precaution, Trinity had tailed her to the café and back, wearing a disguise. Eden had told her to stand down via her earpiece before entering the hotel. The other Valkyrie was now outside in the hallway, ready to step in if anything went wrong. But Eden was almost certain Zack wasn't going to hurt her, and if he tried to drug her and carry her out of here, Trinity would intervene the moment they stepped out of the room.

Still, it took everything Eden had to keep her face impassive and mask her body's reaction to his nearness as she stepped inside the room. She shut and locked the door, then faced him and folded her arms. He stood less than ten feet away, looking around the room, the woodsy scent of his cologne filling her nose, tormenting her with memories of the way it had been between them. Making her yearn to erase the invisible divide keeping them apart now, and feel that hard body up against hers again.

"Okay, we're alone, as requested," she said, all business. The sooner they got this over with and he left, the better.

He faced her, those storm-gray eyes full of suspicion and a heat that threatened to make her toes curl in her boots. "Are we?"

"Yes."

"No cameras?"

Just her earpiece, transmitting everything to Trinity and Rycroft. "Does it matter?"

"Yes." His closed expression bothered her. There

had been a time when he'd been so natural and easy with her. Then she'd had to walk away.

He was definitely going to ask her about why she'd left. She didn't want anyone else overhearing any of that. It was private, and no one else's business.

Reaching up, she removed the earpiece, switched it off, then tossed it onto the dresser beside her. "There. Now what about you?"

"Just my phone. No comms or wires." He pulled it out so she could look at it, then held his arms wide, his expression mocking. "You wanna search me anyway?"

"No." She wasn't touching him. And enough with the pleasantries—she wanted intel. "Do you have any idea who might have hired your friend to kill my handler?"

"Back up. Who are you working for? The NSA? CIA? Rycroft?"

She owed him that much. "When I met you in St. Petersburg that last time, myself. Now I'm part of a team."

"What team?"

She sidestepped the question. "I want to find out who killed my handler and who's targeting me and the others."

"What others?" Frustration burned in his gaze.

Eden eyed him, trying to read his expression and wondering what was going on in his head. He'd been in touch with his CIA contacts. Had doubtless told his handler about this supposed meeting with Rycroft. What was he after? What was his angle?

He gave a hard exhalation. "Look, you blew two of my missions, and I lost a good friend yesterday. In both St. Petersburg *and* Sevastopol my team was working on something way bigger than Terzi, and each time you killed off the only men who could give me the intel I needed."

She wasn't sorry. "First, your friend killed my handler and tried to kill me. Second...I had my reasons for those kills."

His expression hardened, turning him into a remote stranger, reminding her that she'd never known the real him. "Enlighten me."

Being alone together in this intimate space was starting to get to her. She couldn't read what was going on in his head, but she was thinking about being in other hotel rooms just like this one together, and the things they'd done to each other.

Like him pinning her to the shower wall or the bed with his big, hard body. Reducing her to quivering helplessness with his touch, his kisses. The way he'd held her, woken every nerve ending with his hands and mouth before satisfying the molten desire inside her.

It shook her even now, how far she'd let him in.

He was the only man she'd ever lowered her guard for. And dammit, it *hurt* to have this cold wedge of suspicion and hurt between them now. She wished things could have been different back then. That she'd been a different woman with a normal life, free to follow her heart.

But wishing for that was like wishing for the sun to suddenly rise in the west, and though she had regrets, there had been no other option but to leave him behind. She'd done what she'd had to in order to survive.

Maintaining an impassive expression, she held firm. "No. Tell me about your friend."

"John rarely ever did hits, and he had a specific moral code, so if he did this—"

"He did. I saw him."

Zack inclined his head in acknowledgment. "Then he was following orders."

"Maybe he got an offer he couldn't refuse and did it for the money." People did bad shit all the time when the right circumstances were in play, moral code or not.

Zack shook his head, adamant. "No way. He was told to go after you both. The order either came from someone high up in the intel community, or he was fed false information."

"Why are you so sure of that?"

"Because we worked security contracting jobs together after we got out of the military. I spent almost three years with him on and off. I knew his family. He knew mine. We were close. So if someone set him up, then I want them brought down hard."

She understood that need for vengeance perfectly. "I know exactly how you feel."

His expression softened and his posture relaxed. "Did you see who killed him?"

"No. And just to reiterate, it wasn't me." She paused, watching him. This was why she was here. To get answers, feel him out, and then see if he was open to being recruited to their cause.

Their history didn't matter now. Only the mission did, so if Zack could help them, Eden had to try to bring him on board, even if she didn't trust his motives now. "Believe it or not, I really do know how you feel right now. My team is trying to find out who's responsible for all of this."

He frowned. "What kind of team?"

"How much did Rycroft tell you?" she countered.

"Not much, other than mentioning you and setting up the meeting at the café." He paused, watching her. "What are you, Eden? A spy? You owe me that much."

She bristled at his wording, a retort springing to the tip of her tongue. *I don't owe you anything.*

Except she did. What they'd had together was the closest thing to real she'd ever allowed herself to experience. He also hadn't hurt her in Sevastopol when he'd suspected she was the killer. He hadn't hurt her now. And she *had* ruined two of his missions.

Given everything that had happened, at this point

there was no harm in telling him the truth. "I'm a Val-kyrie."

His lack of reaction was telling. He'd already suspected. How? "That…explains a lot," he said slowly. Then he narrowed his eyes, suspicion taking hold again. "Did you drug me that morning?"

"Yes. I'm—we're—being targeted, by the same person or people who had my handler and your friend killed yesterday. It has to be the CIA and it screams cover up." And…

I'm afraid.

She'd never been truly afraid before. Not like this. Knowing someone with powerful connections and resources was systematically eliminating Valkyries and those close to them, was different than anything she'd faced before. And while she and Zack might not trust each other, Trinity and Rycroft were insistent that the team needed his help now, whether Eden liked it or not.

Silence stretched out between them. "Are you going to try to turn me in?" she finally asked.

His gray eyes never wavered from hers. "No."

"Why not?"

"Because I believe you."

A measure of relief hit her, but she was still surprised. Just like that? After everything she'd done? He might be trying to reel her in. Make her drop her guard so he could spring a trap.

"What do you want from me?" he finally asked, calm in spite of what she'd just told him. Solid, strong, ready to face whatever came at him.

"You're an intel expert with lots of contacts. You understand how the Agency operates. We want your help in finding the people behind this." Well, Trinity and Rycroft did. Eden worried this was a disaster waiting to happen.

He didn't answer. God, her emotions were too close to the surface now. She was rattled and wanted to end this now before her resolve to stay detached from him crumbled. Every moment she spent here alone with him made her ache for what could have been.

Zack didn't move, just kept staring at her. "Why did you leave that day?" he finally asked.

Here it was. The moment she'd been dreading most. She raised her chin. "Because I had to."

He gave a slow nod. "Was it all an act?"

She drew a breath, done with this torturous conversation and not about to beg him to join the team. "I've told you everything you need to know about this. You need to decide whether you're in or out. You've got twenty minutes. Text this number if you're in."

She shoved a business card with the number scrawled on the reverse side and handed him back his phone. "If not, forget this meeting ever happened. Don't ever try to contact me again, and stay out of our way."

He nodded, his eyes hardening like steel. "So it's like that."

"Yeah, it's like that." She put her earpiece back in, opened the door and walked out, her throat tight and her whole chest aching.

If this turned out to be the last time she ever saw Zack Maguire, at least he would remember her walking away with her spine straight and her head held high.

Chapter Seven

T rinity was waiting for her down the hallway when Eden came out of the room. "You good?"

"Yeah." A little queasy, if she was honest.

The other woman nodded, her expression shrewd as they reached the door to the stairwell and stepped inside. "Weirdest thing happened earlier—I lost comms with you right after you went inside with him, and they resumed the moment you left."

Eden didn't bother answering, just followed her down to the parking garage under the building. Reaching their vehicle, she slid into the passenger seat and shut the door. While she had the utmost respect for Trinity, Eden didn't care if she and Rycroft were pissed at her for cutting comms. Seeing Zack in private was hard enough without having their past exposed to scrutiny and speculation.

"So what did he say?" Trinity asked as she put on her seatbelt, thankfully letting the other matter drop.

"He didn't know about the hit, or that the hitter was dead. Apparently John was a good friend of his. Said he must have been following orders."

"What about the rest of it. Did you tell him about

you?"

"Yes. He didn't seem surprised by it, only about us being hunted."

"His handler might have tipped him off after Sevastopol."

"Could be." She settled back in the seat, still uneasy about this whole thing. "Why do we need him specifically again?"

"Why, do you have a problem with working with him?"

Eden looked over at her. Trinity obviously suspected something had gone on between them. "You mean, other than his so-called 'friend' killing my handler and targeting me as well?"

Trinity was silent for a moment, the quiet of the insulated parking garage settling around them. "Were you in love with him?"

The sudden jump in topic tripped her up. Her past relationship with Zack had no bearing on their current mission, but Trinity clearly either saw or suspected there was something between them. "No, it was nothing, and it was after my mission was over."

The other Valkyrie's expression remained unreadable. "He's certainly been diligent in his digging about you since whatever happened in St. Petersburg. He's been trying to find you ever since, first with his CIA contacts, then on his own. After Sevastopol he was tasked with tracking you down."

To know all of that, Amber and Rycroft's team must have researched him—which, yeah, of course they would. "He didn't suspect a thing when we were together, and he was just as surprised to see me in the Crimea as I was to see him. And if he's been tapped to find and possibly capture me, why do we want him on the team when he poses a risk to us all?"

"Because we can use him."

Despite Eden's suspicion about Zack's motives, her hackles rose at the implication there, automatically wanting to protect him. "Use him how?"

"Not *use* him. I mean he'd be a good asset for us, because of his current involvement with the Agency. He's got the most recent service with them, the most up to date contacts there, and he has easier access to their intel resources than the rest of us. Except for Amber, but every time she hacks something from them, it increases the risk they'll be able to find us."

"There are plenty of intel specialists we could bring in to do that."

"Yeah, except Maguire has intel on someone we think might be connected to another Valkyrie we've identified," Trinity continued. "Also, and this is pretty damn telling, Zack only agreed to this meeting when Rycroft explained it involved you and told him your real name."

"Yeah, because he wanted to find me." For the CIA? Himself? Because he was still angry with her for walking away? For ruining his missions? Or was there more to it? Dammit, she shouldn't want there to be more to it, but she did.

"Did he threaten you at all?"

"No."

Trinity glanced at the phone in her hand, then back at Eden. "No alerts from Amber about his phone. He's still in the room and hasn't tried to contact anyone. If he wanted you captured, he would have called it in by now."

"I can see how he'd be useful to us. But he's got every reason to want to turn me over. So how can we trust him?"

"Sure you want me to answer that?"

"Yes."

"Because of your history together."

Eden flushed. Trinity and whoever else had been looking into this couldn't know the extent of it. She and

Zack had been careful. "Whatever history he and I do or don't have, is between me and him."

Trinity shrugged. "You wanted to know. Also, Rycroft is one of the best operatives I've ever known, and he can read people like a book. He said Zack was protective of and concerned about you when Rycroft questioned him. That, combined with him wanting to find out who killed his friend means he's motivated, and suggests his allegiance might not be with the Agency. So if he agrees to come on board with us now, chances are he's not going to turn you in later, and this way we'll be able to keep a close eye on him."

Eden didn't like it. She'd never imagined Zack being brought back into her life, and never like this. How was she supposed to work with him and stay objective after everything that had happened? How could she trust him after what had happened?

"How long did you give him to decide?" Trinity asked.

"Twenty minutes." She was torn between wanting to get away from Zack and going back upstairs to tell him everything. That she had continued to see him after that initial op because she hadn't been able to stay away from him. That she had started falling for him, and it still scared the shit out of her. "He's got fourteen minutes left."

"Amber texted earlier to say she's got your personnel file ready if you're interested in reading it when we get back, by the way. She left it in your room at the manor."

"What personnel file?"

"From the Program. She hacked some of their files before they could shut everything down."

Impressive. "Does it say anything about my parents?"

"It will, yes."

An unexpected pang hit her and she looked away,

staring at nothing through the windshield. "I don't remember them. My dad's mom raised me after they died."

"What happened to them?"

"Some kind of an accident. She took me in, kept me until her health gave out. Something to do with her heart. I was put into foster care when she went into a palliative facility."

"I'm sorry."

Eden nodded, glanced at her. "What about you? Did you know your parents?"

"No. The paperwork says my mom was a single parent when she dropped me off at the facility one day. There was no mention of my father. When no one wanted to adopt me I was put into foster care, bounced around from place to place. To tell you the truth, it was a relief to wind up in the Program. For the first time, I felt worthy, even important." She shot Eden a wry smile. "That was back before I realized what I was being groomed for, of course."

Yes. Trinity's experience was way worse than Eden's. Eden didn't know how operatives like Trinity and Kiyomi handled what they did. "Did you have any say about it?" she asked, curious. Because she couldn't imagine candidates ever choosing that kind of life. "They were torn about where to put me after the initial phase. I cross-trained with Kiyomi in several areas, and I think they were grooming me for that specialty. I loved studying botany and toxins, so maybe that's why they put me there instead." Thank God for that. Eden couldn't have done what Kiyomi and Trinity had.

"No, it wasn't a choice."

Her stomach tightened. She'd been so afraid they would force her to become a femme fatale too. Unable to face the thought of having to let strangers use her body time and again. "What about Kiyomi? Did she get a choice?"

"No. Our kind never got a choice."

Eden faced forward again. Her feelings about the Program were so complicated. It had taught her so many valuable things, made her feel like she could do anything, yet it had taken so much as well. "I'm sorry. That must have been really hard."

"You know how they were. They made it seem like being the rarest kind of Valkyrie was the toughest and most coveted assignment. That we were the most elite, like it was the greatest prize to be coveted."

Fucking liars. Brainwashing in all its forms, subtle and otherwise. She could admit to that now. "I'm glad you and Kiyomi both made it through to the other side." Few of that kind survived longer than a handful of years in the field.

Trinity shot her a genuine smile. "Me too. The most rewarding work I've ever done in my life is with you and the others. I feel like I'm part of a dream team, with people who understand me in ways no one else could."

Eden couldn't help but grin. It was true, no one understood her like the others did. "I'm not hating it so far."

"Good. But don't ever cut comms on an op again, okay? You're part of this team now, and we're your backup for a reason."

Before Eden could respond, her phone buzzed with an incoming message. From Zack. Her stomach sank even as her heart tripped in excitement. "He's in."

"Great. Tell him to meet us down here in five. We're taking him to the manor."

God, not only was she going to be trapped in this car with him for the next two-plus hours, but he was going to live in the same damn house as her for the foreseeable future?

Eden sent the message, then lowered the phone to her lap, conflicted. She'd done everything in her power to get over him. She'd left to keep them both safe. Now they would both be in danger, and she wasn't ready to trust him. "He doesn't really know what he's signing up for."

"You need to give him more credit."

Eden didn't want him to be used again or see him get hurt. Didn't want to be hurt by him in retaliation for what she'd done. She couldn't shake the fear that he would turn her world upside down again.

What was she going to do? She'd found the strength to leave him once. If something happened between them this time, she wasn't sure she could do it again.

Trinity reached over to squeeze Eden's shoulder. "It's going to be okay. You're part of our family now, and we take care of each other, no matter what."

She blew out a breath, nodded. "Thanks." Knowing that helped. She'd never had backup she could trust, except for Chris. "Does Marcus even know we're bringing someone else back with us?"

Trinity was busy typing something on her phone. "He does now."

****

Marcus updated his last account spreadsheet and was about to shut down the computer when a new email popped up. The name made him pause, a knot of dread coiling in his gut. He clicked on it anyway.

How's it going, mate? Long time no talk to. Shite's going down here. Wouldn't be surprised if our paths crossed again soon. I know better than to hope for a reply, but I hope all is well with you.

Rory

He read it twice, was tempted to reply and ask for more intel, then closed it and shut the computer down. His gaze strayed to one of the framed photos on the corner of his desk. It had been taken in Syria just prior to the disastrous mission that had cost him nearly everything. He stood in the center of the sixteen-man troop, Karas as a pup sitting at his feet wearing her Kevlar vest. Rory stood to his left.

Of the sixteen men in that photo, only nine had made it home alive. And although Rory and the others didn't hold Marcus responsible for what had happened, he'd cut contact with them all when he'd returned to the UK. It was just too painful otherwise.

Hurried, impatient footsteps that could only belong to Chloe rushed past the study, pulling him from his memories. He waited until she was out the front door and her steps faded into silence before planting his cane and rising from his desk, covering a wince as a sharp pain sliced through his left hip. The surgeons had told him it was a damn miracle he was even walking. But the price for surviving was he'd never have the mobility he once had, and would never be without pain again—mental and physical.

Beside him, Karas stretched and lazily got to her feet, none too thrilled at having her afternoon nap interrupted.

"Right. Let's crack on," he said, striding for the door. He liked Chloe and the others well enough, but he craved solace and privacy—two things in short supply now that his house was full of Valkyries and their significant others.

Through the constant buzz of activity he did his best to stay out of everyone's way and keep to himself. So it was odd that in spite of all the people around and his preference for solitude, he felt more isolated and alone than ever.

It probably had to do with Megan. Now that she had Ty, Marcus didn't see her often. They rarely worked out or rode together these days. He missed the way things used to be, even if it was just a quiet evening together in front of the fire with a proper brew. The bond they'd forged in Syria meant he was more comfortable with her than he'd ever been with anyone else—even his own family while they'd still been alive.

Now she had Ty, and that's how it should be. Marcus wanted her to be happy, she deserved it. All these women did after what they'd been put through, and he was glad to at least offer them his home as a place of refuge while they needed it.

Especially one other Valkyrie in particular that he couldn't seem to stop thinking about.

The hallway was empty. At the back door he and Karas stepped outside together and headed for the stable. Megan often liked to go riding at this time of day. He might be able to catch her before she headed out.

At first he thought it was her sitting on the bench at the top of the path with her back to him, but as he came nearer he saw the woman's hair was black, not brown.

Kiyomi. Bent over sketching something onto a pad in her lap. His pulse skipped a beat and he almost stopped, but kept going. This was his home. He couldn't avoid her forever, and God knew, he didn't want to.

She sat up and looked behind her when she heard the crunch of his boots and cane on the fine gravel. A polite smile curved her mouth. "Hi."

"Ey up."

"You just missed Megan. She and Ty went out with Amber and Jesse to shoot some arrows."

"Ah." He smothered the twinge of disappointment, quickly extinguished by the excuse to talk to Kiyomi. "And what are you up to, then?"

She made a disgruntled sound and looked down at her sketchpad. "I was trying to draw."

Stopping beside her, he studied the drawing. In a few scant strokes she'd captured Rollo as he stretched his head over the door of his stall, ears pricked forward. "It's brilliant."

"Then that makes you a liar," she said with a smile,

and closed the cover. "I'm badly out of practice, but it's just so quiet and peaceful out here and I like the sweet, dusty smell of them." She gestured to the horses.

"Do you ride?"

"No."

"Fancy a go?"

She seemed surprised by his offer. "Now?"

"Aye. I've got a mare so gentle she used to be a children's therapy horse, if you're interested." It surprised him how much he wanted her to say yes. She'd healed physically during her time here, but not the rest of her. There were still shadows in her dark brown eyes he wished he could erase. Because he knew what it was to be haunted by things that could never be forgotten. "I'll talk you through it, hold onto the reins so she can't go anywhere."

A sparkle of amusement lit her eyes, and he was glad to see a hint of the vibrant woman he sensed hidden beneath her quiet reserve. "Promise?"

"Aye." He offered her his hand.

She took it, allowed him to help her to her feet. Savoring the small victory, he released her and led her to the stable. "This is Maple. She's from Canada." The bay mare came right to her stable door and put her head over it to bump her nose into his chest, her eyes half-closing as Marcus gave the white blaze on her forehead a scratch. "Good lass."

"She's beautiful," Kiyomi said softly, reaching up to stroke the horse's cheek. Marcus had never been jealous of a horse before, but he couldn't help but imagine her hand on his skin instead, and lusting after a woman who was still struggling to overcome the trauma she'd been subjected to made him ashamed.

"Aye. You can help me groom her, then I'll saddle her up and get Jack ready."

"Jack?"

"My horse. Short for Jacobite's Revenge."

She laughed softly, the relaxed sound making him smile. "Let me guess, he's from Scotland?"

"Aye."

When the horses were ready, Marcus hooked his cane in the crook of his elbow to bring both animals into the stable yard and took Maple over to the mounting block. After putting a helmet on Kiyomi, he helped her into the saddle. Grasping her ankle to position her foot in the stirrup, he caught the glance she shot him from under her lashes, but she didn't pull away. "I'll hold onto the reins and walk beside you for now, so you can get comfortable," he told her. "Ready?"

At her nod, he led both horses out into the beautiful fall morning, Karas trotting out in front of them. The air was cool and crisp, carrying the scent of damp leaves and a faint whiff of wood smoke. Overhead the sky was dotted with fluffy white clouds, the rays of sunlight slanting through them making the dew-damp grass glisten.

"How do you feel?" he asked, watching Kiyomi closely. She looked relaxed, her posture perfect, if a little stiff. Were her ribs still bothering her?

"Fine so far." She aimed another smile at him, setting off a sharp twinge in his chest. Her smiles were so rare, being given one was like receiving a precious gift.

She was the quietest of the Valkyries here, though she might not always have been that way. Captivity and all the horrors that came with it changed a person.

He didn't like thinking about what had been done to her, or to imagine her doing the kinds of things Megan had told him an operative like Kiyomi would have carried out. She'd endured too much in her years of service to her country. War and espionage weren't pretty. Marcus admired her for being a survivor. Yet the most primal part of him rebelled at the thought of any other man touching her against her will. He wanted to help her, comfort her, protect her…

And offer other things that would probably either revolt or terrify her now.

He rolled his shoulders as a wave of self-loathing washed through him. "Not fine, brilliant," he corrected, leading her up the hill to the lower pasture. Maybe this impulsive decision hadn't been a good idea. He purposely limited his time with her because of his growing attraction, and because she held the power to test the restraint he prided himself on.

The steely core beneath that alluring exterior drew him the most powerfully of all.

He walked the horse up the slope, through the gate, and through the field. Karas loped ahead, then stopped to look back at them. Marcus threw the ball for her and she raced after it. "Ready for me to get on Jack now?" he asked Kiyomi. "I'll keep hold of your reins too if you want, but she'll follow me like a lamb without it."

"Okay."

He hid a smile. She wasn't sure about it but didn't want him to know she was nervous. Handing her Maple's reins, he made sure she was holding them properly before mounting Jack, putting him a few inches above her, then tucked his cane under his arm. Getting on a horse pulled at the damaged muscles in his hips and thigh. Getting off was worse.

"Right, off we go." He urged Jack into a walk, keeping a close eye on Kiyomi as Maple stayed close. "Awright?"

Kiyomi nodded, a grin tugging at her mouth. "She's totally following you."

"Aye, she's a good lass." They rode in silence through the upper pasture toward the hills.

"How is Eden settling in?" he asked a few minutes later. She and Trinity had gone down to London for a meeting.

"Pretty well, I think. It'll take time for her to really trust us, though."

"Aye, trust needs to be earned. The building of it can't be rushed."

The look she gave him was so full of meaning it triggered an echo deep inside him. "No, it can't." She went back to studying the terrain, no doubt reading it like a topographical map. "Where does Megan ride?"

"Through the tracks and bridle paths there," he said, gesturing to the rolling hills beyond it, bordered with lush green hedgerows and copses of trees turning amber and orange in the distance.

"It's beautiful. Can we go there?"

"Course." He angled them across the pasture, cutting toward one of the most used paths. "Reckon you're ready to try a trot now?"

She slanted him a sideways glance. "I can handle whatever you throw at me."

"Aye, I reckon you can." He clicked his tongue to set Jack into a trot, kept a close watch on Kiyomi as he gave her instructions on how to position herself in the stirrups and saddle.

After a few seconds, she broke into a laugh. "It's so bumpy!"

"Want something smoother?"

"Yes."

After giving Kiyomi a few quick pointers, he clicked his tongue and nudged Jack with his heels, sending him into an easy canter. Kiyomi instinctively leaned forward in the saddle a bit, a laugh bursting out of her. The happy sound made his heart swell.

They cantered side by side for a couple of minutes before Marcus slowed them to a walk.

"Did you know you would inherit all this one day?" she asked.

"No. I used to spend time here every summer as a

lad. I didn't know my great-uncle had named me to inherit the place until I was called to hear the reading of his will six years ago."

"It's so beautiful here." The wonder and enjoyment in her expression tugged at him. She made him feel things he hadn't felt in a very long time, woke parts of him he'd thought dead. Without even trying she'd lit the banked fire burning inside him, and it threatened to burst into an inferno at the first hint of encouragement from her.

"We should head back," he said abruptly, earning a questioning look from her.

"All right."

Taking her out here alone might not have been wise, but he didn't regret it. It only made him want more.

The others were unsaddling their horses when they arrived at the stable yard. Megan raised her eyebrows at him in surprise when he and Kiyomi rode up. He dismounted, hiding a grimace as the muscles in his hip grabbed, and came around to help Kiyomi, trying his damndest to disguise the worsening of his limp. "Drop the reins, lean forward and swing your right leg ov—"

Kiyomi swung her leg over Maple's rump and dropped lightly to the ground like she'd done it a thousand times before. Marcus automatically caught her waist to steady her, and just touching her that way sent a bolt of heat through him. He let her go like she'd burned him and stepped back, her scent swirling in his head as she turned to face him, unbuckling the helmet.

She took it off, looking up at him as her shiny black hair fell around her face, those liquid dark eyes fixed on his. "Thank you. I loved it."

"My pleasure." He took the helmet, stepped back so he could think straight. "I'll see to Maple." It came out like a dismissal, and that's how Kiyomi took it. She forced a smile, nodded, then joined Amber, Ty and Jesse as they headed to the house. It took all his discipline not to watch her go.

Megan stood by Rollo's stable as Marcus put Jack in his and started unsaddling Maple. "How'd she do?" she asked.

"She was brilliant." He wished they were still out there together. "How was shooting?"

"I only hit six reds. I'm getting rusty. Think we could put in some practice together this week?"

He smiled, the tension inside him easing. "Aye, I'd like that."

"Me too." She folded her arms and leaned back against the stall, ignoring Rollo as he lipped at her hair. "Did you ask her to ride, or did she ask you?"

Okay, now he was uncomfortable. Megan saw too much, knew him too well, and he had to be more careful about hiding his increasingly intense attraction toward Kiyomi. "I asked her." Pulling off the saddle and cloth beneath it, he strode over to hang them on the wall, knowing this conversation wasn't near over yet.

"She likes you. She trusts you."

Marcus released the saddle and turned to face her. "Aye. I'm glad of it."

Megan nodded, her expression troubled. "It's okay to live, you know. You don't need to keep punishing yourself."

It wasn't what he'd expected her to say.

Unable to hold her gaze, he looked away. Yes, he did need to keep punishing himself. And a washed-up cripple of an ex-soldier was the last thing a woman like Kiyomi needed anyway. She'd wouldn't want him now, and after what had happened in Syria, he was the last person who deserved happiness.

"Marcus."

"Leave it alone," he said, his voice quiet but firm.

Thankfully he was saved from whatever she'd been about to say in reply by the chime of his mobile, alerting him to a new message. He pulled it from his pocket, then tossed the brush to Megan. "Mind untacking Jack and giving Maple a brush down for me? Trinity and Eden are back, and they've brought our newest guest with them."

Grabbing his cane, he started for the doorway with Karas right at his heels. His once empty house was all but bursting at the seams. He had to make sure it remained secure.

Chapter Eight

This was their *headquarters*?

Zack gazed around in amazement as he stood in the entryway of Laidlaw Hall, feeling like he'd entered an alternate universe. Well, what was one more surprise in a day full of them? He sure as hell hadn't expected to wind up here when he'd woken up this morning.

He'd spent the two-plus-hour drive from London mostly making small talk with Trinity, and convincing himself he'd made the right decision in joining the team. He didn't owe the Agency anything, but Rod would rain shit down on him if he'd known what was really going on. Zack was now basically AWOL as far as the CIA was concerned.

Not that his handler or anyone else could track him at the moment, because as soon as he'd gotten in the car they'd taken his phone, switched if off and pulled out the SIM card, then swept him for electronic devices. Zack hadn't protested. They were right to be cautious and he was willing to take whatever consequences came his way, as long as it meant having time with Eden.

She'd barely said two words to him the entire trip, answering only when asked a direct question, and in as few words as possible. She might not love that he'd agreed to join their cause, but too damn bad. They had unfinished business, and if he could help find justice for John as well, then he wasn't going anywhere.

"This way," Eden said without looking at him as she started down the hallway.

He hurried to keep up with her as the owner, Marcus, followed Zack, his cane tapping on the worn stone floors and an Anatolian Shepherd-type dog at his side. Zack still didn't understand how Marcus fit into all this, and why he was letting the team stay here. This place was hundreds of years old and must be worth a damn fortune.

Eden walked out a doorway at the end of the hall into a formal, manicured garden, and along a path that led to a grassy area on one side of the house. He could hear feminine voices and laughter close by, as well as an occasional *thud* every few seconds.

As they rounded the side of the house, Zack stopped. Across a lush, neatly-trimmed lawn, four women were taking turns throwing knives into a target. Out in front of the group, a tall blonde reared her arm back and let what looked like a KA-BAR fly, hitting the center red circle with a solid *thunk*.

The other women started trash-talking. Then the one with chocolate-brown hair spotted them and alerted the others. Four pairs of eyes fastened on Zack.

"All right, fresh meat," the blonde said, grinning as she chewed her gum.

The chocolate-brown brunette rolled her eyes and shook her head. "Don't mind Chloe. I'm Megan," she said, stepping forward to offer her hand.

He shook it. "Zack Maguire."

"Yeah, I know. Welcome." She introduced him to the others, and he was surprised to learn that the other brunette was her older sister, Amber.

"So, Maguire," Chloe said, snapping her gum. "You ready for this?"

"Ready as I'll ever be."

The others snickered and Chloe kept grinning, seeming amused.

"So, these are the others," Eden said, sounding less than thrilled at having to make the introductions. "You'll meet the guys later. Now you might as well get settled in." Okay, and even less thrilled at him staying here. He had an uphill battle ahead of him if he was going to make any headway with her, and he needed to know the truth about what had happened between them.

"Megan will show you to your room, if you're ready to go up," Marcus said in his accented voice, reaching a hand down to scratch behind the dog's ears.

"Sure." He'd rather Eden do it, but he was smart enough not to push too hard for the time being. Seemed she planned to give him as wide a berth as possible while he was here. Unfortunately for her, he wasn't going to allow it. And then there was his dad, who was going to be crushed that Zack's promised visit home wouldn't be happening anytime soon.

He followed Megan back inside and up to the third floor, mentally piecing everything together. From what Trinity had told him, all the guys living here were former military—some SOF—and thoroughly vetted by Rycroft's people before being invited here to join the team. Zack was still fuzzy on all the legal details of this thing, but if Rycroft was heading it up, then he must have found enough loopholes and gray areas to make it work.

"You and Eden are the only ones up here aside from Marcus," Megan told him as they reached the landing on the third story. "Everyone else is on the second floor. Well, Marcus would call it the first floor, because they classify it differently here in the UK. Anyway…here's you." She opened the second door down the hall. "Your room's probably a lot girlier than you're used to, but it's one of the most masculine in the house."

She stepped aside to let him into the room done in a

medium gray tone. A dark, antique four-poster took up most of one wall. His suitcase was already beside it. "This is great."

"Glad you like it."

"Where's Eden's room?"

Megan met his gaze, her curiosity clear. "Across the hall and down two."

He nodded and took a look into the en suite bathroom. Whoa. This was by far the nicest place he'd ever stayed, and it put him close to Eden, so bonus. "So what happens now?"

"We're meeting downstairs in a bit to get everyone on the same page as far as recent developments go. We used to meet in Marcus's study, but it's pretty much the only room left that he can escape from us all now. There are so many of us here now that the library's a better size anyway."

"Lead the way."

She smiled, her eyes full of curiosity. "I plan to."

Down on the main level the library was off to the left, a large room stuffed with built-in bookcases, comfortable-looking furniture, and a bank of tall windows at the far end that let in lots of natural light. The room smelled faintly of wood smoke. Three men and all the women except Eden were already assembled, and they were all staring at him. Sizing him up.

This was where Zack excelled. He was an expert at making people feel comfortable and getting them to talk to him. He went straight over and introduced himself to the guys, even got a couple laughs from them, but when Eden stepped inside a moment later, he swore the air charged with an electric current.

He couldn't take his eyes off her. She'd changed into a feminine, blue top that hugged her breasts. She'd also let her hair down, all those sexy curls falling around her face and shoulders.

She kept her distance, standing at the back of the group and folded her arms, her expression unreadable as she avoided looking at him. All that did was confirm she was very much aware of his presence. Good.

Being surrounded by all these Valkyries wasn't exactly comfortable, but he'd taken way worse assignments in the past. Individually these women were lethal, with a ninety-five-percent success rate on their targets. Together? They could topple powerful organizations and destabilize governments.

This is the shit I saw on the news.

Every one of these women was a force to be reckoned with, legends within the operative and intel community, and here he was with six of them in the same room—had been romantically involved with one for months without realizing it. Unreal.

Eden had duped him completely, and if everything people said about the Valkyries was true—and he was pretty sure it was—then he was damn lucky she hadn't just offed him before walking out of that hotel room that final morning, to protect herself and keep things neat and tidy. It made him wonder why she hadn't simply killed him.

Because she cared about me, at least on some level. It was the only thing that made sense, and before this was all done, he wanted to hear it from her own lips.

"Okay, everyone's here, and you've all met Zack," Trinity said, moving to stand in front of the fireplace where a few logs burned in the grate. "He's been briefed on the basics on the way here, and will be providing his intel expertise, so now I'm going to talk about our latest mission."

She lifted the tablet in her hands and held the screen so everyone could see the picture of the strawberry-blond woman on it. "This is Penny, and she's the last surviving Valkyrie we've been able to identify. Given the state of things and the current security situation facing us all, she's obviously in grave danger. So far all attempts to contact her have come to nothing. But thanks to the intel on the thumb drive Eden's handler provided her, we think we have a possible location for her. Zack will be working with Amber more on this to confirm, and I'll be their link with Rycroft and the analysts Stateside."

"Where's Penny now?" Eden asked.

"Best we can figure, Edinburgh," Trinity answered. "But we'll need Zack to look at the files Chris gave you, and analyze them further with Amber before we can be sure it's a good place to start looking for her."

"Do we know what she's doing there?" Chloe asked, her arm around Heath, a former Pararescueman.

Trinity nodded. "We think she's hunting an escaped war criminal. Both Eden and Zack are familiar with him."

Alexei Popovich.

Eden's gaze shot to Zack, understanding in her expression. "That's why you were at the dinner in Sevastopol. You were gathering intel on Popovich."

"Yes." Until Terzi had mysteriously been poisoned...by her, killing the entire operation.

Trinity lifted an eyebrow at him. "You ready to get to work?"

"Ready." He had a fake cover that would still work and allow him access to some of his old contacts, so he should be able to get answers about Popovich, and maybe Penny as well.

"Good. Once you and Amber verify the likelihood of Penny being in Edinburgh, we'll get moving."

Everyone listened as Trinity handed out their assignments. If they confirmed Penny was likely in Edinburgh, he, Eden and Trinity would fly out tonight on a private jet and start the search as soon as they arrived in the city. From there, it was wait and see, but if anyone had a shot at finding her, it was another Valkyrie.

When the meeting broke up everyone went to the kitchen to grab something to eat, but Eden headed left. Zack followed her outside into the formal garden where she stood near a fishpond close to the stone wall in the far corner.

"You should eat," she said without looking at him as he approached. "It's gonna be a late night."

"I'll get something in a bit." He hated this awkwardness between them.

She blew out a breath as she looked across the garden. "Why did you say yes?"

"Why do you think?"

She eyed him coolly. "If I knew that, I wouldn't have asked."

"Because of you," he said after a beat.

His answer made her uncomfortable enough to look away. "Why, you still thinking about turning me in?"

"You think I would?"

She shrugged. "I don't know what you're capable of now. I don't know *you*."

Yeah, she did. Way more than he knew her, and that put him at a huge disadvantage, especially since she didn't trust him anymore. "That goes both ways, though, doesn't it? Because it turns out I never knew you either."

She was silent a moment, then lowered her gaze to the pond. "Look, I'm sorry for leaving the way I did, and severing contact. But I had no choice."

"Didn't you?"

Those gorgeous honey-brown eyes swung back to his. "Not that I could see. Chris had warned me that Valkyries were being systematically hunted. I had to go to ground."

"Did you know I was a CIA contractor when we met?"

"Yes."

Anger sparked inside him. "Then why didn't you

come to me for help?"

She didn't answer, just held his stare, and her silence told him everything. Because he worked with the CIA she hadn't trusted that he wasn't involved in the hunt somehow. Some part of her hadn't been sure if he might be trying to get close to her to extract intel on other Valkyries, then kill her.

Everything in him recoiled at the thought. He would never hurt her, ever, not even if he'd been ordered to. He couldn't. That wasn't how he was wired.

Pushing aside his frustration, he shoved all that into a box for later. "And now? Do you still think I pose a threat to you?"

Her soft chuckle held a bitter edge that made his skin tighten. "Oh, I know you do. But this is for the greater good, so I don't have any choice but to deal with it." She turned and walked away before he could answer, leaving him standing there and fighting the urge to go after her, have everything out here and now.

Zack ran a hand over his face, hit with a barrage of emotions. But most of all, he felt bereft. Sad for the loss of everything they'd had for that brief time together. That it had all been based on lies.

One thing hadn't changed, however. He wanted to see if another shot was possible for them. To move past everything that had happened before and see if they could start over. To find out if they could have something *real* together now that they both knew the truth.

No matter what had happened in the past, he wanted to reclaim what he'd lost with Eden, more now than ever. He just hoped her feelings for him hadn't all been in his head.

Chapter Nine

"A re you there yet?" Glenn asked the man on the other end of the phone. He was in his car again, the safest place for him to make these kinds of calls. It was six in the morning here, and eleven in Edinburgh. That didn't give the contract hitter a lot of time to find their target.

"Yeah, and I hope you've got a good tip to give me a solid starting point."

"Her legal name's Penny Green. She's been sighted recently in Sweden and the UK. We have reason to believe she's been tracking Alexei Popovich."

"Wasn't he accused of war crimes?"

"Yes. If we're right, she'll be in Edinburgh to target him at some point over the next three days, beginning tonight. Once she does, she'll get out of the country as quickly as possible, probably by boat, so you need to find her before she makes her move. I'll send you his known itinerary in an encrypted file, as well as any up-to-date hits on her from facial recognition."

"What kind of proof do you want when it's done?"

"The usual." Photos and a tissue or blood sample he could use to verify the body was hers. "I'll send you the file now. Keep me updated if you find anything."

"You got it."

"Again, this is between you and me."

"Understood."

Glenn disconnected and continued down the country road, driving away from the inn he'd stayed at last night. Still no word about Eden or the others. The female handler was dead and so was the hitter Glenn had sent after them, but now Eden was missing. Until he found definitive proof otherwise, he had to assume she was still alive.

He'd checked the hospitals and morgues in the area near the hits but hadn't found anything on Eden, and hadn't been able to find any travel information on her either. She'd disappeared, vanished like the ghost she'd been trained to be, and he didn't know how the hell he was going to find her now.

The only thing scarier than having a Valkyrie gunning for you was when she disappeared off the grid. His network of resources was limited now that he was officially off the Agency payroll. Anything he needed had to be paid for on his own dime, so he'd planned all this out carefully.

Hopefully Penny Green would be the key to unraveling the mystery of where the other Valkyries were hiding. For now, he had pent-up energy to unleash.

His personal cell rang, his wife's number appearing on screen. For a moment he thought about ignoring it, but he didn't need any more suspicion on her end. "Hello."

"Where were you last night?" she demanded.

Glenn shoved back the sudden surge of anger at her tone. He was on edge and in no mood for female bullshit. "I told you, I had a late meeting." Not completely a lie. The best liars knew to always stick as close to the truth as possible, and he was an expert.

"Well, are you coming home today?"

"No, not for a few days."

She made a frustrated sound. "You've been promising for weeks that you'd fix the guest bathroom shower before my sister came. I was going to hire someone and you told me not to, that you'd handle it, and she's coming in tomorrow."

What the fuck did he care about a shower or anything else right now? His instincts were jangling, on high alert for the threat he knew was out there but couldn't find.

That's because you won't see it. You won't know it's there until it's too late.

"Glenn?" she pressed.

"Just call the plumber. I don't know when I'll be home."

A few seconds of taut silence passed. "When you retired you promised things would be different, but here you are still having secret meetings and not coming home, not telling me what's going on." She paused. "Are you having an affair?"

That offended him. "*No.*"

"I swear to God, if you're cheating on me…"

"I'm not. Christ, Annie." That's what she thought was going on here? Yeah, he'd been a shitty husband in a lot of other ways over the years because of his work. Yeah, he'd cheated on her once, and look where it had landed him.

He'd been thinking with his dick instead of his brain, had even thought he might be falling in love with the woman, who was a master manipulator. She'd played him like a violin and he hadn't even realized it until it was too late. He was still paying for that mistake, and would never do it again.

"You've been acting weird for weeks now," she continued, sounding dejected.

"I'm not having a fucking affair," he growled. Jesus. Dangerous people were closing in on him, and he was trying to figure out a way to get to them first.

"Then what are you doing?"

"I'm dealing with something. Something important."

"But you're still not going to tell me."

"I can't."

She gave a bitter laugh. "Wow. The more things change, the more they stay the same."

He ran a hand over his face, exhaustion hitting him all of a sudden. He'd barely slept the last few nights. In his twenties and thirties, he could run on almost no sleep. Not anymore. "Look, I'm still in the area, but it's…" *Not safe for me to come home.* "I think you should take Kimmie and your sister up to the lake for a few days."

Another tense pause filled the line. "Why, what's going on?"

"I can't tell you." For her own safety, and their daughter's. "I think it might be a good time for you to be at the cabin with your parents." Her parents had owned it for decades, and that way she and their daughter would be surrounded by people, making them a less vulnerable target.

"Jesus, Glenn, what the hell's going on?" Fear was evident in her voice.

His past sins were catching up with him. And when they did, he didn't want his family to wind up collateral damage. "It's going to be fine. I'm taking care of it." He didn't want to cause her more alarm than he had to. And he sure as fuck didn't want her to know what he'd done.

"When are you coming home?"

"As soon as I can. But I can't give you a timeframe on this." Not until he ended this potential threat.

"Are you safe?"

"Yes." For now. "I love you."

She sighed. "I love you too. You'll update me when you can?"

"Yes. Kiss Kimmie for me."

An uncomfortable tension spread through his gut as

he ended the call. How fucking ironic that with all the things he'd done on ops for the Agency, he'd never been worried for his family's safety before, and now that he was retired, he was. This whole thing was haunting him, never giving him a moment's peace. It had been a long time since his days as a field officer, and even longer since he'd been in the military. He'd worked damn hard to stay in shape and maintain his skills. He could still hold his own with the best of them.

If the Valkyries came for him, he would be ready.

He headed for the highway, watching closely to make sure he didn't have a tail following him. At the gun range he took his weapons out of the trunk in their cases. Shooting was a perishable skill, it degraded without consistent practice. He'd made sure not to let that happen.

The range officer broke into a grin when Glenn walked in. "Bennett. Back for more already?"

"What can I say, I'm addicted."

"I know the feeling."

He took Glenn through to the range out back, watched as Glenn set up his rifle. "Want me to spot you?"

"Sure." He'd start with the long gun, then move to close quarters-style shooting with his pistol after.

Lying prone on his belly with his cheek pressed to the stock of the rifle, the butt of it tight to his shoulder, a sense of calm overtook him. Everything else faded away as he stared through the scope at the target in the distance and adjusted the focus.

Finger on the trigger, he cleared his mind of everything but the center of the target, letting muscle memory and training take over. Exhaling, he waited until all the air had left his lungs, then fired. A metallic ping sounded a second later.

"Hit, right center," the range master said, then grinned at him. "Man, I love watching you work."

Glenn ignored him, focused on the target. He'd

missed the center by several inches, when he needed to be hitting dead center on the first shot every time. He adjusted his scope again, readied for the next shot.

He didn't care what the Architect thought or said. If the remaining Valkyries were working together, it was only a matter of time before they uncovered the truth. His gut said that time was now. He had to stop them, keep sending hitters out every time he had a lock on one of them, and be ready for anything.

Glenn was done waiting, so he'd taken control. It was a race against time now, a case of kill or be killed. He was *not* going to be brought down by the same operatives he had helped create.

****

Eden pulled the hood of her coat down lower over her forehead as she climbed the steep, narrow stairs up Advocate's Close in Edinburgh's Old Town. She paused at the top, taking in the sound of the people walking past and the rain hitting the stone pavers beyond the archway.

The imposing structure of St. Giles' Cathedral stood directly across from her, looming over the street. She stepped out onto High Street and turned right toward the castle, making her way up the incline toward the next location she had to check.

The old city center was still busy for a rainy fall evening. Groups of tourists hugged the front walls of shops on the sidewalk as she passed them, trying to stay dry. A lone piper stood near the top of Castle Hill, the mournful skirl of his pipes drifting through the air as the incredible silhouette of torch-lit Edinburgh Castle rose above the gloom behind him.

She scanned the street constantly, alert for any sign of a threat or someone following her as she made her way to the flat she needed to check out. The unit was half a block up on the third floor of a tall stone building built in the mid-seventeen-hundreds.

Ducking into the alcove, she took the spiral stone staircase to the fifth story, her blade strapped to her calf beneath her jeans and her pistol securely tucked into its holster in the back of her waistband.

According to Amber this flat had no security camera outside it. Eden checked anyway to verify that before approaching the bright cobalt blue door and peering through the window beside it. The Roman blind was drawn but there was enough room in the small gap at the bottom for her to see inside. The window looked directly into a small living room and kitchen, lit by the lantern hanging overhead in the entryway.

Inside, the place was immaculate, no shoes or other items in the foyer to the left, no dishes in the sink or anything on the counter. It was a rental unit in a prime location, and booked constantly. The cleaners had come in after the most recent guests had checked out that morning, but as far as she could tell, no one else had arrived yet, least of all Penny. A Valkyrie would never have left a gap at the bottom of the blind for someone to see inside.

Eden stepped back to glance around, having already decided this place was a dud. She doubted Penny would stay here. It was too close to the Royal Mile, too many people around who might see her.

She pulled out her phone and sent a text to Trinity and Zack.

Location delta clear. Heading back now.

At the bottom of the stairs she stepped back out into the cold rain and made her way across the wide street, the sound of the pipes following her. Edinburgh had atmosphere in spades but she didn't have time to stop and appreciate it.

They had to find Penny before she got to her target and put herself at serious risk of getting killed. Her cover was likely blown. Popovich had his own private security detail, and so did a lot of other men he was here to meet with. The likelihood of Penny walking away after killing him was almost zero.

On the other side of the Royal Mile, Eden turned down Victoria Street, passing the brightly-colored shops and restaurants on her way down to Grassmarket at the bottom of the hill. She passed more cafés and restaurants, then took King's Stable's Road past St. Cuthbert's, crossed Princes Street and finally made her way up Charlotte Street.

Her jeans were soaked from the lower thigh down as she let herself into the flat their team had rented for the night. She pulled off her wet coat as Trinity emerged from one of the bedrooms, phone in hand. "I struck out too. Zack just texted that he's on his way back now. Hope he had better luck than we did."

Eden didn't like that he'd been sent out on his own tonight. Amber was monitoring his phone and movements, but he could buy a burner or have face-to-face meetings with someone and they would never know. Zack was invested in finding out who had sent John to kill her and Chris, then had him killed, not necessarily anything else. "Yeah, let's hope."

Time was ticking, and their best hope of finding Penny was probably locating her target and then lying in wait for her to show up. Much as she didn't like it, with his connections and social skills, Zack had the best chance of determining Popovich's whereabouts.

Another mistake was in thinking that with the initial tension broken between them, things would get easier. She'd been wrong. It was increasingly difficult to be around him with every minute they spent in each other's company. He was so much like he was when they'd been together. He *seemed* sincere about his commitment to the team, but she was still skeptical about his motives.

"Any of the locations you checked seem likely for her to rent?" Trinity asked.

"No, none." According to the most recent intel Amber and Zack had analyzed, Penny had been in hiding for months and had a long list of enemies, including the war criminal Popovich. He was due at a meeting in Edinburgh in the morning, so logic dictated he was probably in the city already.

If they were going to save Penny, it had to be tonight.

Two rapid knocks on the door signaled Zack had arrived. Eden steeled herself but the moment he stepped inside and their eyes met, it was suddenly hard to breathe.

Since seeing him in London she'd been trying not to think about them together, and failing miserably. Everything reminded her of him, and the memories were so damn vivid. His smile, the deep sound of his laugh. The way he'd looked at her, like she was the most beautiful, incredible woman in the world. His *touch*. Lighting up her whole body with only the graze of his fingertips. The feel of him on top of her. *Inside* her.

Now every time she saw him it was like a punch to the gut. She ached for him still, and part of her desperately wanted to find out how much of what they'd shared was real, and how much was lies. She'd told herself it was mostly lies, to make it easier. But not knowing for sure was eating away at her insides.

"Find him?" Trinity asked, standing.

Zack nodded, wiping rain from his face. It glinted on his dark hair and few days' worth of growth on his face. "He's at The Balmoral with a security team. My contact there said things have been calm there all night. When I fished a little, he didn't seem to know anything about Penny, but there's a dinner Popovich is scheduled to be at in two hours."

"And you're sure your source is reliable?" Eden asked.

He turned those piercing gray eyes on her, and something tightened in her chest. "Yes."

The conviction in his voice and the sincerity in his expression looked so damn real. "And your handler? Did you call him back yet?" Amber had alerted them that Zack had been contacted two hours ago.

Zack nodded, not seeming surprised that she knew about it. "He offered me another contract, which I turned down. He knows I'm in Edinburgh, but not why, or with who."

"Did he fish for any information about us?" Trinity asked.

"No. And even if he had, I wouldn't have given it to him." His gaze swung back to Eden. "I ditched the burner outside the Balmoral."

She relaxed a little more, though she'd feel even better once Amber had confirmed what the conversation had entailed. And if there had been a problem, Amber would have alerted them already. "We've only got one location left to search for Penny. If she's not there, we're gonna have to start all over from scratch." And in a hurry, too. If Penny planned to target Popovich at the dinner tonight, that didn't give them much time to intercept her.

"Let's get going, then," Trinity said, pulling on her coat and tucking her weapon away. This time they all wore earpieces to communicate with one another. "You two go together and approach from the east. I'll go in from the west."

Eden turned for the door without looking at Zack, shoving aside the tumult inside her and locking into op mode. He was trained. If shit went down, he could handle himself.

The rain had eased up slightly, now falling in a steady rhythm instead of a chaotic downpour. Streetlamps and headlights glistened off the wet cobbles as they walked up the street together, heading for Stockbridge, just north of Edinburgh's New Town.

It started out comfortable enough. But with each passing minute, everything left unsaid between them weighed heavier and heavier, until she was struggling to maintain her vigilance through sheer determination alone.

"Think she'll be there?" Zack finally asked a few minutes later, halfway to their destination.

"Hope so." The sooner they intercepted her and got her out of here, the sooner they could switch gears and start focusing on finding the masterminds behind all this death and destruction.

"And none of you know her?"

"No. But there used to be more of us, so I'm sure someone did."

A man stepped out of the shadows as they reached the opposite sidewalk. Zack instantly shot out a hand to grasp Eden's waist and stepped in front of her, but the man merely hunched deeper into his hoodie and kept walking.

The protective move was so foreign to her, she didn't know how to react. Then she shrugged out of Zack's hold and continued up the street, annoyed at how easily he threw her body and mind into chaos. One simple touch even with the barrier of clothes in the way, and her whole system was humming with awareness and need. If he ever touched her with intent, she wasn't sure she'd have the strength to stop him.

Thankfully he maintained a bit of space between them for the rest of the journey. Less than ten minutes later they'd reached the row of flats that followed the curving line of the road that bordered a small oval-shaped park across the street. Eden headed around back to the alley behind the long building, just as a lone female figure emerged from the shadows at the far end.

Trinity.

With Zack right behind Eden, she headed for the rear

steps of number nineteen. At the bottom she turned to signal for him to stay put, then two faint pops suddenly broke the quiet.

She and Zack both spun around to face the rear of the flat.

Eden tapped her earpiece. "Suppressed gunshots," she whispered to Trinity, scanning for signs of movement.

"Copy. I'll head around front."

Eden's pulse kicked up as she stared at the back of the flat through the gloom, Zack just behind her. Then a crash came from inside.

If Penny was inside, she was under attack.

Drawing her weapon, Eden charged for the back door. Before she could reach it Zack shot past her, pistol in hand as he drew his foot up and kicked at the old lock. Two kicks and the lock gave. He shoved the door open with his shoulder, swept the entrance with his weapon. "I'll go left," he whispered.

They surged inside, scanning the darkened interior. He went left, Eden went right.

She crept forward slowly now, rocking her weight from heel to the ball of each foot as she searched her side of the main floor. Streetlamps cast a faint glow through the windows on either side of the front door, spilling over the hardwood floor.

A sound captured her attention. Something moving just out of sight in the room closest to the front door.

She and Zack both stopped. Eden whipped her weapon around the corner and peered into a small sitting room. Then froze.

A woman lay sprawled out on her stomach on the floor. Still alive, hands weakly moving over the hardwood as if she was trying to pull herself forward, a dark trail of blood marking her slow, painful progress. The killer could have gone out the front door while Zack was kicking the back one open.

"Sweep the rest," she said to Zack, then holstered her weapon and rushed over to kneel beside the woman.

Her head was turned toward Eden. There was just enough light coming through the edges of the blind covering the window to allow her to see the woman's face.

Eden's heart sank. *No*... "Penny?"

The woman's eyes lifted to hers, the labored sound of her shattered breaths filling the room. Strawberry-blond hair, brown eyes, freckles. Right build. A pistol lay just out of reach of her right hand, and she held what looked like a go bag in her left.

Jesus, no. "It's Penny," she told Trinity and Zack. "She's hit bad."

"I'm pursuing the shooter," Trinity said, her voice uneven as she ran. "Thirty-ish male, dark hoodie and jeans, heading west."

"Copy," she answered, already doing an assessment on Penny. She'd been shot twice, center mass. Both rounds had gone out through her back, leaving larger exit wounds. Eden grabbed the bag in Penny's hand and rummaged through it, finding some bandages and pressure dressings they always took with them on missions. "Just stay still," she told Penny, keeping her voice calm even though her heart rate was elevated.

"G-gone," Penny wheezed.

"The shooter?"

"Place is clear," Zack said, coming up behind her. "Where's she hit?"

"Chest. Call an ambulance."

"Already did." He knelt beside Penny and helped Eden turn her over onto her back. But there was so much blood already.

She leaned over Penny, held that shocked, anguished gaze. "Penny, we're here to help you. I'm Eden, and this is Zack."

Penny opened her mouth. Blood spilled from the corner of it, dripping onto the floor. Eden pulled on a pair of latex gloves in the go bag and pressed down harder on the entry wounds, letting Penny's weight and gravity press on the exit wounds. She'd lost too much blood. The bullets had hit her lungs, and probably her heart.

"Penny, who shot you?" she asked, leaning close, willing the other woman to hold on. She needed an IV immediately to keep her blood volume up before her heart gave out. The ambulance was Penny's only chance. "Did you see him?"

Penny's eyelids fluttered. Her lips moved, then she grimaced and choked on her own blood.

Shit. Immediately they rolled her onto her side to try and make it easier for her to breathe. "Who shot you, Penny?" Eden said urgently. "Who came after you?"

Penny jerked, a terrible rasping sound locking in her throat, then convulsed, her body desperately fighting for oxygen.

No, no, no… "Penny, stay with me. The ambulance is almost here." Anything to get Penny to hold on. "I need you to fight, Valkyrie."

Even as the convulsions grew weaker, those brown eyes lifted to lock with Eden's, a heartbreaking flare of recognition there.

Eden bent to cup Penny's face in her hands. "That's right, sister. I'm one of us. Loyal Unto Death. I'm not leaving you."

Through the agony and fear, surprise filled those wide brown eyes. And then tears. Penny stopped struggling, her chest barely moving now. But she held Eden's gaze, the hope and relief there heartbreaking as it mixed with something else. Resignation.

She knew she was about to die, with a fellow Valkyrie beside her.

Too late. Too fucking *late*!

"We've found you," Eden said, putting on a reassuring smile. If that was the last thing Penny saw on this earth, hopefully it would bring some measure of peace. "You're not alone anymore."

That stare remained locked with Eden's, but then the light in Penny's eyes changed. Dimmed. Her features went slack, her lids half-closing, eyes staring at nothing as the life drained out of her.

"Fuck," Eden snapped, easing back onto her heels, her chest about to explode. They'd found Penny, but too late, and now she was dead. "She's gone," she said to Trinity, voice hoarse.

"Dammit. Okay, I'm coming back to you now. Meet me in the back and bring Penny out. We're taking her home."

Home. Where was home, for any of them? "What about the shooter?"

"Tell you in a few minutes."

Heartsick and suddenly so damn tired, Eden swallowed and pushed to her feet. "Copy that." She could feel Zack watching her, still kneeling beside Penny.

"I'm sorry," he said quietly.

Eden nodded, staring down at the other Valkyrie. She was young. Mid-to-late twenties, maybe. She might not have known Penny personally, but Eden still felt like she knew her. They were all sisters in a way, with only each other to count on now.

She set her jaw. It wasn't fair. Wasn't right. If they'd shown up a few minutes earlier, they could have gotten her out safely. If they'd gotten here in time, they could have whisked Penny onto the plane waiting on standby and given her protection. A new life.

"I'm going to find some blankets to wrap her in," she said, ruthlessly shutting off her emotions. They had to be out of here by the time the ambulance arrived to avoid any more problems.

She found some upstairs in a linen closet. When she came back down, Zack had already positioned Penny on her back, hands clasped at her waist, and he had closed her eyes.

Steeling herself, Eden handed him a blanket. Together they wrapped Penny up, and Zack carried her to the back door.

"I'm here," Trinity announced a moment later through Eden's earpiece.

A silver van was parked on the sidewalk, its side door slid open.

Eden checked up and down the street to ensure no one was watching. "Hurry," she said, wanting to be away from here, and for this awful night to be over.

Zack rushed out with Penny in his arms and climbed into the back. Eden shut the side door, then hopped in the front passenger seat and slammed the door. "Go."

Trinity took off up the alley. "Amber's cancelled the ambulance and is calling in a clean up crew."

"What happened to the shooter?" Eden asked, eyes on the road. She couldn't stand to look back and see Penny wrapped in those blankets where Zack had laid her on the floor.

"Ran his motorcycle into the side of a truck a block away."

"Suicide?"

"Maybe. I've got his prints." Trinity turned onto a main road and accelerated. "Did she tell you anything?"

"No. She was too far-gone. Hitter shot her twice, center mass."

Trinity was quiet for a few moments, the spray from the wet tires and the whir of the windshield wipers the only sounds in the vehicle. "We'll transport her back Stateside for burial, and make sure she's honored."

Eden glanced at her in confusion. Valkyries were ghosts long before they died. And when they did, there was no one to mourn them, no grave to mark their final resting place. "Honored? With what?"

Trinity's hands flexed on the steering wheel. "With a star on the wall in the CIA memorial at Langley, same as the others."

Chapter Ten

Zack waited until they were back at the manor house before approaching Eden.

She'd spent the short flight from Edinburgh with Trinity, talking to Amber on the phone. They'd tried to determine how the hitter had found Penny, and who he was. Upon landing they'd left Penny's body at the airport, to be transported back to the States on another flight. Trinity had set it up with Rycroft, who would handle the burial.

"It's been a long night," Trinity said as they reached the front door just before midnight. "I'm turning in for a while. See you guys in the morning."

"Sure," Eden said as they stepped inside. The house was quiet, everyone else asleep except for Amber, who was working in her room. "I'm going up too."

Zack caught her arm to stop her from leaving. "Can I talk to you a minute?"

She gave him a wary look, then nodded. "Fine. One minute."

What he had to say would take longer than a minute, and he wanted privacy. "Let's take a walk."

For a moment he thought she'd refuse, but then she

nodded and stepped back outside.

"Are you okay?" he asked as they took the gravel path along the back of the house. She had to be upset about Penny, tough act or not.

"Yeah. Just disappointed and angry."

Zack still wasn't sure how much of the real Eden he'd known back when they'd been together. She was closed-off now, so different than the relaxed, carefree woman he'd known. He wanted to know this one too, so much it wound him up inside.

It had rained all night in Edinburgh, but here the skies were clear. A bright half-moon lit their way as they headed around the side of the house and up the lawn toward the pasture bordering the stable. He had so much to say. God, where to start?

He kept his hands in his coat pockets, an extra deterrent to keep from touching her. There was no point in delaying this conversation any longer. Keeping it inside was killing him. "I looked for you after you left me," he said quietly, unable to stand the distance and hurt and lies between them a second longer. "I never stopped looking for you."

She stopped beside him, staring out at the moonlit hills surrounding them as the silence spread. "I didn't want to hurt you. Or to put you in danger."

"You knew what I did, who I was. But you didn't trust me, or that I could make that decision for myself?"

She finally looked at him, and the impact of her gaze nearly drove the breath from his lungs. In that moment he was finally seeing her for who she truly was. A woman who'd spent her life as a weapon, moving from one op to another, never getting close to anyone. Except him. "It was too dangerous. For both of us."

He absorbed that in silence for a moment. He was sick of lies and secrets and half-truths. "Was any of it real?" *Please say some of it was real.*

Her expression shuttered before she broke eye contact and stared out at the surrounding hills. She was silent for so long he didn't think she would answer. Then, "I was more real with you than I've ever been with anyone else."

It came out so quietly he barely heard her, but her words made his heart pound. "How real?"

She slanted him a look but didn't answer.

He pushed. "Which is the real you? The woman I knew, or the one standing in front of me now?"

"Both," she said after a moment. "The one you saw was the one I always wished I could have been."

The answer made his whole chest hurt. She'd never been free to be who she wanted, who she truly was inside. The Program had taken away her choice. He couldn't imagine living like that, hated that she'd had to. "Then that must mean you felt safe with me before."

She still wouldn't look at him, but nodded. "You made me wish my life could have been different."

His whole body tightened. It took all his restraint not to reach for her, pull her close and ease the burning ache in his chest. To take away the loneliness he sensed in her. "Maybe it can be now."

"No, it can't." She met his gaze again and he could sense the battle now, the yearning pitted against her need to stay detached. "How much of it was real with you?"

There was no point in lying. He still wanted her, more than ever. "All of it. Except that I was working for the CIA. Which you already knew about." He'd been more authentic with her than anyone else.

"It's not a good idea."

"Why the hell not? I know the truth about you now, and I'm still here. I set my career aside to help you and this team, and even though you don't trust me completely, I haven't turned any of you in." What more did he have to do to prove himself to her?

Eden exhaled and shook her head, her dark curls

bouncing against her shoulders. "Christ, I was stupid to stay with you as long as I did."

"Why?" he demanded. Why was she denying herself the possibility when the proof of the others was right in front of her?

"Because I should have gone to ground immediately when the threat against me first broke, but I didn't. I broke all the rules to be with you, and it almost got me killed."

"What do you mean," he said, a chill spreading through him.

She let out a hard exhalation. "Someone must have seen me go into the hotel at St. Petersburg. They caught up with me partway to the train station, would have shot me dead if I hadn't noticed him at the last moment and acted first."

Jesus. "I didn't know."

"I know. But I was playing with fire every time I met you. I knew it, and kept going back for more anyway. I won't make that mistake again."

Refusing to accept that, dying to touch her, Zack took her by the upper arms and turned her to face him. "Then tell me you don't still feel it," he challenged, holding her gaze. "Tell me you don't still want me."

"It doesn't matter what I want."

The hell it didn't. And that wasn't a no.

Desperate to get through to her, break through that barrier she hid behind, he cupped her head in his hands and covered her lips with his. She stiffened, her hands going to his chest, but instead of pushing him away she gripped the tops of his shoulders and kissed him back.

It was like a chemical reaction. Just like it had always been between them.

Zack groaned and hauled her to him, pulling her as close as he could while he slanted his mouth across hers, relearning the feel and taste of her. She didn't hold back, her fingers sliding into his hair as her tongue stroked his, those firm curves plastered to the front of him, making him hard all over.

It had been so long. So damn long since he'd been able to feel her, lose himself in her. The sensual, urgent way she kissed him set his whole body on fire.

"Eden," he groaned. "I missed you so goddamn much. It tore me up not knowing what happened to you, or what I'd done wrong."

"Stop talking," she gasped out.

No way. He'd bottled this up for long enough. Now that he had her in his arms again he couldn't hold it in. "I want to lay you down right here," he said between kisses. "Want to strip you and pin you right here in the grass and make you come with my tongue."

Eden moaned and kissed him harder. She'd never been shy about what she wanted with him. God he missed the way she let go for him, the sounds she made. He would never get enough.

His hands moved over her restlessly, greedy for the feel of her, mapping every curve. Knowing the truth about her had only made the hunger worse.

He wrapped an arm around her hips, locking her to him, his other hand now splayed in her thick curls. This was real. No matter what they'd pretended before, this amazing heat and connection between them was real and all the more intense because they both knew the truth about each other now.

She rubbed against him, seeking more. Zack skimmed his hand up her ribs to cup a breast, triumph soaring inside him when she arched and gasped, momentarily breaking the kiss.

They stared at each other, faces inches apart. He drank in the arousal on her face, the way her eyes slid shut when he rubbed his thumb across the nipple straining against the thin fabric of her sweater and bra.

"Zack," she whispered, gripping his hand as she

pressed her forehead to his shoulder.

The vulnerable edge to her voice pierced him. He gathered her to him, held her close while he kissed her temple, her cheek, the side of her jaw. Her body was taut with a pent-up need he would kill to satisfy, her breathing ragged. "What?" he murmured.

Her fingers dug hard into his back, her short nails pricking him through his shirt. "I can't think straight around you. I can't do this again." She sounded miserable. "I can't afford to be that weak again."

He closed his eyes and hugged her tighter, the protective, possessive part of him refusing to let go. "I want you back, Eden. I'll never stop wanting you back."

"Wanting's not enough, and you don't even know me."

Yes, he did. She'd just told him he'd seen a side of her that no one else ever had. And that meant everything. "Then let me in so I can."

She made a frustrated sound and pressed her head harder into his shoulder, her breath creating a warm patch on his shirt. "I've never…"

"Never what," he whispered, wishing he knew what to say, what to do that would make her let go of her fear and mistrust and open herself to him again.

"Only one person really ever knew me, and now she's dead because of it."

Her handler. Zack caught her chin in his fingers and tilted her head up until she looked at him. "I'm not afraid, Eden. I want to know you. Everything, good and bad."

Her half-smile was sardonic, a little sad. "You might not like what you find out."

He liked both versions of her, for different reasons. The sweet, sexy woman he'd known before, and this strong, fierce one before him now. "Give me a chance. Give *us* a chance."

She searched his eyes, the torment in her face tying

him in knots. Time and actions were the only thing that would ever convince her he was for real, but with everything so crazy right now, he might not have much time left to show her.

Eden tugged him back down for another kiss, and he stopped thinking at all. A slow, heartfelt kiss full of so much tenderness, heat and longing it made his heart clench. Because there was no misunderstanding what it meant.

She was saying goodbye to everything they'd had. Everything they could be.

Easing back, she lowered her gaze and stepped away. "We'd better go back, tomorrow's going to be another busy day. We both need to sleep."

She wanted to escape him, have time to reinforce her protective walls. He wouldn't force her to stay, but he wouldn't give up either. "Eden." He waited until she made eye contact before stepping forward to cup the side of her face. "I'm on your side. And I'm not going anywhere."

She stared back at him for an endless moment, her expression almost resigned, then turned away and headed back toward the manor.

Zack let her go, his whole being protesting having to watch her walk away.

****

Kissing him had been a colossal mistake.

Eden scowled at herself as she reached her bedroom door on the way to breakfast the next morning. Why the hell had she done it? Annoyance pricked at her like needles. A few fancy words, a couple of kisses, and she'd caved. Pathetic, and now she couldn't get him and the things he'd said out of her head.

She'd been up half the night thinking about everything. Zack. Penny. The others.

This entire situation had thrown her world off kilter, and when she and Zack had finally been alone last night, her resolve to keep her distance had collapsed the moment his lips had touched hers.

He wanted to be with her, and he was after more than a fling. But how the hell could she open her heart up and bare herself to him when everything they'd shared before had been based on lies?

She didn't know how to do that. Dammit, letting Zack in so deep last time had almost gotten her killed.

Kiyomi smiled at her from the table as Eden entered the breakfast room. "Hey. Get any sleep last night?"

"Not much." Eden helped herself to the silver coffee pot in the center of the table. "You?"

"Some, but not much after I heard the news. Anyone else up yet?"

"I heard someone moving around outside my room a while ago."

"Marcus. Apparently one of the neighbors' sheep got through part of the fence on the northeast side of the property, so he went out to deal with it." She studied Eden over the rim of her teacup. "You okay?"

She nodded. "Angry, though. And I feel guilty. If we'd gotten there sooner, we could have saved her."

Footsteps sounded on the stone floor in the hall. Amber walked in, followed by Trinity and Zack.

Eden's eyes locked on him, a warm, flipping sensation hitting her low in the belly as she took in the sight of him in dark, snug jeans and a charcoal-colored collared shirt that hugged his powerful chest and shoulders.

"Morning," he said, his deep voice sliding over her like a caress. Weakening her decision to stand firm on not getting involved with him again.

"Morning." Wrenching her eyes away, she busied herself with buttering toast someone had set out in silver toast racks.

"I just talked to Megan," Amber said, reaching for two boiled eggs perched in cobalt blue glass eggcups. "She and Ty aren't coming up until later, but I'll fill you guys in on what I told Trinity before I came down."

Eden stilled and focused on her. "About Penny?"

Amber nodded. "From recent communications and other files I accessed from her phone, I think she somehow knew about us. It looks like she'd been trying to make her way into England. She started in Finland and moved into Scotland, had searched bus schedules going to York."

That was only a few hours' drive away from them. Eden's hand tightened on her coffee cup. "She was trying to find us?"

Amber's face was somber. "I think she wanted refuge. And maybe to join us. How she found out about us, I don't know yet."

Setting her cup down, Eden sat back, feeling ill. Minutes. Mere minutes had cost Penny her life, had made the difference between death and rejoining her Valkyrie sisters, who would have protected her.

"What about the hitter?" Zack asked.

"It took some digging," Amber replied. "Someone buried his info deep, but he's a contract officer with ties to the CIA." She held up her phone to show a picture of him.

"I don't recognize him," Zack said, frowning at it.

Suspicion shot through her before she could stop it. Eden forced it aside, reproving herself. Zack was a contract officer with no true loyalty to the CIA. He'd lost a good friend in this, had volunteered to be here. If he'd wanted to turn on them he could have easily done so the moment he'd first arrived at the manor, alerting his former handler and superiors to their location if he'd wanted.

Unless he's playing the long game. Biding his time, trying to win her trust, using their past to try and get close to her again, make her lower her guard…

Not everyone's a threat, Eden. You used him *before, remember? Not the other way around.*

Except Zack Maguire still remained a threat. Last night had shaken her, showing her just how weak she was with him. And the things he'd said. That she didn't have to be alone anymore. That she could have him and a shot at something real if she'd just take the chance.

It tantalized her, tormented her with everything she'd longed for and never believed was possible, calling to the woman she'd allowed herself to be with him for those few brief months.

"Jesse does," Amber said, drawing their attention. "And this guy is also connected to two names on the list of possible suspects involved with the Program recovered from your handler," she said to Eden, then said a name that meant nothing to her. "He hasn't worked an op in a while, but the ones he *has* done have been connected to both those names."

The news settled like a rock in the pit of Eden's stomach. "So that's how he found Penny. The source or leak must be in the CIA itself."

"Looks like," Amber said, reaching for a piece of toast. "And we're going to use every resource available to us to find whoever's responsible." She started to say something else, but stopped when her phone rang. "Excuse me," she said after checking it, and walked out of the room.

"I'm gonna get changed so I'm ready to go if we get a lead," Kiyomi said, tossing her napkin on the table and standing. "See you guys in a bit."

"Sure." Eden forced a piece of toast down after Kiyomi left, aware of the silent tension crackling between her and Zack, then stood. "I'll see you later."

He shot out a hand, snagged her wrist as she turned away. Before she could pull free, he'd tugged her into his lap. She stiffened at the feel of those hard thighs beneath her bottom, the heat of his chest against her side.

Holding her gaze, he reached up to stroke his fingertips across the nape of her neck. Tingles exploded along her skin, tightening her nipples and sending an instant rush of heat between her legs. "I didn't sleep much." He traced a fingertip beneath her eye. "And from the looks of those shadows, you didn't either."

"Let me up."

He didn't. "Did you think about what I said last night?"

How could she not? She was *still* thinking about them. "And if I did?"

One side of his mouth twitched at her curt tone. "Then I'm grateful." His fingertips caressed her cheek, every subtle stroke laden with the promise of what he could offer her, memories of mind-melting pleasure and a sense of security that made her whole chest tighten. "Spend some time with me. We can start over, get to know each other all over again. The real us."

She huffed. Oh, he knew her plenty already. Including everything about her body. "Little late for that, wouldn't you say?"

He grinned at her meaning. "Okay, maybe. How about we pick up from where we left off, then? We'll fill in the gaps as we go."

The offer was so damn tempting she wanted to say yes.

That gave her all the incentive she needed to push to her feet, unable to ignore the way her body cried out for him. Need and love were two different things. Just because the first one was real didn't mean she could trust him with her heart, and losing him the first time had hurt so much she wasn't sure she could handle it a second. It was safer, smarter to shut the door on that chapter and move forward.

Zack caught her hand. "I meant what I said. I'm not going anywhere, and no matter how long it takes, I'm going to prove I'm worth the risk." The heat and certainty in his eyes made her stupid, needy heart skip a beat.

She opened her mouth to tell him he was a cocky bastard, but yanked her hand free when she heard footsteps in the hallway. A second later Chloe strode in, long blond hair up in a ponytail, already chomping away on some gum even though it was only six in the morning, and wearing a T-shirt that read: *Fuelled by ADHD and caffeine*.

She glanced between the two of them, the fierce look on her face telling Eden she meant business. "I just heard about Penny, and I only wanna know one thing. Who are we taking out next?"

"I'm guessing someone on the list my handler gave me," Eden answered, resolve hardening inside her like steel as she walked out of the room.

Zack would always hold a piece of her heart, but she'd be stupid to give him any more of it. They were teammates on this mission, nothing more. If she wanted to stay clear-headed and find Chris and the others justice, then that was the way it had to stay.

Chapter Eleven

Glenn arrived early at the country club and did a quick perimeter check just to be sure it was safe. He was armed as he went in to take his seat at a table in the back to await his contact. This meeting was time critical. Ten minutes ago, he'd received confirmation about last night's op in Edinburgh.

Penny was dead, but the other Valkyries were all still unaccounted for.

At least the hitter was dead too. One less thing to worry about as he formulated his next step.

He almost dropped his gin and tonic when he looked up and saw Alex fucking Rycroft walk in. The man's silver gaze locked on him and stayed there while he crossed the private room toward Glenn. What the hell was *he* doing here?

"Bennett," Rycroft said, helping himself to the seat across the table. "Been a long time. Mind if I join you?"

Maybe this was coincidence. Maybe it had nothing to do with the Valkyries. He played it cool. "I'm actually expecting someone—"

"I won't stay long. I'll just catch up with you while you wait." He leaned back in the chair like he planned to stay for a while. "So, how've you been? Retirement treating you okay?"

The intensity of that gaze made nerves come to life in the pit of his stomach. "Yeah. You?"

One side of Rycroft's mouth kicked up. "Can't quite kick old habits, I'm afraid. Still have my fingers in all sorts of pies. Guys like us never really retire, am I right?"

It was suddenly hard to swallow. The bastard knew something. Or at least had heard something. No way he was here right now by chance. And if Rycroft was sniffing around... Fuck. "Yeah." He set his drink down, his mind working fast. "What are you doing here?"

"Lunch meeting." He glanced around. "Nice place. You come here often?"

"No." Only when he had someone to impress...or make an impression upon.

"Ah." He focused back on Glenn, and those eyes held a glint that turned the buzzing in his gut into a swarm of angry hornets. "What do you do to stay busy these days? Still working the odd case, off the record?"

Glenn hadn't risen through the ranks of the Agency the way he had by allowing himself to be intimidated or letting pressure get to him. Still, Rycroft was one of the few people on this earth who could make him nervous. "Nah, that's all done." He put on an easy smile. "I travel with my family. Play a lot of golf."

"Golf? Huh. I heard you've been playing a lot of something else lately."

Glenn would have had to be in a coma to miss the message.

They're watching me. They know.

He put on a puzzled frown, shoved down the spurt of panic that shot through him. Rycroft was tight with Trinity Durant and Briar DeLuca. Were they suspicious of him? "Really? Where'd you hear that?"

Rycroft shrugged. "Around. You know how it is. Our

world is pretty small."

Yeah, it fucking was. People you thought were friends and allies could turn on you in a heartbeat if it meant saving their own skins. Had someone sold him out? He couldn't read Rycroft, other than the subtly implied threat underlying the conversation.

Someone else walked into the restaurant. Not Glenn's contact. Rycroft glanced back, then faced Glenn. "Well. I've taken up enough of your time." He pushed his chair back and stood, held out his hand. "Good to see you."

Glenn gripped it, holding that eerily knowing gaze. "Yeah. Take care."

"You too." He let go and walked away.

Glenn stared after him, his heart hammering against his ribs. He waited two minutes before leaving through the back entrance and hurrying to his car. There was no sign of Rycroft, but the man would definitely be watching, and there were plenty of other vehicles around. Any one of them might have someone watching him or waiting to follow him. He checked beneath the vehicle and looked under the hood for any signs of tampering or explosives before getting in it.

After texting his contact to cancel the meeting, he drove west for an hour to ensure he wasn't being followed before he deemed it safe enough to stop. Not trusting that Rycroft hadn't bugged his car, Glenn got out and walked to a secluded side street before using a burner phone to place another call he didn't want to make.

"It's me," he said when the Architect answered.

"You're fucking kidding me. What the hell is *wrong* with you?"

His pulse raced frantically in his throat. "Alex Rycroft just showed up at what was supposed to be a secret meeting with one of our colleagues. They're watching me. They know." He rushed to get it all out before he was hung up on. "Penny's dead—"

"I'm aware."

He paused. Aware of which part? He didn't bother asking, because he wouldn't get an answer. "But the others are still out there. Eight of them, and Rycroft has close ties to two." He listed them all by name. "...Chloe and Eden, and—"

"Kiyomi."

The way the name was said was odd. Full of interest and a sort of pride that struck Glenn as weird. "Yeah, and if they're doing what I think they're doing, then we're both fucked."

"I'm not fucked," the Architect flung back at him. "But you will be if you don't quit with this bullshit. You hear me? Don't. Ever. Call. Me. Again."

"*Hey*," he snapped. "I'm not taking the fall for this. You got me into this mess, and you're gonna help me make it go away. Because if I go down, I promise I'll take you with me."

A shocked laugh answered him. "And here I thought even you weren't stupid enough to threaten me."

The line went dead.

Glenn flushed hot with anger, then cold with dread as the buried threat hit home.

He ran a hand through his hair. Fine. He hadn't wanted to do things this way, but it looked like he had no choice. He'd hoped this day wouldn't come, but deep down he'd known it would. That one day that shit would come back to haunt him. He'd just never imagined it would go down like this.

After destroying the burner phone, he tossed it in a nearby garbage bin and got back in his car. On the way to the airport he called his wife at the lake, knowing she'd be out in the boat this time of day, and left a message. "Just calling to let you know something's come up last minute, and I have to go out of town for a while. I'll talk to you when I can. Give Kimmie a kiss for me. Love you both. Bye."

He had to act now and cover his tracks better going forward.

But even as he planned his next move, unease coiled inside him like a venomous snake. At this point he had to assume that at least Trinity and Briar were investigating him and his contacts, and that they'd gotten Rycroft involved too. If they'd joined up with the remaining Valkyries, with their combined skills it wouldn't be long until they uncovered everything he'd tried to bury, and come after him.

Finding the women was the hardest part. Using contract hitters was expensive and posed its own risks. The more he did it, especially against the same target group, the higher the chance it would eventually be traced back to him.

That left him one choice. He needed to take care of this personally if he wanted to eliminate his enemies and stay ahead of the threat. Right now he had two possible targets within reach. Briar and Trinity were somewhere close by, because their men were based out of Quantico.

Getting to either one of them was incredibly risky. Briar was married to the FBI's Hostage Rescue Team commander, and both she and her husband were trained snipers. Trinity, one of the deadliest Valkyries in her own right, was engaged to one of the HRT's sniper team leaders.

But Briar and DeLuca had a kid. A daughter, if he remembered correctly. He'd heard that since becoming a mother, Briar had been out of the game. There was a chance she might not even be involved in any of this.

Since he didn't have time to delve into that at the moment, he'd start with Trinity. She still did contract work for Rycroft occasionally.

Glenn turned the car around and headed back toward

Virginia, a plan taking shape in his mind. First Trinity, while her fiancé was away. Once she was dead, he would rip apart everything she'd left behind. Every phone call or text, to find out who she'd been in contact with, and go from there.

The only way to end this was to find the nest, and destroy it. Because if they found him first, there was no place on earth he could hide from the wrath of the Valkyries.

****

Zack took the rifle Ty offered him and loaded in a full magazine, ready to unleash some of his frustration by putting a pile of rounds into the target downrange. The guys had invited him out to the private shooting range located in a pasture over a mile from the manor house, and he was only too happy to join them. It was bordered by a farmer's field, and apparently Marcus's neighbors were all aware of the range so no one would be concerned or call the cops when they heard shots.

"Ready to do some damage?" Ty asked.

"Oh yeah." Eden had made a point of avoiding him since the meeting that morning, because of their kiss last night, and it was driving him crazy.

She still wanted him, whether she liked it or not. He'd made her lose control for a moment, and she hated that.

Zack understood it, but he still wasn't sorry. He'd never be sorry for it, because finally being able to hold her and kiss her after so many months without her had made him feel more alive than ever.

"So, you're with Eden, huh?" Heath asked, handing Zack a pair of earmuffs.

"Not with her."

Heath and Ty looked at each other, then back at

Zack. "No?" Ty said.

Zack shook his head. "Used to be. Not anymore." Not in the way he wanted to be. He wanted it to be the way it used to, minus the lies or secrets between them. No holds barred, everything out in the open so they could start fresh and take a stab at something real. "How does this all work, anyway? With the ladies. Are we their backup, or...?"

"We're whatever we're told to be," Heath answered with a wry smirk.

"Pretty much." Ty laughed and clapped Zack on the back. "Don't worry, you'll get used to it."

"I mean, it's not like I have a problem answering to women, of course," Zack added quickly, wanting to make that point clear. "But I've never worked with a team like this one before."

"Brother, we know just how you feel," Ty said. "What's the story with you two, anyway? You didn't know what she did when you were together?"

"No."

"Not even a little?"

"Not a single clue." It still amazed him how she'd hidden everything from him for that long. She was one hell of a liar. And an actress. Though of course he'd lied too, by omission.

"Must have been eye-opening for you when you found out." Heath's blue eyes gleamed with humor.

"Yeah. She dove out of my car as I was driving her away from the place where she'd just murdered the guest of honor in front of everyone." He'd never forget it. "I got out to run after her, and she doubled back and stole the damn thing while my back was turned. Left me standing there on the sidewalk like a dumbass."

Ty hooted, rocking back on his heels. "That's awesome."

Zack couldn't help but grin, because it *was* kinda

funny. Now. "Didn't see that one coming."

"Don't feel bad, we've all been there."

"Yeah? What happened with you?"

"Megan escaped her cell during SERE training and scared the shit out of me by showing up unannounced at my campsite in the middle of the forest one night," Ty answered.

"Holy shit." Having seen and learned what he had about the women so far, that wasn't a stretch. "What about you?" he asked Heath.

Heath grimaced. "Chloe cornered me outside a train station and put a knife to my junk."

Zack's eyes widened. "Seriously?"

Heath lifted a shoulder. "She only nicked me a little, just to make a point—pun intended. Wasn't the greatest start, but it left an impression."

"I'll bet. Hell, sounds like I got off easy," Zack said.

"Are we shooting here, or just shooting the shit?" Jesse strode over from his ATV with a rifle in his arms.

"Tell him what Amber did to you on that highway outside Damascus," Ty said to him.

Jesse shot him a frown. "Why?"

"Because, we're comparing notes about how badly we underestimated the ladies when we first met."

Jesse turned his gaze on Zack, a fond look on his face. "It was a motorcycle chase. We were on a highway, and I couldn't catch her. Came around a bend going full tilt, and there she was standing in the middle of the road pointing a weapon at me."

Yeah, Eden had let him off easy compared to the others. "What did you do?"

"Dumped my bike. Wound up like road kill on the side of the road. She drove off and left me lying there all beat to hell and feeling sorry for myself. Bike was completely trashed, so I had to hitch a ride back into the city and start hunting for her all over again."

Zack shook his head, impressed and glad he'd only been drugged and left behind. "You can bet I won't underestimate any of them ever again."

Jesse nodded. "Smart man. Each of them are incredible in their own right. But together?" He whistled, his expression saying it all. Their enemies were in deep shit.

"I can imagine." It was sexy, though. Knowing Eden was that capable in so many different areas. What other secrets had she hid from him?

"So, we doing this, or what?" Jesse said.

"Always busting our balls," Ty said, smirking as he put on his earmuffs.

The four of them shot until they were out of ammo, then loaded back onto the ATVs and started back for the manor house. Testosterone got the better of them, and turned the journey back into a race approximately six seconds in.

Ty shot out in front initially, pursued by Jesse. Always game to be part of the group, Zack gunned his ATV to catch up, only to be cut off by a rooster tail of dirt kicked up by Heath.

They jockeyed back and forth on a different and longer route back, trying to cut each other off in their quest to come in first. A quarter mile from the outbuilding where the ATVs were kept, Zack saw his chance and took it, flooring it up an incline to the top of a hill, then veering sharp left toward the others.

Ty jerked his ATV out of the way just in time to avoid a near collision. Zack whooped as he flew past, holding a fist up with his middle finger extended.

"In your dreams, cheating bastard!" Ty called after him, but Zack was too busy laughing to reply.

His laughter died a quick death, his smile vanishing when he spotted the lone figure leaning up against the side of the stone shed in the distance.

Eden pushed away from the wall when he slowed

nearby, standing with her hands in the pockets of her leather jacket while she watched him. None of the other women were here, just her. Had she come to see him?

He quickly parked the ATV inside and came back out. "Hey," he said, testing the waters.

"Hi. You guys have fun?"

"Yup. I won." Winning was way more fun than losing, and he intended to win Eden no matter what it took.

"He didn't. I let him," Ty said on his way past into the shed.

Zack grinned at Eden. "I totally won."

Her lips quirked, her amber eyes steady on his. "Feel like taking a walk?"

"Absolutely."

He fell in step with her as she headed across the field, ignoring the telltale grins he got from the guys. "Everything okay?" he asked when they were out of earshot.

"Fine. I've just been thinking a lot about what you said."

"Which part?"

"All of it. If we're going to be teammates, then we have to be able to trust each other."

He nodded. "Agreed." Though he didn't want to be *just* teammates.

"It's not easy for me to do, especially since you're still involved with the Agency."

"I'm not—"

"You're still connected to your handler. So yeah, you are." She leveled a look at him. "Are you really from Indiana?"

"Born and bred. You?"

She looked back out over the fields. They were covered with a light mist in the distance. "Amber says I'm from coastal Georgia originally. It's in the file she compiled for me from the ones she hacked off the Agency's servers."

Amber's abilities with that laptop of hers were insane. He hoped they would help uncover who was responsible for John's death. "But you don't remember?"

She shook her head. "I only have bits and pieces of memories from before."

Before she'd entered the Program. "Do you remember your family?"

A fond smile softened her face. "My grandma. My dad's mom. According to my file, my parents died in an accident with a logging truck when I was three. My grandma raised me after that until she got too sick to take care of me, and then I went into foster care. Do you still have family back in Indiana?"

"My dad and his wife. They've been together for almost thirty years now. Both of them have been breathing down my neck about coming home for a visit. I haven't been home in almost seven months. I need to make it happen sooner rather than later."

"And your mom?"

"I don't really see her much. She's in Wyoming with her fourth husband. Never really was into family."

She absorbed that with a nod. "Tell me one thing I don't know about you."

"Okay. I'm actually an introvert."

She shot him a disbelieving look. "Please. I've never seen anyone work a room like you can."

He lifted a shoulder. "It's the truth. I prefer quiet alone time to social gatherings and events."

"You come across as the opposite."

"I have to, for my job. It's a learned skill. My dad's a huge socializer, always has been, because of his business. He dragged me to all kinds of functions growing up, trying to force me out of my shell, and then made me take drama in high school. Guess it worked to some extent."

"Huh. Interesting. I think I used to be more outgoing than I am now. It was trained out of me. They wanted us to be solo operators, never forming any kind of bonds and whatever."

"They wanted you all to stay isolated."

"Made us easier to control," she said with a surprising lack of bitterness.

He decided to change the subject. "Okay, your turn. Tell me one thing I don't know about you."

She thought about it a moment. "I used to love to garden. When I was a kid my grandma taught me all about gardening in her yard. We had flowers and a vegetable patch. I've always wanted to take it up again, but I'm never in one place long enough to bother."

It was such an interesting and unexpected layer to her. "You left me a flower that day."

"Mmhmm."

Since she didn't offer anything more, he shifted gears, though he was more curious now than ever. If she loved flowers so much, then it must have had some kind of meaning. Or maybe he was overthinking it. "What kind of garden do you want?"

"A poison garden," she said without pause.

The answer and the smile on her face made him do a double take. "What?"

"A garden full of poisonous plants."

"Why?"

"Because toxins are my specialty, and some of the most toxic plants remind me of my grandma's garden. Foxgloves, nightshade, oleander... I've learned about so many others since then. I think it would be cool to have a garden that everyone sees as beautiful, without realizing everything in it's deadly."

"Wait. I just remembered something. The night we stayed up watching that nature documentary together while eating dessert. You went off on tangents telling me all about the different venomous creatures. You knew way too much about the venom of puffer fish and the blue-ringed octopus. I thought you were just a giant nerd, but there was more to it, wasn't there?"

"Yes." She smiled a little. "I'm what you'd call a font of knowledge about all things toxic to the human body. What different substances will do, the symptoms they can elicit. What concentration and dosage to give, and various ways to administer them in order to get the effect I want."

Zack stared at her for a moment, then chuckled. She'd given him a major clue about what she was, and he'd been clueless. "You are something else."

Eden grinned at him, seeming pleased by the compliment, and he saw a flash of the woman she'd been with him before. "Cool idea with the garden, no?"

"Yeah, as long as it wouldn't kill anyone by touching something they shouldn't."

"Touching? Nah, nothing that severe. Maybe hives and a rash, or some vomiting."

"You sound way too excited about that," he said in amusement.

A shrill whistle sounded behind them just as Eden pulled her phone from her pocket. Zack looked over his shoulder to see Ty waving them back.

"It's Amber," she said. "There's a meeting at the house in ten minutes, because Trinity's gotta go somewhere."

Zack turned around to face the house and gave her a playful nudge with his elbow. "Race you."

Eden grinned. "No."

He arched an eyebrow. "You afraid of losing?"

"To you? Nope." She took off.

Zack tried to go after her, but his foot slipped. He stumbled, his heel coming out of his shoe.

Eden darted away from him with a throaty laugh that told him she'd stepped on the back of his shoe on purpose. It was the second time she'd left him in the dust. "I don't think so!" he shouted, shoving his foot back into his shoe to race after her.

She was fast, and fit. He had to go all out to catch up with her, reaching her just as they crested the final hill before the manor. By the time they got to it, they were both laughing, and it felt fantastic.

They slowed before the gravel path leading around the side of the house into the back garden, and his heart was beating faster from more than the run. He liked this Eden even more than the previous one, and seeing her laugh and have fun with him gave him hope that he was beginning to earn her trust. That they still had a chance together.

Trinity was waiting at the back door for them. "There you guys are. Come on, we're all waiting."

Zack and Eden followed Trinity into the library. He stood off to the side with Eden while everyone waited for Trinity to start.

"Okay, I just got off a call with Rycroft," Trinity began. "He met with former CIA Deputy Director Glenn Bennett less than an hour ago. You'll recognize him as being on the list of possible suspects we're looking at, verified by the thumb drive Eden's handler gave her."

Zack had read up on him last night in the files Amber had showed him, to keep abreast of the current investigative work she was working on, and to take his mind off that kiss with Eden.

Bennett had retired two years ago, and most of what he'd done during his tenure with the Agency had been buried deep. Some of it so deep it appeared to have vanished altogether. Amber and the team of analysts back in the States were still digging, but it seemed like Bennett might have been involved with the Valkyrie Program somehow.

"Rycroft thinks he's dirty, but we don't know if he's directly involved with us in the past or present, and he's definitely not the Architect we've seen mentioned in several memos Amber has from her original hack of the system," Trinity continued.

Zack had seen that term mentioned several times in various places in the files Amber had shared with him. The Architect could be anyone, but whoever it was, it was someone with influence and authority. Almost certainly a man, given the nature of the Valkyrie Program, and likely former military—maybe intel or SOF. Someone who had clout in the upper hierarchy of the CIA's leadership.

"Bennett's on the move. An encrypted phone called his wife's cell number shortly after the meeting with Rycroft. The message he left for her said he had to go out of town for something—we think because Rycroft spooked him. We think he might be involved with the murder of Eden's handler, and subsequent hit on Zack's friend. We're not sure where Bennett is going yet, but I'm taking a team to D.C. in anticipation of getting a location on him. I want all of you to go with me, except Kiyomi, who will stay and monitor things here."

Zack glanced at Eden, who didn't react to the announcement, watching Trinity intently.

"Once we get Bennett's location, we're going to capture him and extract the intel we need. If he's dirty, we turn him over to Rycroft to deal with. Any questions?" Trinity finished. When no one spoke, she continued. "Good. Everybody go pack a bag and meet me out front in ten. Kiyomi, keep working the intel on the other suspects."

"You got it," Kiyomi answered.

Everyone dispersed to get to work. Zack followed Eden up to the third floor, stopping her before she could reach her room. Going after the former Deputy Director of the CIA wasn't an average op, even by Valkyrie standards. "You ready for this?"

"Of course. You?" She studied his face. "Because

you don't have to do this."

"I'm going with you," he said firmly. He was staying as close to her as possible to make sure she was safe, and fighting for her. For them. "I want to find out whoever's behind all this shit and make them pay."

A little smile teased the corners of her mouth. "Never saw this side of you before. I like it."

Zack cupped her cheek in his hand and bent to kiss her, but she blocked him with a solid hand on his chest, taking a step back. "No. That's off the table for now," she told him. "We're teammates, and there will be no blurring of the boundaries."

Holding back a growl of denial, he stared down into her eyes. *For now* meant there was hope. He would just have to wear her down. "I won't give up on us."

She held his gaze for a few heartbeats. "We need to keep our heads on straight," she warned. "It's the only way we're going to come out of this alive."

With that she disappeared into her room, her defensive shields stronger than ever, and all he wanted to do was to rip them down.

Chapter Twelve

"Hey, there's my girl!" Trinity beamed and crouched down to hold out her arms as little Rosie toddled precariously toward her.

"She still walks like she's drunk," Briar laughed, hovering over her daughter to catch her if she fell.

The transformation in her friend was incredible, and beautiful. Briar had been one of the hardest and most lethal snipers the Program had ever turned out. While she would always be deadly, motherhood had softened her entire personality. Briar lived for her daughter and, after a rocky start that had shaken her, now adored being a mom.

That was why Briar was taking Rosie away for a while. Valkyries were used to taking a stand and fighting to the end. But with the current security situation facing them all, ensuring Rosie's safety was as important as completing their mission.

Trinity caught Rosie and lifted her into the air for a big hug, making smacking kissing noises against the toddler's neck. "You did it, clever girl." It was four in the morning UK time, she was jetlagged as hell, but it was all worth it when those little arms closed around her neck and Rosie chortled in her ear.

A sharp pain stabbed through her chest, so intense and unexpected her lungs seized for an instant. She forced a deep breath, locked the grief in the vault inside her, and focused on the sweet baby in her arms.

"You gotta be wiped," Briar said. "Want something to eat quick before I go? Matt made a lasagna I pulled from the freezer last night. I can warm you up a piece."

Trinity grinned at her. "You still can't cook?"

"Please. I barely have time to shower with this little one underfoot, and you expect me to cook?" She snorted. "And she's being sweet right now, but Rosie hasn't eaten her snack yet, so we'd better feed her before she realizes she's starving. Then we can get going."

Trinity carried Rosie to her high chair and set her in it. The suitcases were ready to go by the back door, awaiting departure for the airport. After Eden's handler and Penny had been murdered, it was no longer safe for Briar and Rosie to stay here when it was so easy for enemies to find them.

Trinity and Rycroft had told Briar and Matt what was going on, and as a precaution their friends had decided it was best for Briar to take Rosie to San Diego and stay with Matt's parents in an undisclosed location until the threat level reduced.

"But I can cut up fruit and stuff," Briar said as she walked into the kitchen, then aimed a smile over her shoulder at Trinity. "Still good with a blade."

"Yeah? Not rusty? And how's your shooting?"

"Meh, I haven't been to the range lately. Too busy, and the guys have been out of town a lot recently, so Matt hasn't had much free time anyway. When we do get free time together these days, we nap."

That made Trinity laugh. "Oh, my, what a difference a year makes."

"Tell me about it." She smiled at Rosie. "Good thing I love you, little stinker."

Another bittersweet pang hit Trinity. She was happy for Briar, and her friend knew how lucky she was to have Rosie.

But it underlined the stark reality that Trinity would never have a baby of her own.

She rubbed her thumb over her diamond engagement ring, thinking of Brody. Even now she sometimes still couldn't believe he was hers. He'd been more than patient with her. They'd been engaged for two years and she just kept putting off setting a date for the wedding.

It was wearing thin on him, she could tell, slowly eroding the foundation of their relationship, and their conflicting work and travel schedules kept them apart for long stretches of time. They were slowly drifting apart and she was afraid the distance was only going to grow, because she couldn't give up on this mission, couldn't give up on the others when they needed her.

With her back to Trinity, Briar pulled items from the fridge and started cutting them while Trinity amused Rosie with a game of peek-a-boo. "So, what's the latest from headquarters?"

"We've brought on two new members."

"Including Eden?"

"Yes, and Zack's an intel specialist. I don't know the details, but they've got a history together neither of them are forthcoming about."

"Ooh, juicy. Sorry I'm gonna miss out on all the fun when you guys go hunting."

Before Rosie, Briar would have been the first one to volunteer to be on their team, doing anything and everything to get the job done, up to and including giving her life. Now everything had changed. "We'll miss you. But we'd all rather know you and Rosie are safe." All the others understood.

A brisk knock came at the back door.

"I'll check it," Trinity said, hand on the weapon in

the holster at the small of her back. Not that she expected to find an assassin on the other side of the door. Killers didn't usually knock first.

Her heart flipped when she found her fiancé standing on the doorstep. She unlocked the door and whipped it open to throw her arms around him. "What are you doing here?" she breathed. He was supposed to still be on the flight back to Quantico.

His warm chuckle fanned her temple, the strength of his embrace making her eyes sting. "Wanted to surprise you."

"Boss gave him the rest of the day off," a familiar voice said from the direction of the driveway.

She peered over Brody's shoulder to smile at Matt DeLuca, Briar's husband, wearing his cherished Chargers cap and carrying a duffel. "Did he?"

"Yeah. He's the best boss in the history of bosses." He raised his eyebrows at Brody. "Right?"

"He's a prince among men," Brody answered, grinning down at her.

Trinity took his face in her hands and kissed him, her heart about to explode. It had been weeks since they'd last seen each other, their contact limited to texts and brief calls. "God, I've missed you."

"Missed you too."

They all went inside together. Rosie stopped eating her snack and broke into a huge smile when she saw her father walk in.

"Rosie cheeks," he called, feigning openmouthed astonishment as he went to her, arms wide.

"Dada!" Rosie cried, bouncing up and down in her seat, little fists opening and closing.

He pulled her out of her high chair and covered her face with noisy kisses, earning an endearing belly chuckle. "How's my sweetheart, huh? Ready for your first plane ride?"

"God, I hope she's a good flier," Briar said. "Can you help me get her diaper bag together?"

"Sure." Matt turned to Brody. "Take her for a minute."

Rather than balk or look uncomfortable, Brody took Rosie from him and settled her against his broad chest in the crook of one muscular arm. "Hey, lady. You've grown again since I last saw you." Rosie reached up to pat at his short beard with her tiny hands, and Brody smiled down at her with such warmth...

It hurt so much Trinity had to leave the room.

She ducked into the powder room to collect herself, fighting back the sadness and...grief clawing at her. When she came back out a minute later with a smile on, Briar and Matt were gathering up everything by the back door.

They said their goodbyes, then Briar tugged her aside, her dark eyes serious. "Keep me updated about what's going on. Whatever happens, if you need me, just call. I'll be on the next flight out with my gear."

That Briar would even contemplate leaving Rosie behind and put herself in danger to back Trinity and the team up, was everything. "Thank you." She hugged Briar goodbye, hiding a smile at the momentary stiffness in her friend before Briar returned the embrace. Briar had come a long way since meeting Matt.

Brody grabbed his bags and climbed into the front passenger seat of Trinity's SUV as she got behind the wheel.

"Sucks that Briar has to take Rosie away," he said. "Matt's so attached, I've never seen him so happy."

"Same with Briar. After those first few weeks she just blossomed. She's an incredible mother."

"Yeah, she is." She glanced over at him, her belly flipping. He never failed to take her breath away. "Tired?"

"Yeah. But not *too* tired." Grasping her hand, he

raised it to his lips for a kiss, a grin tugging at his sexy mouth.

She laughed softly. "You're never too tired."

"Nope. Not when I've got the sexiest woman on earth beside me."

Trinity smiled, but his words had her all up in her head. Brody was the most family-oriented man she'd ever met. She was an orphan with no relatives. Meeting and falling in love with him, being welcomed into the Colebrook clan, had been hard for her. Was still hard.

No matter how often he told her he loved her, no matter that he'd put a ring on her finger, she couldn't shake the thought that she just didn't fit into his family. He wanted to make it official and marry her, but she wasn't convinced he would truly be happy if they did.

She was...damaged, and no amount of time or love would change that. That's why she'd held off on naming a date. While they were just engaged, there was still a chance for him to back out if he wanted to, without all the legal mess necessary after marriage.

She'd never considered herself a coward, but in all honesty, part of her was basically waiting for the day he woke up and realized he'd be better off without her.

"How long you in town for this time?" he asked as she drove away from Matt and Briar's place.

"Not sure. We're following a promising lead right now. If we get a location, we'll be going after our target."

"Who's the target?"

"Former Deputy Director of the CIA."

Brody gaped at her. "Jesus Christ, Trin."

"I know. But even if he's not directly involved, he knows something. We need to find out what."

"And the others?"

"Everyone but Kiyomi and Marcus are here, along with our two newest members."

He was silent a long moment, watching her. "You

staying tonight?"

She wanted to. She desperately wanted to, given how strained things had become between them lately. "Wish I could, but no. I've only got a few hours."

He didn't say anything else on the way home, but she could feel the silent tension rolling off him, and her own stomach tightened in response. This mission couldn't have come at a worse time for them, but she couldn't stay.

Knowing she'd disappointed him yet again, she braced herself for cool indifference once they reached the house, but the moment he locked the door behind them, Brody grabbed her and pinned her up against the wall. Relief and desire hit her all at once. She wound her arms around his neck, staring up into his beautiful brown eyes.

His mouth came down on hers, and it was like a lit match touching accelerant. Heat exploded between them, punching through her whole body. She lost herself in the moment, in him. His taste, his scent, the feel of that long, lean and powerfully built body straining against hers.

They tore at each other's clothes, dropping them in a messy trail on the hardwood floor as he wrapped one arm around her hips and carried her to their room, kissing her with a desperate passion she shared. Her back hit the duvet and he came down on top of her, his urgency making the need sharper, deeper.

He used his intimate knowledge of her body to his advantage, doing all the things that shot her arousal to red-line level. She was on the verge of exploding when he entered her with a single hard thrust. He was relentless, restricting her movements with his weight while hitting all her sweet spots in a bid to push her up.

Then he held her there, his eyes full of molten heat as he pinned her beneath him. "Say you need me." His voice was raspy, full of need.

"Need you," she gasped out, quivering.

He gave her what she needed. She flew over the

edge, soaring, her cries ringing off the ceiling. All she could do was cling while he surged in and out of her, low, throaty groans of pleasure tearing from his throat before he shuddered and moaned aloud, his whole body cording.

Slowly they came back to earth together. Trinity cradled him to her, sliding her fingers through his hair, tracing the muscles in his back and shoulders.

After a minute he withdrew, rolled to the side and pulled her into his arms, tucking her face into the curve of his neck. "I love you," he murmured, sounding half-asleep.

"Love you too," she whispered back, her throat tightening. She did love him. More than anything. But this mission wasn't something she could walk away from. She *had* to do this, had to see it through. And thankfully Brody loved her enough to never stand in her way.

He fell asleep within minutes, but she couldn't. Gently extricating herself from his embrace, she used the washroom and then went into their walk-in closet to pack a new bag.

Catching sight of her naked reflection in the full-length mirror hanging on the wall, she stopped to study her reflection.

She was no longer the firm-bodied femme fatale the Program had created so many years ago. The operative who had seduced and killed dozens of targets. That life was over now, yet she would always bear the scars.

Her gaze dipped down to the curve of her belly, lower, to the hysterectomy scar just above her pubic bone. A constant reminder of what had been taken from her. A reminder of a cold, sterile room and a stainless steel table beneath her. Restraints around her wrists and ankles. And blindingly white lights overhead.

At the time she'd believed them. That it was for the best. She'd given her consent, not understanding how much it would matter to her now.

They'd taken so much from her. She wouldn't let them take anything else—not from her, and not from the others.

Looking down at her left hand, she touched her thumb to her ring one last time. This mission to go after those behind the Program put her relationship with Brody in jeopardy, but she couldn't walk away now. For better or worse, she had to see this through, no matter the cost.

She slipped the ring off and set it in her special jewelry box on the shelf.

"I knew I should have gotten you a size smaller. That way it would be harder for you to take it off," he said in a wry voice from behind her.

She focused on Brody in the mirror, leaning a thick shoulder against the doorway. He'd given up on pushing her directly about getting married, switching to the occasional pointed remark tempered with humor. "You know I can't wear it on—"

"I know." He crossed to her, no hint of anger in his tone or expression, but she knew it disappointed him that she wouldn't set a date, and her taking her ring off was a reminder of that. Wrapping his thick arms around her middle, he set his bristly chin on her shoulder and met her gaze in the mirror. "You okay?"

He somehow knew that seeing Rosie today had been hard for her. "Yeah, fine." He'd told her over and over that it didn't matter if they couldn't have a baby together. That he'd be totally fine adopting one day if that's what they both wanted. But that wasn't the point.

"When this is all over, you'll go away with me for a while? Just the two of us."

God, he was so wonderful, putting up with her. "I'd love that."

"Good."

Silence stretched between them, and it made her uneasy. "You know why I have to do this, right?" It was important for her to know that he understood.

He ran a hand over her hair, kissed the side of her jaw. "Yeah, I know. Just be careful. You're the only fiancée I've got."

She gave him a smile, her heart twisting at the unspoken yearning in his eyes. For just a moment she let herself imagine standing in a wedding gown, Brody before her in a tux while a small gathering of his family and their close friends looked on.

She would be proud to become the wife of such an incredible man. But not yet.

Before she could make that final commitment to him, she had faceless enemies to eliminate...and personal demons to conquer.

Chapter Thirteen

The most frustrating part of conducting an op was the waiting.

Glenn walked through the back exit of the condo building and headed for the staircase, reining himself in. He hated waiting. Always had, even back when he'd been a Paramilitary Operations Officer with the Agency.

Killing Trinity Durant was a risky enough venture, but trying to target her when her HRT sniper boyfriend was there too? Suicide.

Much as it annoyed him, he'd just have to wait for an easier opportunity. He'd planted an undetectable tracker on her vehicle. He'd follow her progress via his phone, then do some recon at different times to find out when she was at her most vulnerable. When that chance came, he'd strike.

The hallway was deserted save for one cleaning person entering another room with her cart and vacuum cleaner when he walked past. This place was expensive and exclusive, affording him total privacy. He'd checked in under an alias as a precaution. No one knew he was here, or why.

He paused at the door to his room to ensure it hadn't been tampered with in the short time he'd been gone. The little slip of paper he'd wedged between the top of the door and the jamb was still in place.

Stepping inside, he glanced around. The side table lamp was on as he'd left it, and the bathroom door was still a few inches open. He locked the door and removed his concealed holster from the small of his back, a wave of relief and fatigue hitting him.

He'd served his country for his entire adult life. The Valkyrie Program had been his proudest contribution to the security of it. He was a patriot, full stop. Oftentimes that meant operating in shades of gray as far as legalities went. When he'd helped the fledgling Valkyrie Program come into existence, he'd seen the beauty of it. Female assassins could go places men couldn't. Were often over-looked until it was too late. The whole thing had been a stunning success.

Glenn had never thought of the women as his "crea-tions" the way the Architect did, but he was proud of what they'd accomplished together. Having to kill the opera-tives he'd helped produce was a last resort, yet a necessary one.

He tossed his jacket on the back of the chair and be-gan unbuttoning his shirt as he headed to the bathroom for a shower. Stepping inside, he flipped on the light switch.

He barely caught the flash of movement out the cor-ner of his eye, then an elbow slammed into the side of his head an instant before he could block it. Pain exploded through his skull. He grunted as lights exploded before his eyes, raised an arm to deflect the next blow and spun to face his attacker.

A fist caught him in the kidney. He struck out, a snarl of rage and agony bursting free, and landed a punch to the assailant's ribs. The attacker let out a muffled groan and danced back, giving him a second to regroup and get his first good look. Slightly built, dressed in dark clothes, a mask covering the face.

"Who the fuck are you?" he snarled and lunged forward to throw another punch.

The attacker dodged it, caught his fist and used his momentum to throw him over their hip. He slammed into the side of the tub with a loud thud.

Ignoring the pain and his hazy vision, he shot to his feet.

An arm locked around his throat from behind, applying strong pressure.

Blood hold. He had seconds to break it before he lost consciousness.

He tried to shove a hand between his head and the forearm. A blur of movement flashed in his peripheral vision, just enough for his bulging, painful eyes to see the knife coming at him.

The military-style blade slashed across his throat, a deep line of burning fire. He clutched at the wound as blood spurted everywhere. His shoulder hit the wall, his eyes darting to the mirror to catch sight of his killer.

A pair of familiar green eyes stared back at him for a moment, burning with triumph and hatred.

Shock detonated inside him. *No...*

His knees thudded against the floor. He toppled over, his frantically racing heart only speeding up his death.

He lay there gasping for air he couldn't suck through his severed windpipe while his blood spurted and pooled on the bathroom floor.

Rough fingers pried his jaw open. A searing hot pain flashed through his brain. More blood sprayed.

The light went out. His killer stepped over him, leaving him to die alone in the darkness.

A silent scream reverberated in his head. *Valkyrie...*

****

"Amber's sure it's him?" Zack asked her.

"Yes." In the rental house living room, Eden slid another full mag into one of her cargo pants pockets and checked to make sure all of her hair was still hidden beneath the wig.

Instead of long ringlets she now had a straight, chin-length bob in chocolate brown that covered her ears. That and the baggy clothes she wore would help conceal her identity from anyone else searching for her with facial recognition software. "She hacked into some facial recognition program and got a hit on Bennett leaving the building earlier."

"Hacked it from where?"

"No idea. And probably best we don't know." Amber was a force to be reckoned with. That she'd even been able to steal the files she had from the Program as the people in charge had been trying to burn everything was impressive.

"Still gonna ask her later."

"You do that." He and Amber had become pretty chummy in the short time they'd known each other. Zack's intel expertise and Amber's tech wizardry were a potent combination. The two of them had spent the entire flight across the Atlantic with their heads together, going over various things.

The unwelcome twinge of jealousy pissed Eden off. Amber was happily committed to Jesse, for Chrissake, and she had to spend time with Zack to prepare for this mission. There was nothing at all improper going on between them, yet a few times when Eden had looked up the aisle at them, she'd been tempted to wedge herself in the seat between him and Amber just to get his attention. To show that she had something to offer to the hunt as well.

Op time, she scolded herself. *Get your insecure head out of your ass and focus.*

This was why she and the others had been relentlessly trained not to get involved with anyone on a mission. They screwed with your head, even when you weren't actually with him anymore.

She straightened as Zack slid his sidearm into the holster beneath his armpit. "Good to go?" She wanted to get moving. Trinity was already scoping out the building, and Eden wanted to limit the amount of time she and Zack were alone.

"Yeah." He swung his leather jacket on and started for the door. "I'll drive."

Fine with her. She'd be able to watch everything more carefully without her attention divided.

She started for the door but stopped when Zack grabbed her elbow and turned her to face him. "What?" she demanded, annoyed. *Let's just do this already.*

Zack stared down into her eyes. "You be careful. Don't take any unnecessary chances. If it doesn't feel right, just get out. Hear me?"

Eden hated being told what to do. But from him it was merely annoying because it was kind of sexy in an alpha, protective way. She'd never had anyone in her life who cared about her like that before, except Chris, and that was different to the vibe Zack was giving her now. He didn't like her being in harm's way, wanted to protect her. It reminded her of how he'd been when they'd been seeing each other last year.

Even his grip right now. Firm but gentle, combined with the concern on his face. Little things, like a hand on the small of the back when walking through a crowded room or space together. Him entering the room first, keeping hold of her hand so he wouldn't lose her in the crowd, or keeping her on the inside of the sidewalk, away from traffic. They'd told her a lot about the sort of man he was.

"You don't need to worry about me. I can take care of myself," she told him. She'd gone up against scarier targets than Glenn Bennett, and she wasn't even going to kill him.

Yet. But if she found out he'd been involved with Chris's murder, he was a dead man.

Her job was to take him off guard and tranq him so Zack could carry him out, and together they would drive their prisoner back to the safehouse for questioning. Eden loved the idea of Bennett bound and blindfolded, waking up in total darkness to find her, Amber and Trinity there to interrogate him.

"Too bad, because you don't get a say in that," Zack said, no give in his tone or expression.

She firmed her jaw. "Can we go now?"

He waited a beat before releasing her. She couldn't help but admire the figure he cut as he walked out to the street to where the rental car waited. Broad shoulders, jeans hugging his strong thighs.

She shook herself and aimed for the front passenger seat. Zack opened the door for her and held it while she got in. "Thanks," she muttered, wishing he would stop being a gentleman and pretend she was nothing but a teammate.

"Welcome."

They didn't talk on the drive to the building. A swanky one located close to the business district. Not a place likely to be frequented by Bennett's normal crowd, she was sure, and at least he was smart enough not to stay at a hotel.

That was as far as her respect for him went, however. If he was dirty, she would tear him apart.

Zack pulled up to the curb in front of the building. "I want to come in with you."

She turned to face him. "No. That's not the plan, and you need to realize that I can handle myself."

"It's not that I don't think you're capable," he argued. "It's that I don't like you going up there without backup. Bennett was former Paramilitary Ops, and before that, SOF."

"Just do your job, and I'll do mine," she muttered, and exited the car.

Taking a deep breath, she pushed the annoyance from her mind and focused on the task ahead. Zack would park around the side of the building and watch the back exit, then wait for her to contact him via their earpieces. Trinity was keeping watch from the south side of the building in case Bennett figured out what was happening and tried to escape. Amber and Jesse were nearby, monitoring things from a van.

She smiled sweetly at the doorman and gave him the name and unit number of someone Amber had discovered was away. "I'm here to water her plants and feed her fish while she's in Cabo." She handed him her ID, the name on which Amber had added to the approved visitor list.

He glanced at it, checked in with the front desk via radio to confirm, then smiled. "Come right in."

"Thank you." *And don't mind the noise on the eleventh floor in the next few minutes when I knock Bennett's ass out.*

She took the stairs, only running into one other person on the way up. At the door she paused to make sure no one was around. Bennett was well-trained. She'd only have a second to catch him off guard and administer the syringe. Trying to get him to open the door for her was too risky, so she was going in.

Pulling out the little electronic gadget Amber had given her, she placed it beneath the lock and waited for the combination to appear on the tiny screen. She entered it, thankful for the near whisper-quiet mechanism as it unlocked.

She hid the syringe in her left fist, ready to strike, and gingerly opened the door a crack.

Total blackness greeted her, sending a prickle of unease across her skin.

Was Bennett asleep? She slipped inside and stood there in the dark as an eerie stillness settled around her.

Then the smell hit her. Blood. Lots of it.

Whipping out her penlight, she risked turning it on. The bed was empty, still neatly made. She took a step further into the room and turned toward the bathroom.

Jesus.

She tapped her earpiece to activate it. "Bennett's dead."

Chapter Fourteen

Eden's heart sank as she stared down at the body sprawled on the bathroom floor. Bennett had been their best hope for getting intel about Chris and people involved with the Valkyrie Program. That lead had died with him.

"What?" Zack said through her earpiece.

"He's lying on the bathroom floor with his throat slashed. It looks like a slaughterhouse in here." No way this was random. Not this kind of a murder, and with a man like Bennett.

She moved the beam of light up from the body, careful not to step in his blood. It spattered the wall, the sink. She spun back around to face the bedroom, looking for signs of an intruder. "Does Amber still have the security cameras locked in the building?" If not and the killer was still here, whoever it was might know she'd gone into the room.

"Yes," Trinity responded.

"There's no sign of forced entry."

"I'm on my way to you," Zack said. "Don't move."

Eden didn't answer, busy sweeping the room. The curtains were drawn tight, and nothing was out of place.

Bennett's jacket was draped on the back of the chair and his weapon was lying on top of the dresser. "Room's clear. I'm going to check for bugs and cameras."

"Copy," Trinity said.

As she was finishing up a few minutes later, Zack spoke. "I'm at the door."

Eden drew her weapon anyway as she approached the door, angling her body toward the peephole in case anyone out in the hall was thinking of taking a shot through the door. But Zack was alone.

She let him in and stepped back. "Room's secure," she said as she locked the door behind him. "Turning on the light." She flipped the switch, flooding the room with light.

Zack stepped past her to look in the bathroom. "Holy shit," he murmured, taking it in.

Eden stepped up beside him. "Yeah."

Rage. Looking around the bathroom, the killer's uncontrollable rage was palpable.

She took in everything with a critical eye. The killer had planned this well, slipping into the room unnoticed to lie in wait, and surprising Bennett. "Whoever it was, was waiting in here for him and took him by surprise. They—" She stopped, her gaze halting on the lump of flesh she'd missed during her initial sweep.

Bennett's severed tongue lay on the cold tile floor, inches from his face, his half-open eyes staring at it. He might have still been alive when it was cut out.

"This was personal," Zack said quietly. "The killer knew him, and either was afraid of him talking—"

"Or was punishing him for something he'd already said." It was a vicious attack, yet planned with care. The killer had been cautious initially, planning the details, leaving no sign of a break-in. Then they had seen Bennett and lost control, letting the anger take over. So much anger that they hadn't cared about leaving a giant mess and risking leaving evidence behind. They'd wanted to send a message. A warning to someone else?

Eden didn't see any bloody footprints on the bathroom tile or the carpet leading to the door. "Throat was slit from right to left, in a single, deep stroke." No hesitation. "The killer was comfortable with using a knife, likely left-handed. I don't see any visible shoeprints on the floor," she said to Trinity, and leaned over Bennett's body to peer into the tub/shower.

It was immaculate except for the spray of blood on the outside of the tub portion. "The killer must have hidden in the tub behind the shower curtain. Looks like Bennett made an initial effort to struggle, but from what I'm looking at in here, he didn't see the knife coming until it was too late."

"Understood," Trinity said. "Amber's reviewing the security footage now. You two get out of there."

"On our way." She stopped to check Bennett's jacket pocket, took his wallet, keys and phone while Zack quickly checked through the small bag Bennett had packed. "Anything?"

"No. Let's hope we get something good off his phone."

"We need to check his vehicle." He'd parked it beneath the building.

Zack stepped in front of her on the way to the door, one hand on the weapon beneath his jacket. "Stay close."

She didn't waste energy arguing, just stayed close as they entered the hallway and hurried for the nearest stairwell. Much as she didn't like admitting it, she felt better having him with her as they rushed down to the underground parking garage.

"Just heard from Amber," Trinity said to them. "Security footage during a twenty minute window around the probable time of the murder is corrupted."

Given that, it seemed like they were dealing with a

pro, and possibly more than one person. Sounded like the killer might have a team behind them. But then what about all the evidence and the body being left behind? If it had been a pro, they must have taken precautions not to leave DNA behind.

"Copy. We're going down to the garage to search his vehicle." Amber had sent them the make, model and plate number of the rental earlier.

"Okay. Alert me when you're on the move again."

"Will do."

Zack stayed in front as they entered the garage. There were six levels, but they were in luck because they found Bennett's rented Nissan parked one level down, near the bottom of the ramp. She unlocked it. He stood watch while she went through the interior, then checked the trunk.

"Nothing. It's clean." Hopefully Amber would find something useful on his phone.

"Let's get moving. We've been down here too long already." He led the way again as they started for the turn in the ramp.

"On our way to our vehicle," she said to Trinity.

"Street's clear. I'll rendezvous with you back at the house."

"Got it."

Zack looked back at her as they reached the turn. "I'll bring the car up—"

A blue Tesla whipped around the corner. They hadn't heard it because the engine was so quiet. It veered toward Zack at the last moment.

Eden caught him around the waist in a flying tackle, knocking him out of the way at the last second. They hit the concrete with a thud and rolled, but the Tesla was reversing at them.

"Move!" Eden shouted, shoving to her feet.

She planted her hands on the trunk of a car parked

beside her and vaulted over it just as the Tesla's back end whipped toward her, missing her by a foot. As she landed on the other side, she grabbed her weapon and spun around in time to see Zack on the other side of the ramp, pistol aimed at the Tesla's rear window.

Two shots exploded through the garage. The driver sped up, disappearing around the corner behind them.

Eden ran for him. "Go, *go*." Together they raced up the ramp. The incline was only a hundred feet long, but they weren't fast enough. Seconds from reaching the top, the Tesla came roaring up behind them. "Look out!"

She dove right, rolling and slamming into the concrete wall. The Tesla shot past into the street and screamed around the corner. "Trinity, take that asshole in the blue Tesla out," she snarled, climbing painfully to her hands and knees.

"On it."

Zack ran over and took her by the shoulders, anxiously scanning her face. "Are you hurt?"

"No." He lifted her to her feet and she scanned him in turn. "You?"

"I'm fine. Let's get the hell out of here."

They hugged the wall as they ran to the top of the ramp, pausing there to check for the Tesla. "Are we clear?" she asked Trinity.

"I see it. Just turned east heading toward the front entrance of the building," Trinity responded. "In pursuit now."

Eden ran with Zack down the sidewalk, both of them watching for new threats. She almost ran into his upraised hand, inches in front of her face. "Stay here," he told her. "I'm not letting you anywhere near this thing until I'm sure it's safe."

She opened her mouth to argue but he'd already turned around for the rental vehicle. Things were tense enough without them arguing, so Eden stayed put, guarding him while he checked it out.

"All right, we're good," he called out, and she hurried to the car.

He already had the engine running. As soon as she shut the door, he shot away from the curb. She checked the side mirror, then swiveled to look behind them. "Anything?"

"No. Trinity?"

"Lost it around the next corner. It's headed east."

They were headed east.

She and Zack looked at each other, then Eden spun around—just in time to see the blue Tesla veer out from behind the truck between them.

"Hang on," Zack said, and hit the gas. He yanked the wheel to the left, passing the car in front of them before veering back in front. Horns blasted as he hit the brake just in time to whip around the next corner.

The Tesla followed as Zack picked up speed, weaving in and out of traffic. There was so much of it. Innocent bystanders were going to get seriously hurt. "Fifty meters and closing fast. We need to get off this street."

"Working on it," he muttered, dodging cars and trucks as he raced to get them away from the Tesla. He took a hard left on a stale amber light, tires squealing. She braced herself against the door, then jerked against the seatbelt when Zack suddenly hammered the brakes to avoid smashing into the back of a minivan.

They both grunted, their heads snapping back when the car behind them rear-ended them. Wincing, Eden turned to look behind them. The Tesla was only three cars back and coming on fast. "Zack—"

He cranked the wheel hard and took off before the other driver even knew what happened. The traffic up ahead was even thicker, ending in a lineup at the next light.

"Hang on," he warned and cranked the wheel again, spinning them into a sharp U-turn.

More horns blasted, three cars colliding with a metallic crunch as they swerved to avoid them. The Tesla mimicked them, pulling a tight U-turn and coming up behind them.

Zack turned right, trying to get them on a road with more room to move, but it was no use. "You're gonna have to take out the driver," he said to her.

Firing her weapon at a moving target with so many innocents between them was a last resort, but they needed to get rid of this asshole if they were going to make their escape.

"Ready." She rolled down her window, pistol in hand. "Bring him in closer."

Zack's face was grim as he eased up on the gas. Eden watched the Tesla in the side mirror, tracking its progress as it neared, counting down to when she would pop her head out the window to fire behind them.

Four. Three. Two—

A black car barreled out of a side street just as they passed it, hurtling toward the Tesla. The Tesla swerved an instant before they collided and was slammed into by a passing delivery truck.

"Your tail's clear," Amber said through Eden's earpiece.

Holy shit. Eden grinned. "It's Jesse and Amber." Jesse was behind the wheel. "Great timing," she told them.

"Even better, that driver's going to be all over that intersection camera footage for me to look at," Amber replied.

"Everyone okay?" Trinity asked.

"Yes," Eden said.

"Good. Pull over, give Bennet's phone and wallet to Jesse, then you and Zack go back to the house. Amber and

Jesse will meet me at RV point Charlie to go through the phone, surveillance and traffic cams. I want to know who our killer is and find out who the hell that driver was working for."

"Roger that." Zack drove for a couple minutes before turning onto a quiet side street and pulling over. Eden got out and handed over Bennett's stuff, then they swapped cars. By the time she and Zack got back to the safehouse in Jesse's rental, the adrenaline crash had hit her.

"You all right?" Zack asked as the garage door closed behind them.

"I'm okay." Just tired, and right now she needed distance from him. "I'm gonna take a shower."

Inside she stood under the hot spray, letting it ease the tension in her neck and shoulders. Her palms stung from where she'd scraped them on the pavement, and she was going to have a few bruises as well. That rear-ender had been far more than a love tap. She was gonna feel it in the morning.

Leaving her hair to dry naturally, she pulled on a sweater and a pair of yoga pants before walking into her bedroom. She stopped a foot past the bathroom threshold, her heart doing a terrified backflip.

Zack stood between her and the bed, his stormy eyes sweeping over her like a physical caress.

They stared at each other, the space between them suddenly filled with erotic memories. They pressed in on her along with the quiet, making her pulse thud in her throat.

Say something, she silently ordered him.

"For those first few months after you left, I saw you everywhere," he said, his deep voice stroking over her skin. "On the street. In airports. Restaurants. Once I even ran out of a meeting because I thought I saw you on the sidewalk outside."

His words made her feel small. "I'm sorry I hurt

you." She hadn't wanted to.

He came toward her. Eden forced herself to remain still, holding that molten pewter gaze.

Don't touch me. Please don't touch me.

She was weak where he was concerned. If he touched her, she didn't think she had the strength to pull away. And that would be a disaster, for both of them.

Stopping inches from her, taunting her with his scent and nearness, he lifted a hand to cup the side of her face.

Eden sucked in a breath as a thousand tingles raced over her skin, scattering her thoughts and pulling her nipples into hard points.

"We both lied to each other back then," he murmured, his face inches away. "But for me what we shared was real."

She scrambled to shore up her defenses, growing weaker with each heartbeat he stood so close. This was too dangerous. They'd both been hurt too much already, and this could only lead to more heartbreak.

"I can't give you what you want," she whispered back. "I can't give you normal."

His eyes darkened, the pupils expanding until they almost swallowed the irises as a solid arm locked around her waist. "I don't want normal. I just want you."

His mouth came down on hers, obliterating everything as a sudden tidal wave of need crashed over her.

Chapter Fifteen

Eden stiffened, fighting the onslaught of need pumping through her in a last ditch effort to pull away. But instead of devouring her mouth as she expected him to, Zack wound his arms around her and buried his face in her neck, crushing her to him.

Her hands stilled on his shoulders. He was holding her so tight. As if he was afraid she would be torn from him at any moment. Eden closed her eyes, her heart twisting. Against her better judgment she leaned into him, resting her head on his chest. His heart thudded beneath her cheek.

"I *missed* you," he whispered. "Missed you so damn much."

Oh God. She hadn't expected this. Had no defense against it, his words piercing her.

Unable to say it back to him, she slipped her hands around his ribs to his back and held him to her, telling him how she felt without words. Her chest felt tight, his desperation taking her completely off guard. She'd never imagined she'd affected him this much. Had never guessed he'd truly missed *her*, and not just the sex.

His fingers dug into her back, holding on tight as he

nuzzled her neck. A shiver swept through her, her body humming, skin alive with sensation as he skimmed his way up to her jaw. He dropped warm, fervent kisses over her face, his lips pausing an inch from hers.

She shouldn't let this continue. If she was smart she would end this now and retreat until they were both thinking straight, but that wasn't an option with him so close and holding her like he never wanted to let go. His honesty and openness made it impossible to walk away.

This might be their only time together without any barriers between them, no lies or pretense. She wanted to feel what it was like to be real with him. She'd dreamed of it so many times, would grieve for him all over again after this was over, but even the threat of the coming pain wasn't enough to stop her. This was worth the pain.

With a ragged sound she turned her lips to his. Heat detonated in her belly, her core.

Her hands found their way into his hair as he slanted his mouth across hers. Zack didn't plunder, didn't take. He gave. Heart-stopping, soul-wrenching kisses, his hands cradling her head. The touch of his tongue to hers made her gasp and plaster her body to the length of his. She wanted closer. Skin to skin, as close as they could get.

"Eden, fucking *touch* me," he rasped out, the desperation and yearning in his voice shredding the last wisps of her control.

She couldn't touch enough of him, couldn't get close enough. It was like she'd been slowly dying inside since the day she left him, and now she had suddenly burst back to life.

A seam ripped as she drew his shirt off to expose the raw power of his upper body. He groaned and clenched his fist in her hair as she rubbed her face against his chest, kissing and licking as she went.

The world went dark for a second as he pulled her sweater over her head. She brought his mouth back to hers, moaned at the way he caressed the inside of her mouth, one big hand cupping the back of her head while his other undid her bra. He cradled one breast in his palm, his thumb sweeping over the hard nipple.

She shuddered, rolled her hips against his and moaned again at the rigid length of his erection. It had been so damn long, felt like years instead of months, and she'd never forgotten how he could light her body up.

She wound her legs around his waist when he hoisted her into the air and turned to the bed. He came down on top of her, claiming her mouth in a deep, thorough kiss even as he pulled her pants down her legs. The heat of his hand cupping her stole her breath, then his mouth was closing over her nipple, lips and tongue caressing.

Closing her eyes, she allowed herself to sink into the sensations, not just the pleasure he was giving, but the feeling of being wanted, of being *safe...*

A soft, needy cry burst from her when his fingers stroked her sensitive folds. She was wet and throbbing, shuddered and bowed her back when he at last touched her swollen clit. "Zack," she gasped out.

"Yes." He remembered exactly what she liked. He gave it to her, building the pleasure, heightening the anticipation as he finally kissed his way down her belly and settled between her thighs. She'd thought about this so many times, but he was even better than she remembered.

The first touch of his lips had her gripping his hair tight, and then his tongue settled over her, stroking her most sensitive spot. Driving her wild before sliding inside her, making her push against his face, hungry for more.

Zack held her upper thighs and proceeded to make her mindless, twice bringing her to the edge before stopping suddenly.

"Oh, God, don't stop—make me come," she blurted, trembling, barely able to breathe for the unbearable ache between her legs.

"I want to be in you when you come. Wanna feel you clench around me," he rasped, shucking his jeans and coming up with a condom.

Eden levered up to reach between his legs, taking his rigid length in her hands. He jerked taut, a low groan coming from his throat as she squeezed and stroked.

One big hand plunged into her hair, tipping her face up to meet his kiss. She sucked at his tongue, stroking him the way he loved best, reveling in every twitch of his muscles, every raw groan she pulled from him.

He pushed her hands away, rolled the condom on and pressed her flat on her back, kneeling between her thighs. He stroked himself with one hand as he teased her with the other, gliding along the side of her clit, keeping her on edge until she was squirming and gasping for breath.

Just as her vision began to haze over he finally stretched out on top of her and blanketed her with his weight, his cock sliding between her folds, his belly and chest pressed to hers. Those gorgeous gray eyes stared down into hers, searing her with their heat and intensity, then he thrust home, burying his length inside her with one single thrust.

Eden cried out and squeezed her eyes shut at the perfection of it, the heat and thickness of him as he filled her. His mouth came down on hers, tongue driving into her mouth as he began to move. Smooth, firm strokes, the muscles in his shoulders and back flexing.

She clung to him, opened herself fully to him as she surrendered to the pleasure of it. He shifted higher, changing the angle, allowing her to wriggle around to just the right position and allow her friction against her clit, his weight and strength pinning her down.

"Move with me," he whispered, his voice sliding over her like dark, soft velvet.

Her arousal shot higher, the tantalizing promise of release looming at the edge of her consciousness. She sought it with single-minded need, her body tightening, reaching...

Zack slipped a hand between them to find her clit with his fingertips, rubbing in gentle circles while he rode her, stroking her inner sweet spot at the same time. "Let go for me, Eden."

Her breath halted, her body arched, and the orgasm ripped through her, a blinding wave of pleasure made all the more intense by the desperation they shared.

Above her he stiffened, his mouth lifting from hers. She forced her eyes open, mesmerized by the sight of him like that, riding the knife edge of ecstasy, the muscles in his chest and shoulders standing out, eyes squeezed shut and his face contorted into an expression of sensual agony.

Eden wrapped her arms around him, set her feet flat on the bed and rolled her hips, stroking him with her core.

His eyes flipped open, met hers for a single heart-stopping moment. They slid closed again, his ragged groan filling the silence as he drove deep and shuddered over and over, helpless in her embrace as she'd been mere moments before.

Breathing hard, he came down on his elbows, his head dropping to her shoulder. Eden gathered him to her and closed her eyes, her body warm and melted like chocolate left in the sun. She stroked his broad back as the silence settled around them, her mind allowing her a few seconds more peace before reality intruded into the perfection of the moment.

The sting of tears made her keep her eyes shut. This couldn't last, because she didn't believe he could ever be hers. And if they never got to the point where they could be together and make it work, at least she would remember this moment for the rest of her life.

His weight lifted, and she sensed him looking down at her. "Hey," he murmured, cradling her cheek in his hand.

Eden turned her face away, afraid the tears would leak out. The soft, tender kisses he scattered across her face made it even worse.

She swallowed the lump in her throat, forced the welling emotions back through sheer force of will and curled into him when he withdrew gently and rolled them onto their sides. If he tried to talk about them or their future, she couldn't take it.

"What's wrong?" he asked, smoothing his hand up and down her bare back.

"Nothing." Just that he was tearing her heart apart, making her wish for a future that might not be possible. She couldn't let herself dwell on fanciful dreams while they were dealing with everything else.

Eden cuddled closer, shutting off her brain, refusing to think about anything but right now. It was all she could handle for the moment.

Zack gave a low, contented groan, reached back to switch off the bedside lamp, then gathered her tight to him. "You feel so damn amazing."

She kissed his chest in response, not trusting herself to speak, unwilling to spoil this with words better left unsaid. Instead she drank it all in: his protective embrace, his delicious scent, the warmth and feel of his naked skin against hers.

In the darkness she lay listening to his breathing change, first evening out, then deepening. He twitched twice as he drifted off, his arms loosening around her.

Only when she was sure he was fast asleep did she carefully extricate herself from his arms and leave the room.

Chapter Sixteen

Zack stirred, his brain waking up before his body did. He rolled over and reached for Eden as his eyes opened in the dimness, but his hand met empty covers.

He jerked up onto his elbow and looked around, dread and disappointment flooding him. The bedroom door was closed and faint gray light coming through the edges of the blind told him it was still early, before seven at least. She'd been cuddled up against him when he'd fallen asleep last night. He hadn't even noticed when she'd left the bed.

He sat up and reached for his jeans, willing his heart to slow down, memories of the last time she'd ghosted on him swirling through his head. What if she left again?

No. If she'd left him, she still wouldn't have gone far. There was no way she would walk away from this mission and the others, even if she regretted last night. He sure as hell didn't, other than not noticing when she'd snuck out on him. It was rare for him to sleep so hard. He must have been more exhausted than he'd realized.

All caught up in his head, he hurried into the hallway, checking the other rooms. He stopped short in the kitchen doorway, relief sluicing through him. Eden stood at the stove with her back to him, cracking eggs into a pan.

She was still here. He could breathe again. God, he wanted to go up and wrap his arms around her from behind, nuzzle the side of her neck, but now he wasn't sure if it would be welcome or not.

"Morning," he said.

She looked back at him, her expression guarded, and gave a little smile. "Morning." She went back to cooking the eggs. "I just put the coffee on before I started on the eggs. I was going to bring you a plate."

He melted a little. "As in breakfast in bed?"

"Yes." Her cheeks flushed a bit as she stirred the eggs. Scrambled. Because she remembered that's how he liked them? "We didn't have any bread, though." She turned off the burner and slid the pan aside.

"Coffee and scrambled eggs is fantastic." The sweet gesture surprised him. They'd never stayed anywhere but hotels together, so he'd never seen her cook before. "Do you like to cook?"

She shrugged. "Sometimes. But not every day."

"Me neither." Encouraged that she wasn't trying to avoid him, Zack approached her, watching for any telltale stiffening of her spine. She tensed slightly, stopped him by turning around to face him, spatula still in hand.

Her gaze traveled over him, taking in his bare chest, then back up. Just having her eyes on him had blood shunting south.

She studied his face a moment. "You thought I left." A statement, not an accusation. There was a touch of disappointment in her eyes, though.

Yeah, he had. And now he felt bad. "Well, it's not the first time you've snuck out on me," he teased, adding a grin to lighten the mood. "But hey, at least you didn't drug me this time."

Her lips quirked and if he wasn't mistaken she

smothered a laugh as she turned back to the stove. "You and I have serious trust issues to work through, Maguire."

"Yeah. But I'm willing to put in the work to get through them." He closed the distance between them and settled his hands on her waist. Her abs contracted beneath his fingers but she didn't push him away as she scooped eggs onto a plate and handed it to him.

"Just eat your breakfast and behave yourself."

He couldn't resist leaning in to run his nose up the side of her neck. "You smell so damn good," he murmured, gratified when goosebumps rose on her skin, her nipples hardening to points beneath her T-shirt. He resisted the urge to touch them, allowed himself only three soft kisses along her neck before letting her go and reaching for the cupboard to get mugs out. "Do you really like your coffee black?"

"Yes." She aimed him a sideways glance, her eyes laughing at him. "Why would I have lied about that?"

"I dunno why you Valkyries do the things you do," he answered, filling both mugs and carrying them to the table. She came over with two plates of scrambled eggs and sat across from him.

It was so much like before, the quiet intimacy of sharing breakfast with her, just the two of them. Except now they knew each other's deepest secrets, so the intimacy was ten times as intense. He held out his fork. "Cheers."

A slow smile curved her mouth. He'd done this every time they'd eaten together in whatever hotel they had stayed in. "Cheers." She tapped her fork to his and dug in, her eyes warm as she gazed at him.

Taking that as a good sign, he started the conversation with something non-personal. "Where are the others?"

"Stayed at different places last night. Safer if we all split up for the moment."

"Any word on the driver last night, or Bennett's killer?"

"Not yet. Trinity said she'd call when she's got something for us."

"Yeah?" He gave her a heated look that was only partially teasing. "How long do we have, do you think?"

She wagged her fork at him. "Not long enough for what you're thinking."

He blinked in mock surprise. "What am I thinking?"

"X-rated things."

She wasn't wrong. "You sleep okay last night?"

"Pretty well. You?"

"I was out cold." And she didn't look like she'd slept that well. She had shadows under her eyes. What time had she left the bed?

"What?' she asked when he kept staring at her.

"Tell me something about you that's different from how you were before with me."

She considered it for a moment. "I don't like flashy clothes. I prefer this look." She tugged at the snug T-shirt she filled out beautifully. "It's comfy and practical."

"Hmm. And you're definitely shier than you were before." When they'd first met she'd posed as a classy, breezy, and stylish flight attendant. Elegant clothes, sophisticated makeup. In reality she was far more subdued.

Her lashes lowered, a slight flush turning her cheeks pink. "I can't be when I'm on a job, but... Yes."

It was charming. And adorable. "I never would have guessed."

Those gorgeous amber eyes lifted to meet his. "Never would have guessed you were an introvert."

That made him chuckle. "Touché. What else?"

"I hate wearing makeup. And heels. God, I hate heels."

"You wore them every day we were together," he said in surprise.

181

"I know, but I always ditched them as fast as I could, and I usually got a nice foot rub out of the deal for my troubles."

A startled laugh burst out of him. "You were using me for foot rubs, too?"

"You give awesome foot rubs, and I told you, while I was with you I got to be a different version of me. The one I never got to be in real life," she said with a smile, then sobered. "Tell me the truth. Are you disappointed with the real me?"

He would have laughed, but her expression was dead serious...and there was concern lurking in her eyes he wanted to erase forever. "No. In fact I prefer this version a hundred times more. The other you would have bankrupted me eventually," he teased. "All those fancy hotels and dinners and room service."

They shared a smile, remembering how it had been, then her phone rang. She pulled it out and answered, her expression turning grave. "And Bennett?" She listened a moment. "Okay, understood. Eighty minutes. Bye."

"Trinity?" he asked as she set the phone down.

"Yes. The Tesla driver made it a few blocks from the scene of the accident before a cop found her."

"*Her?*"

"Yes. They took her to the hospital, but she died on the operating table from internal injuries."

The news surprised him, and was also cause for concern. That woman had definitely been gunning for them last night, or Eden at least. On the plus side, there weren't a lot of female hitters around, so maybe she'd be easier to ID. "Any idea who she was?"

"Not yet. Amber's looking into it, along with Kiyomi."

"Maybe she killed Bennett."

"Maybe. Chances are she's connected to his death in

some way if she was waiting for us when we left the building. Anyway, we can't stay in the city any longer, there may be other hitters coming for us, and the cops definitely will be. Trinity's scheduled a flight for us eighty minutes from now at a small airport outside of town."

"Where are we going?"

"Back to the UK. Rycroft's team and Amber are working on altering the flight plan and route to confuse anyone who might be on to us and hoping to follow."

Good. Because they couldn't risk leading anyone back to base.

Eden stood and grabbed her plate. "We need to sanitize this place."

He leaned over to grab her arm before she could turn away. "Wait." He took the plate from her and set it on the table. "I'll help you wipe everything down in a minute. But first, come here a sec."

Ignoring her protests, he tugged her around the small table and drew her onto his lap. She was rigid at first, but when he wrapped his arms around her and tucked her in close, his chin resting on her shoulder, she slowly relaxed. "I really do like the real you better than the fake you," he murmured against her hair. "The real you has the best of both versions."

She grumbled, clearly uncomfortable with the compliment, then sighed and leaned into him more. "We're all in danger now, especially the others and me, and I don't want you hurt or killed because of what you've been dragged into."

"I wasn't dragged into anything, I volunteered."

"Before you knew the whole truth of what's going on."

"Doesn't matter."

"Yes, it does. *You* matter."

"And you don't?" Bullshit to that. He'd—

She pushed up to glare down at him, her eyes blazing

with frustration…and a hint of fear. "Don't you get it? We're up against an unknown threat from a faceless enemy with powerful connections, unlike anyone you've ever confronted before. You have family that care about you. I don't. No one will miss me if I die. The others and I, we're…"

He put a hand over her mouth to stop her from continuing, afraid the word expendable had been about to come out. She wasn't fucking expendable, and neither were the others.

"*I'd* miss you, goddammit," he fired back, outraged that she would ever think she mattered so little to anyone, least of all him. "Don't you get that? I don't ever want to hear you say that shit again. That's Agency bullshit, drilled into you by the same people who made you into a weapon they could use and dispose of when it suited them. Fuck that. Fuck *them*."

Her anger faded, the look in her eyes replaced by something bordering on exhaustion. "Zack, you don't know me. Not really. And you don't know the things I've done. If you knew the truth…"

He wasn't going to listen to any bullshit excuses she threw out to put distance between them. "We've both done things we'd rather forget in service to our country. But I know and admire the most important things about you." She looked away but he took her face in his hands, forced her to look at him. "I know you're brave and smart and determined, and that I got to see a softer, freer side of you that no one ever has before."

Her eyes filled with torment at the last part, but she didn't deny it.

She'd let him in that much before. He needed her to let him in completely now. "So you're not a saint, and guess what, neither am I. But I know you're dedicated and talented, beautiful, sexy, and loyal. And that's more than enough." It had to be enough.

She closed her eyes. "Zack…"

He slid a hand to her nape, drew her head down so her cheek was pressed to his. "You matter, Eden. To me as well as the others. And if you think I'd walk away from you when you need me most, then you don't know me at all."

She groaned and gripped his shoulders, squeezing tight. "Wanna know something about me that I really hate?"

Yes. He nuzzled her. "What?"

"Crying. So if you make me cry right now, I'll punch you in the face."

It shocked a laugh out of him, then he kissed her cheek. "Thanks for the warning. But just remember what I said, okay?" He took her chin in his hand, tipped her face up to search her eyes. "I'm not leaving you. No matter what you say or do." And he had a feeling she'd fight this more before everything was said and done.

A tiny smile tugged at her mouth, and a spark of hope ignited deep in his chest. "You're probably gonna regret this."

"No way." He kissed her, savoring the feel of her lips, rediscovering the real Eden for a few stolen moments before pulling back. "Come on. Let's get this place wiped down and get outta here."

They grabbed their things, wiped down every room they'd been in, then stuffed the sheets into a garbage bag to take with them. They paid special attention to anything they might have left prints on: light switches, buttons, door handles.

He checked their exterior perimeter to ensure it was safe, then went into the garage and got in the car with her. She navigated while he drove, using a custom app on her phone that showed other team members' locations. "Trinity's got the others with her. She'll be turning in behind us in another two blocks."

Sure enough, as he passed the intersection two blocks up, a gray minivan appeared behind them. "That her?"

"Yes."

They drove straight for the small airport twenty minutes away, still in the metro area. Only a few cars were in the lot, small planes sitting on the tarmac near the little terminal building. There was no sign of their jet. "When's our ride coming?"

"Soon." She searched the surrounding sky.

He pulled through the open gate and headed for the parking lot. Trinity had just pulled in behind them when the screech of tires made him snap his head around.

A black Camaro was racing straight at them.

Zack cursed and cranked the wheel.

The tires squealed on the pavement as he spun them in a tight circle. But just as he aimed for the exit, the barrel of a rifle appeared through the Camaro's open side window and opened fire.

Chapter Seventeen

One moment the barrel of the rifle appeared through the Camaro's window. The next, Eden was yanked facedown in Zack's lap.

Bullets peppered the back of the car as Zack sped away, shattering the rear window and windshield. She shifted to draw her weapon but Zack's hand on the back of her neck kept her cheek pinned to his thigh.

"Stay down," he growled, ducking down in his seat as he raced through the lot, trying to see through the fractured windshield.

Eden twisted free, leaned back and slammed the soles of her boots against the ruined windshield. She kicked it twice, three times, until it finally came loose. She shoved it out with one last push, and it flew over the hood as Zack took a hard left. "Where are the others?"

"Headed for the other exit. Another car's behind them."

Shit. She risked sitting up enough to see in the side mirror. The Camaro was racing after them. "How did they know we were here?"

"No fucking idea." He swerved through the gate and

shot across the road, cutting off traffic. Horns blared and tires screeched. Zack hammered the brake to avoid slamming into a car and veered left, trying to get them free.

He shot through the next intersection, leaning on the horn to make the stopped traffic move out of their way. "Come on. Come on, dammit, *move!*"

Eden turned around in her seat to look behind them. The Camaro whipped down a side street and disappeared from view. "They're gonna come at us from the right somewhere up ahead."

"Not if they can't find us." Zack took the next left turn and gunned it through a fresh green light.

Eden searched around. Were they in the clear? "I don't see them—"

The Camaro shot out in front of them from another side street.

Zack cursed and jerked the wheel, but the Camaro rammed into their back right quarter panel, spinning them around. The squeal of tires and the deep blast of a rig's horn was Eden's only warning, then they slammed into the side of a semi cab.

Stars exploded before her eyes as the seatbelt snapped hard across her chest and hips, the back of her head hitting the headrest a split-second later.

"Eden," Zack said urgently.

"I'm fine," she said, reaching down to unbuckle the seatbelt. They were pinned in now, unable to drive away. Where was the Camaro? Where was—

Zack grabbed her around the ribs and yanked her sideways out of the car. "Get behind the engine block!"

They dove for cover behind the front of the hood just as shots rang out, pummeling the opposite side of the car. People were screaming now, leaping out of their vehicles and racing for the sidewalk, the frightened masses scattering in all directions.

"How far away?" Eden asked him as she scrambled

up on one knee, poised behind the engine block. It would provide them a decent amount of cover for a bit longer, but they couldn't stay here. Cut off from their teammates and all alone with a rifleman closing in, they were sitting ducks. "Did you see?"

"Out of pistol range." His gray gaze met hers. "We're gonna have to run for it and fight our way out."

The gravity of it settled deep inside her. She'd been in danger before, had escaped death many times, but this moment was different. Before, she'd always been alone. Before, she'd never had anyone else to worry about. Now there was Zack. And she didn't want him to die. Not like this, not in front of her, and not when he was in this mess because of her.

Eden tensed and ducked lower as a spray of bullets raked across the hood and punched into the side of the rig.

"You head around the front of the rig on three," Zack told her, his face set, gaze intense. "I'll be right behind you."

Cold speared her gut at the way he said it. Like he had every intention of staying behind to make sure she got clear. Like he was prepared to sacrifice himself to ensure she lived. "Don't you dare do anything stupid or heroic."

"You go on three, and I'll cover you. One." He put a hand on the center of her back. "Two." He shifted behind her, so close she could feel the warmth of his body, and she prayed it wasn't the last time she would ever feel it. "*Three.*"

He shoved her forward, but she was already moving, sprinting around the front of the rig's cab. Bullets plowed into the side of it, missing her by inches. Pedestrians screamed and panicked, clogging the sidewalk.

More shots rang out, hitting metal somewhere behind her. She shoved through a knot of people cowering in front of an alley and ran for cover behind the corner of the first building she came to. As soon as she was out of view she risked a glance behind her, looking for Zack.

He wasn't there.

"God*damn* you, Zack," she whispered, terror flooding her. She stayed behind cover, coming up with a new plan. No way would she keep running if he was still back there, and she didn't have time to try and contact Trinity and the others to ask for backup.

Dammit. She snuck another peek around the corner, but still couldn't see him. Was he okay, or had he been shot? *Oh, Jesus, please not that—*

More shots rang out, telling her he was still alive, but pinned down somewhere. She eased forward, ready to break from cover and attempt a rescue mission, but caught a blur of motion at the edge of her peripheral vision. Her heart careened in her chest when she saw Zack dart out from behind another truck and race toward her.

"Go!" he yelled, waving her forward with one hand, pistol in the other. "Two shooters! They've split up, one on either side!"

She spun and ran down the alley, reassured when his racing footsteps echoed behind her seconds later. Another street loomed up ahead. She slowed as she reached the corner of the building, pressed her back to the side of it as Zack raced up beside her.

Lightning quick, Eden ducked around to check the alley. Bits of concrete exploded inches from her head.

Zack yanked her backward so hard she fell on her ass, heart hammering. Shit, that had been close. But those bullets hadn't come from a rifle. The sound hadn't been right.

He grabbed her head in his hands, searched her face. "Are you okay?"

"Yes. Shooter's to the right, hiding between the wall and a Dumpster. Pistol, not a rifle."

He glanced behind them down the alley they'd just run up. "Other one's going to come in behind us, try to box us in."

Well, there was no way they were making it back the way they'd come with a rifle trained on them. That left them only one option if they didn't want to stay here and wait to get shot. "We'll take this shooter out, then run like hell before the one with the rifle shows up." They had no idea where the other shooter was, but probably close. They might only have seconds to get out of here.

He stared at her for a second. "Okay. I'll go high, you go low."

"On my mark." She stood and knelt at the corner of the building while he crossed the alley and stood with his back to the wall, giving them a wider combined angle of attack. She waited several heartbeats, holding his gaze, straining to listen for any sounds of movement coming up the alley. "And...*now*."

She whipped around the corner, spotted the shadow beside the Dumpster, and fired two shots at it. Zack fired at the same time from his position.

The shadow dropped.

Eden ran toward it, weapon aimed, ready to fire again. She could hear Zack moving behind her but didn't look back, leaving him to guard their six because all her attention was on the threat in front of them.

The shadow moved slightly. Eden fired two more shots but nothing came back at them.

Putting on a burst of speed, Eden raced for the shooter. "Face down and let me see your hands," she snarled.

A muffled groan came from beside the Dumpster.

"Face down, now," Eden snapped, less than twenty feet away now.

Still nothing.

Eden reached under the Dumpster to grab whatever she could get hold of—a wad of material—and pulled.

Dragging the person out, she let go, shocked when

the woman glared up at her. Young. Barely in her twenties if Eden had to guess. What the hell?

The woman's weapon lay fallen out of her reach. Eden snagged it, stuck it in her waistband as she flipped the woman over onto her back and straddled her. Blood poured out of the shooter's abdomen, wetting her black cargo pants.

"Who are you, and why are you after us?" Eden demanded, Zack slightly behind her and off to the side, guarding them. She did a quick search for other weapons, froze when she saw the mark on the woman's left hip in the gap above the waistband. Not a brand like hers. A tat. But it was a stylized symbol, eerily similar to hers.

What the *hell*?

"Who are you?" Eden snapped, out of patience.

The woman didn't answer, eyes burning with resentment, lips white with pain.

"Talk," Eden demanded, grabbing the woman's jaw.

Dark blue eyes remained locked with hers in defiance. Then those white lips curled into a half-smirk that sent a warning prickle across Eden's nape, and a telltale crunch sounded as the woman bit down.

"No—" Eden grabbed the woman's throat, trying to stop her from swallowing, but too late. "*Shit*," she snarled, the distinctive bitter almond smell hitting her a split second before the convulsions started. Shit, shit, shit.

She jerked back.

"What the hell," Zack said, starting forward as if he was going to try to help the woman.

"No," Eden said sharply, flinging out an arm to stop him. "It's too late, the potassium cyanide's already mixed with the hydrochloric acid in her stomach." The woman vomited, still convulsing. "Hydrogen cyanide can be inhaled and absorbed through the skin. Don't touch it—"

"Look out!"

She jerked around at his warning shout, weapon up,

her heart seizing when saw a man fifty feet away aiming a rifle at them.

She was dimly aware that Zack had dropped to one knee as the men fired simultaneously.

Eden held her breath and fired twice as gunfire roared through the narrow alley. Bullets peppered the Dumpster behind her, missing her by inches.

The man holding the rifle fell to his knees, rifle still in his grip, and toppled sideways.

Eden raced at him, weapon aimed at his chest, and fired again. He jerked as the bullets hit him but didn't fall. Before she could fire again, a bullet plowed through his forehead.

He dropped like a ragdoll, his hand going lax around the rifle.

"Mother*fucker*," she breathed, her heart banging against her ribs. She hadn't even known he was behind them, would be dead right now if Zack hadn't alerted her and fired when he had.

She kicked the rifle away and reached down to roll the man to his back. "Not gonna get anything out of him," she muttered, turning on her haunches to look at Zack.

He stood not fifteen feet from her, pistol hanging loosely at his side. His face was pale, his eyes almost haunted as he stared at the dead man.

"What?" she asked. "You know him?"

"He's my handler."

Eden whipped back around to stare at the man in shock, then turned to Zack. "Are you—" She stopped breathing when she saw the blood soaking the front of his shirt. "*Zack.*"

"I'm okay," he said, pressing a hand to his side as he moved to lean against the brick wall beside him, as though he needed it to prop him up.

She reached him in three strides, took his weapon and grabbed the front of his shirt, searching for the entry wound. Oh, Jesus, if he'd been gut shot…

He hissed in a breath, his face contorting with pain. "Really, I'm—"

"Shut up," she ordered, picking up the sound of distant sirens approaching. They needed to get the hell out of here, the cops would be here within minutes. "Just shut up and sit down." She helped him slide down the wall, kept him propped up with one hand on his shoulder while she reached for the blade at her calf and cut his shirt open.

A wave of relief crashed over her when she saw he hadn't been hit in the stomach, but his waist. There was no spurting, indicating the bullet probably hadn't hit an artery or an organ.

She pressed his ruined shirt to the wound, earning a growl and a black look. "Stay still. I'm calling for an extraction." With one hand she reached back to pull her phone from her hip pocket and dialed Trinity.

"Are you guys okay?" Trinity said upon answering. "We're tracking you now."

Eden scanned the alley. No one else had shown up yet, but it was only a matter of time and there could be more shooters. "We need immediate extraction. Do you have our location?"

"Yes. What happened?"

"Zack's been hit."

"How bad?"

She was surprised to see her hands were shaking. Her breathing was choppy, her stomach muscles quivering. "Critical, but not life-threatening." She hoped.

"Hang tight. We'll be there in under five minutes."

Eden slipped the phone back into her pocket and pressed both hands to the shirt, blinking hard. Shit, she needed to hold it together. If more shooters or cops came after them—

"Hey," Zack said gently. His bloody fingers curled around her wrist as he cupped her cheek with his free

194

hand.

Eden blinked fast, trying to stem the rush of tears, but it was no use. Didn't matter that it shamed and embarrassed her, she was fucking crying while he was the one bleeding all over the place.

"I'm okay, sweetness."

Sweetness.

The endearment threatened to split her wide open. He'd called her that for the first time the night before she'd walked out on him.

A sob caught in her throat. She squeezed her eyes shut and shook her head, unable to speak. No, he was *not* okay, he was fucking bleeding from a bullet wound that might have done more damage than she realized, and could have killed him.

"Come here," he whispered, drawing her head to his neck.

She went willingly, pressing her face to his skin, soaking it with her tears.

ZACK HELD EDEN close, absorbing the feel of her and trying to ignore how much the wound in his side hurt. "Don't cry." It shredded him to see her so upset.

"I hate crying," she choked out.

"I know." When she released a shuddering breath and kept her face pressed to his neck, he hugged her tighter, soaking up her embrace.

"I'll punch you for this later," she muttered.

He cracked a half-grin. "Please don't. I'm in enough pain already." It felt like someone had punched a hole through him and then filled it with salt. No, aimed a flamethrower at it. It burned like hell, but he was still alive, and that wasn't the part that hurt the most anyway.

Rod had shot him. Tried to kill him, and would have killed Eden too if Zack hadn't brought him down first.

Zack couldn't even look at the body.

How had Rod found them? Zack had known Rod was interested in finding Eden on the night of the Sevastopol op, but he'd never imagined his handler had been this involved in the hunt. Maybe Rod had known about him and Eden from the start, and used Zack to find her and the other Valkyries.

His stomach rolled. "Christ, this is my fault."

Eden lifted her head, wiped hastily at her face with the back of one bloodstained hand to frown at him. "What?"

"If Rod found us here, then it must have been because of me." The bottom of his stomach fell out as something worse occurred to him. "Shit, what if he somehow found where headquarters is?"

"He couldn't have, or they'd have hit us there instead of here. Now stop talking." She glared at him. "You're making yourself bleed more."

He hid a wince. "I'm gonna be okay, sweetness," he murmured. He'd been damn lucky, though. The bullet had missed his belly only because he'd been moving when Rod fired. An inch or two higher or to the right, and it would have blown his kidney apart.

"Yes, you will," she told him, "because I'm going to make sure of it."

The vow touched him. He leaned his forehead to hers. "Are you gonna nurse me back to health?"

She paused, blinking at him. "Sure."

"Sure? So enthusiastic." He grimaced as fire swept through his side, bit back a growl and focused on her through the pain. "And what about us?"

"What about us?" Her attention was on her hands, pressed tight to his entry wound.

He could feel the blood leaking down his back, soaking his pants as it dripped down his leg. "Are you gonna give us another chance?"

She pulled back, scowling at him. "That's dirty.

You're trying to take advantage of my weakened emotional state."

Yup. "I'll play dirty if that's what it takes to get you back."

"I said I'd nurse you. Now be quiet and stay still. Trinity will be here in a couple more minutes." She glanced around, but no one had wandered down the alley yet. Wouldn't be long until the cops came, though.

He shifted, his legs a bit unsteady. "We should move."

"No. You're staying put, I don't want you to bleed any heavier than you already are. There might be other shooters out there, and amazing as I am, I can only carry you so far if you keel over on me."

"You'd carry me out?"

She met his gaze, her eyes full of outrage. "You really have to ask me that?"

He smiled. Yeah, she cared. More than she wanted to admit, to him or herself. "I won't give up on us, Eden."

"So you've said. Now shush and no more talking. We'll get you to a medical facility—"

"No."

She glared at him. "Yes."

It was too much of a risk if anyone else was coming for them. "Only if Heath says I need to."

She huffed out an irritated breath. "Fine. Now be quiet and focus on slowing your heart rate."

Her phone rang. The sheer relief on her face made his heart squeeze as she answered, looking around. "Where are you guys?" She lowered the phone an instant before someone came around the corner.

He relaxed when Megan, Ty and Heath appeared, weapons in hand as they scanned the alley. "You guys all right?" he asked.

"Yeah, we took out two shooters before the rest scattered, but we gotta get you outta here and haul ass," Ty said. He moved past them to the female hitter while Megan approached Rod's body and Heath hurried toward Zack.

"How you doing, man?" the former PJ asked.

Zack was damn glad to see him. "Hanging in there."

"He's talking too much," Eden said, shooting him a warning look. "Says he won't go get checked out anywhere unless you tell him he has to."

"Is that right? What a stubborn bastard," Heath said, crouching down in front of Zack as he ripped open a bandage he'd brought. "Let's take a look."

While Heath started his assessment, Zack looked over at Megan. "You need to check him," he said to Megan, nodding toward Rod's body. "See if you can find a phone or something on him." They needed to tear apart Rod's contacts, find out who had ordered this and who'd known they'd been here. And *how*.

"Any idea who he is?" Megan asked as she searched Rod's body.

"Yeah. My handler."

Chapter Eighteen

Megan cranked her head around to stare at Zack, then Eden. Her fellow Valkyrie's grim expression confirmed what Zack had said. What the hell?

Turning away, she crouched beside the body and quickly checked it. It was clean except for one item in his left hip pocket. "Got a key, but nothing else."

"Key to what?" Eden asked. Heath was still busy with Zack, and Ty was sweeping the other body.

"Motel, looks like." She shoved it in her pocket, stood and hurried back to the patient. "Can we move him?" she asked Heath, unsure how serious the wound was. Zack had lost a lot of blood.

"Gimme two secs," he said, winding a tensor bandage around Zack's middle. When he was done he stretched Zack's right arm across his shoulders and lifted him to his feet. "Up you go." He steadied Zack a moment. "Can you walk?"

"Yeah."

"Let's move," Heath said.

Ty came back. "Got nothing. But she's got a tat on her left hip you might be interested in." He showed her the picture he'd taken of it on his phone.

She? Megan jerked her gaze to his in shock, then

looked at Eden. "You saw?"

"Yes. Now let's get the hell out of here."

Ty took point down the alley. Megan walked behind Eden and Heath, who had their arms around Zack to assist him. "Just a half block up," she said as Ty turned the corner.

The sidewalk was busy with people but only a few glanced at them as they rushed for the street. A white minivan idled at the curb. Chloe sat behind the wheel, her jaw working away on her gum, and slid the side door open for them as they approached. "Good to go?" she asked.

"Yep," Heath answered, helping Zack inside the middle row beside Eden while Ty hopped in the back and Megan rushed around to take shotgun.

"Okay, where are we headed?" Chloe asked, pulling out onto the road.

"Wherever Trinity is," Megan said.

"New airport with Jesse and Amber," Chloe answered, expertly maneuvering them through traffic. "Trin's diverted the plane there, but it's a twenty-minute drive from here."

Megan examined the key she'd taken from Zack's handler and entered the name on it into her phone. "If Zack can handle it, I need to make a stop on the way."

"I can handle it," he replied.

"So where to?" Chloe asked.

"Little motel off the I-95," Megan said. "I wanna see if our hitter left anything behind that might be of interest."

"I'll go with you," Eden said, and Megan wasn't about to argue. With so much shit raining down on them, extra backup was more than welcome.

Chloe stopped two blocks east of the motel. Megan hopped out with Ty, handed him and Eden latex gloves before heading for the motel. The key was for a room facing the rear parking lot on the second floor.

Ty stood watch downstairs while she and Eden went

up the stairs. Megan slid her gloves on, went straight to the correct door and checked it to make sure it wasn't rigged in any way before opening it. Eden stepped inside behind her and shut the door.

Housekeeping had been here recently. The bed was neatly made and there were fresh towels folded in the bathroom. "Check the closet," she said to Eden. "I'll look in here."

"There's a bag in here," Eden called out. "Nothing in it but dirty clothes."

All the obvious places in the bathroom were empty too. But Zack's handler would be more discerning than most if he'd been planning to come back here after today's hit. If he'd left something behind and intended to collect it later, he would have taken the trouble of hiding it.

Megan pushed the cupboard doors wide under the sink and laid on her back with her penlight in her mouth. Nothing caught her attention but she was undeterred, reaching up to feel along the wood trim beneath the counter top, and behind the sink where it met the wall.

Her fingers bumped something solid and rectangular attached to the wall. Something stuck there with Velcro. *Bingo.* "Got something." She pulled the phone free and crawled out of the cupboard to examine it.

Eden came to the doorway. "Burner?"

"Yep. But if he went to the trouble of hiding it, then there's something on it he doesn't want anyone to find. Unfortunately for him, my sister can make this sing like a soprano." She checked a few other places as well, the inside trim along the ceiling in the closet, then the underside of the bedside table and dresser drawers. Behind the bed and TV.

She found another phone stuck to the underside of the shelf of the entertainment unit. "I can't wait to see what that asshole has on these," she muttered, putting it in an empty pocket.

They didn't find anything else. Before leaving, they did a final sweep to check for bugs or cameras, anything that might have recorded or transmitted their presence. The room was clean.

"What about the female hitter's tat? Did you recognize it?" Megan said to Eden as they moved to the door.

"No, but I don't like it. Think there's another version of the Program going on?"

"At this point I wouldn't rule anything out."

Ty was waiting for them at the bottom of the stairs. He wrapped an arm around her waist as they walked across the parking lot, heading for the place where Chloe would pick them up, his head moving back and forth as he scanned for any more signs of trouble. "Get anything?" he asked her.

"Oh yeah. Amber can uncover all his dirty little secrets on the flight back."

Chloe pulled up to the rendezvous spot as they arrived. "Plane's on the ground and getting refueled."

Trinity, Jesse and Amber were all there at the airport waiting for them next to the jet when they arrived. "What'd you get?" her sister asked.

"Something to keep you occupied on the flight." Megan handed the burners over.

Amber rushed straight up the steps into the plane. Jesse smirked in chagrin and followed her.

Heath and Ty helped Zack up the stairs into the cabin while Eden watched anxiously from the base. Trinity held them back with a gesture as she spoke to Chloe.

Megan stepped up beside Eden, too curious to wait any longer. "Can I ask you something?"

Eden glanced at her, then up at Zack as he entered the plane, distracted. "Sure."

"Were you guys together before?"

That pretty amber stare came back to her. "Yes."

Ah. She'd wondered, but Trinity had never said. "Are you together now?"

Eden's expression filled with torment. "I don't know. I want to be, but—" She stopped and looked away, embarrassed.

Megan let it go, feeling bad for her. She knew what it was like to feel torn between head and heart, duty and desire. How hard it was to trust an outsider. How hard it was for them to *hope*. But she also knew how rewarding and freeing it was to let a deserving man in. And from everything she'd seen so far, Zack was deserving.

"So I just got an interesting tidbit from Rycroft," Trinity said as she strode over to them with Chloe. "His analysts got intel on the driver of the Tesla from the morgue. And it seems she had an interesting tat on her left hip as well." She held up a phone.

Megan cursed under her breath when she saw the picture. The tat was the exact same one as the dead female's in the alley. "So what are we dealing with here? Another hit squad for the CIA?"

"Doubtful it's with the CIA. There's been so much heat on them since they scrambled to dismantle everything to do with us. No way they'd go down that road again with all the scrutiny they're still facing."

"Then what?" Eden asked with a frown. "The dead woman in the alley is barely out of her teens. Early twenties at most."

"Same with the driver last night," Trinity said, reaching out to place a hand on Eden's shoulder and giving her a warm smile. "I'm just glad you and Zack are okay. Now go take care of your man."

"He's not my man," Eden said, looking uncomfortable. But her eyes shot anxiously to the open cabin door as she turned and headed for the stairs.

"He's totally her man," Chloe said with a chuckle

when Eden was out of earshot. "And on that note, I'm going to find mine," she said, aiming for the stairs.

Just then Ty appeared at the top of the steps. He jogged down them, his gaze swinging from Megan to Trinity. "Pilots have clearance. You guys ready?"

"Yes," Trinity answered as she headed for the stairs.

Megan started to follow her, but stopped next to Ty and waited for the other Valkyrie to disappear inside. Ty searched her eyes, concerned. "What's up?"

"Nothing." Something had clicked for her today.

The two of them had had so many close calls together, and there would undoubtedly be more before all this ended. Ty had been with her through thick and thin since coming back into her life. She trusted him without reservation and would be utterly destroyed if she lost him.

Life was guaranteed to no one, least of all them. So what the hell was she waiting for?

He frowned. "Must be something."

She remembered what he'd told her once. That he wanted her to come to him when she was ready.

Say the word, and I'll get down on one knee and ask you properly.

"Okay, there is something." Megan wound her arms around his waist and smiled up at him. "I think we should get married."

His eyes widened. "What?"

"As soon as possible."

A startled smile broke across his face. "Are you serious? I—" He stopped, dropped to one knee in front of her and took her hands.

"No, hey." Laughing, she pulled him upward, spying Chloe and Trinity's curious faces pressed to the windows above them, watching with interest. "You don't need to do that. I already said yes."

Ty wrapped a strong hand around her nape and kissed her. "I've got witnesses. You can't take it back."

She grinned up at him, her heart swelling with love and pride. "I won't take it back." Everything would be all right as long as she had Ty.

Her head whipped around when she caught sight of two vehicles racing into the parking lot. Must have tracked them via CCTV feeds or maybe a drone.

A surge of adrenaline shot through her. "Shit, we've got more company. Let's go," she yelled up into the cabin as she tore up the steps. Ty was right behind her to yank the hatch shut and lock it. "We gotta go *now*," she told the pilots. "Right now."

When she turned around, Trinity and Chloe were peering through the windows on the other side of the plane. "Two cars," Trinity announced.

The engine noise increased as the pilots powered up and began moving the plane forward.

Ty was right beside Megan as they hurried to a window across the aisle from the others as the plane turned. "This is gonna be close," she muttered. They had maybe thirty seconds before the first vehicle was within easy firing range.

"Yep," Ty said, settling a hand on her hip, the solid weight of it reassuring her.

Megan reached for his hand and gripped it tight. Whatever happened, at least they were together.

Chapter Nineteen

"Okay, let's lay you down here so Heath can doctor you up more," Jesse said as he helped Zack into the small bedroom at the rear of the cabin.

Oh, yes, thank God for the bed in the back.

Zack kept one hand pressed to the entry wound and entered the cabin, then gingerly stretched out on his uninjured side while Heath pulled on a new pair of gloves and came to crouch beside the bed with his med ruck. The bandages he'd wrapped around Zack earlier were completely saturated. He dripped blood onto the sheets as Heath unwrapped his waist.

Zack clenched his teeth at the sudden, intensified burn as the air hit the wounds.

"We're gonna need an ultrasound done on your left kidney when we get to the UK," the former PJ said, reaching for his ruck. "In the meantime, I'm gonna put in some stitches for now. Don't have any lidocaine on me, but I think I've got a fentanyl lollipop in here somewhere if you want it."

"Nah, I'm good."

"You sure? No shame in it."

"I'm sure." These guys barely knew him. He wasn't gonna pussy out and suck on a damn lollipop just for some stitches. But he wasn't gonna look while Heath put them in, either. "Go ahead."

"Got a tongue depressor here. Wanna bite down on it?"

"Just sew me up," he said curtly, sick of bleeding all over the place and just wanting it over with.

"Okay."

Turned out that having his hide stitched back together without any anesthetic sucked, he decided a few moments later. Heath held a penlight in his teeth while he sewed Zack up with the curved suture needle. Having a needle stabbed into torn flesh wasn't any fun, and neither was the thread as it pulled through—especially when Heath just kept going. And going.

"How many stitches are you putting in me?" he bit out.

"Enough so you don't leak all over the place," Heath responded around the penlight. "Shoulda taken the lollipop."

Zack was clenching his jaw and trying to think of something else when Eden walked in a moment later. "Hey, how you doing?" she asked softly, coming to kneel in front of him so they were at eye level. She took one of his hands, her eyes full of concern as the engine noise increased and the plane started forward.

Christ, she was beautiful. Just looking at her eased his pain. "Good."

She looked at Heath. "Did you give him any pain meds yet?"

"Nope. Just about done with the stitches now. When was your last tetanus shot?" he asked Zack.

"Can't remember."

"Okay, so you're getting one of those, too."

Awesome. What was one more needle stick on top of everything else he'd just gone through?

"How bad was the exit wound?" Eden asked, peering anxiously at Heath's hands as he worked.

"About twice as big as the entry wound. He's missing a decent size chunk out of his hide, but he's lucky. Shock wave could have pulverized his kidney."

Eden stroked her thumb across the back of Zack's hand while Heath tied off the last suture and then gave him the tetanus shot in the side of the ass.

He'd barely withdrawn the needle when hurried treads came up the aisle on the other side of the door, then Trinity yanked it open a second later. "Get ready for immediate emergency takeoff."

Eden shot to her feet and spun to look out the small window as Zack bit back a groan and pushed up on his right elbow. "More shooters?" he asked, tensing.

"Two vehicles racing for us," Trinity answered, moving to watch over Eden's shoulder.

"They're coming up fast," Eden said, her posture stiff. "How long until we're on the runway?"

"Under a minute, hopefully."

Zack thought fast as Heath wound a fresh bandage around his waist. "Have we got any rifles on board?"

"A few," Trinity answered, "but if it comes to that, we're in deep shit."

The plane turned sharply. Zack shot out a hand to keep from rolling off the bed and the engines powered up more.

"They're coming right at us," Eden said, turning and dropping to her knees beside him. "Hold on." She wrapped an arm around his shoulders to brace him, Heath keeping him steady on the other side.

Zack couldn't hear the approaching vehicles over the noise of the engines, but then the sharp crack of gunfire punched through it. He grabbed Eden and held her close, ignoring the fresh wave of pain.

She let out a hiss as rounds hit the back of the plane. "How bad?" she asked Trinity. "Can you see?"

"No, but... Shit, hold on."

More rounds raked across the fuselage.

The jet kept going, picking up speed, then nosed upward. Zack closed his eyes, helpless to do anything to protect Eden. If any of the rounds had clipped the fuel or hydraulic lines—

Trinity pushed back from the window and reached for the door, leaning forward to counteract the angle of the plane's nose. Heath tied off the bandage and squeezed Zack's shoulder once. "You're good to go. Hang tight." He was up and out of the cabin as the plane started to climb.

Zack started to get up but Eden pressed him down onto his right side with firm hands and a warning look. "Stay here."

"No." He pushed upright, needing to be ready. The plane had sustained significant damage. If they had to do an emergency landing, then he needed to be ready to get Eden out safely within seconds of touching down.

"*Yes.*"

Done with arguing, he swept her aside with one arm, a surge of adrenaline masking the worst of the pain in his side as he struggled to his feet.

The plane dropped sharply, knocking him off balance. He hit the bed on his good side, bit back a howl of agony as fire shot through him, registering another sharp prick in his hip too late.

What the hell? He jerked his head up to stare at Eden in astonishment, taking in the syringe held in her hand. "You *drugged* me?" he accused.

"It's for your own good. Now lie down before you rip open your damn stitches," she ordered, pressing him down once again.

He opened his mouth to argue but whatever she'd hit him with was already pumping through his system, making his limbs heavy and his entire body drowsy. His grip on her eased, his muscles going lax. Then he smelled it.

Smoke.

Eden's head snapped up as she smelled it too.

"Jesus, are we on *fire?*" he said. His voice was already slurred.

"Dunno." Her expression was tense.

Oh, Christ. The plane was burning and he was too weak to move.

Through his rapidly blurring vision he barely made out Eden's silhouette as she raced through the door and shut it, the scent of smoke filling his nose as the blackness closed in.

EDEN SHOVED ASIDE the sharp twinge of guilt and raced up the aisle to the others. Everyone had their faces pressed to the windows, looking at the aft portion of the aircraft. "How bad is it?"

"Bad," Trinity said, staring out her window, tension visible in her face and the line of her shoulders. "I can see smoke and flames coming from the tail."

"Pilot's requested an emergency landing," Ty added, grabbing Megan and pushing her into a seat to strap her in. "Better buckle up."

Shit.

Eden spun and ran back down the aisle, leaning forward to counteract the downward angle of the plane. She didn't like the sound of the engines, either. The smoke was getting thicker in the cabin, a harsh, acrid stench that burned her eyes and nose, filling the air in a dark cloud.

Zack was lying on his back on the bed, out cold.

The smoke was the biggest threat to him at the moment, and he was closest to the source. Eden grabbed him under the shoulders, wrenched his torso upright until he was in a seated position. The door banged open behind her and Ty was beside them an instant later, hoisting Zack over one broad shoulder to carry him out.

Eden followed, shutting the door behind her to try and contain the worst of the smoke, then rushed after Ty, leaning back to keep from stumbling during the steep descent, and shoved armrests out of the way so he could lay Zack down. The two of them quickly strapped him down tight across the chest and hips with seatbelts, then Eden scooted in beside him to buckle into her own.

"Thanks," she said to Ty, who was strapping in across the aisle from her beside Megan. God, they were dropping so fast her stomach was floating up into her ribcage, like the first big drop on a roller coaster.

"No problem."

A second later the cockpit door swung open and the copilot craned his neck to shout at them. "Brace. Heads down, stay down."

Eden leaned forward and laced her fingers behind the back of her head. She coughed at the smoke irritating her lungs, then reached down and grabbed hold of Zack's shoulder. It was for the best that he was unconscious. There was nothing he could do to save them, and if they were about to die at least he wouldn't suffer the fear and pain.

The scream of the engines was the only sound other than occasional coughing, everyone otherwise silent as the pilots tried to get them on the ground safely. She didn't know how close the nearest runway was.

Just when her heart started to climb into her throat, the plane leveled off. The engines changed pitch. Seconds later, the wheels hit the ground with a thud. Eden grunted, the force of the impact slamming her chin into her knees, knocking her teeth together. They bounced twice, then stabilized, and the pilots hit the brakes hard.

Oh my God, we're still alive.

The thought was still running through her head when the plane came to a sudden halt, more smoke pouring through the cabin.

"Everybody out," Trinity ordered.

Eden needed no further encouragement. She ripped off her seatbelt and reached for Zack's, ready to get the hell out of this deathtrap.

****

Voices swirled around Zack as he struggled up through the heavy weight of the blackness surrounding him. He was bouncing.

He struggled to clear the cobwebs from his brain. Something was wrong. Something bad had happened. He hurt. There was danger.

Shots hitting the plane. Smoke.

Fire. The plane on fire with Eden in it.

Zack sucked in a gasping breath and tried to shove upright, the world spinning around him. Pain shot through his side, but he was frantic to find Eden.

"Uh oh, someone's awake, and he does *not* look happy about it."

He squinted up at the source of the familiar voice. A woman's face came into focus. Long blond hair. Brown eyes. Jaw working as she chewed.

Chloe. "Did we crash?" he mumbled, sounding drunk and feeling worse.

"Almost."

What? He struggled to turn his head and look around. Ty and Heath were carrying him using a blanket. "Where's Eden?"

"Whoa, take it easy, brother," Ty said. "She's fine. Everyone's fine."

He'd believe that when he saw her for himself, and not before. "Where is she?"

"I'm right here." Her face appeared above him, and Zack quickly scanned her for signs of injury. She didn't seem hurt. She even smiled down at him as they carried him...somewhere.

"You *drugged* me," he accused. "Again. While we were on *fire*," he added for emphasis. "What is *wrong* with you?"

She didn't look the least bit sorry. "You were being stubborn. Refused all pain meds and wouldn't stay lying down even though you'd just been shot. It's your own fault."

His own— He dragged in a calming breath, wincing as it spread flames up from his wound. "What's going on?"

"Assholes shot our plane full of holes," Chloe answered, happily chomping away on her gum. "The tail section caught fire."

And Eden had rendered him useless in the back. They were having more words about that later. As for right now...

He glanced around in confusion. Ty and Heath were bouncing him so fucking much, making his already woozy head spin. "Where are we?"

"Quantico," Eden answered. "They gave us clearance to do an emergency landing."

"Yeah, it was touch and go for a bit there, but it's all good," Chloe said cheerily.

All good... Holy hell. And he'd been unconscious through everything. "Where are we going now?"

"New ride," Chloe said. "Man, Rycroft was pissed that we got the last plane shot up." She grinned, the light in her eyes a little unnerving. "Epic."

Yeah. Epic.

"Do yourself a favor and lie down," Heath said from behind him, carrying the weight of Zack's head and upper body. "The dose Eden gave you'll be in your system for a few hours yet."

Zack aimed a scowl at her but she didn't see it, focused on something else up ahead. "Who's that with Trinity?" she asked.

Zack lifted his head to see Trinity embracing a big guy dressed in ACUs.

"Her fiancé, Brody," Chloe answered, as if it should be obvious.

"She's engaged?" Eden said in surprise.

"Yep, he's the HRT sniper team leader. They're based here in Quantico," Ty said.

"Oh, wow, would you look at that," Chloe breathed. "The legend himself must be seeing to this part personally."

Zack craned his neck to follow her gaze. A tall man stood waiting for them at the foot of another jet's stairs. Graying hair. Pissed off expression. "Who is it?"

"Rycroft," Ty answered.

A few seconds later, Zack found himself staring up into a pair of intense silver eyes. "Maguire. Good to meet you at last," Rycroft said.

"Yeah, you too," Zack said, feeling lame as he took the hand offered him.

"You gonna make it?"

"Think so."

"Good." He looked at the others. "If you guys have had enough excitement for one day, maybe you could manage not to get any bullet holes in this one." He nodded at the jet.

Chloe's snicker floated after them as Heath and Ty carried him past Rycroft and into the jet. Eden followed them into the back. This rear cabin didn't have a bed, just a long, padded bench built into the wall. They set him down on it.

Eden placed a firm hand on his chest. "Don't even think about sitting up." She lifted the syringe in her hand.

"I got another full dose here, and I'm not afraid to use it."

"What the hell did you give me, anyway?"

"Ketamine."

Holy fuck. "That's a horse tranquilizer!"

"It's a commonly used anesthetic for both people and animals," she corrected.

Jesus. "I'll stay put this time, because this time we're not fucking on *fire*," he growled back, fighting to stay awake. The drug was powerful, trying to suck him back under.

To his surprise, she laughed. A low, husky laugh that did something funny to his heart. "You seriously gotta do something about those trust issues, babe."

The teasing comment and *babe* part made his black mood do a one-eighty. If she was teasing him that he was the one with trust issues, then did that mean she'd finally gotten over hers?

Chapter Twenty

This time the takeoff was without any issues. Eden stayed with Zack in the back, making sure he was as comfortable as possible. When he finally slipped back under soon after they'd leveled off, she left him to sleep and went to join the others. Everyone was crowded around Amber's seat, where she was bent over her laptop.

Megan looked up at her as Eden came up the aisle. "How's he doing?"

"Sleeping." She nodded toward Amber. "What've we got?"

"She's compiling all the data we've got so far, and working on the burner I gave her. You still have yours?"

Eden stepped into the row in front of Amber, took the second phone from her pocket and handed it over. "I want to tear apart this guy's whole life," Eden said to her. "Find out everything we can, so we can nail the bastard who sent him after us."

"Oh, we will," Amber promised, focused on her laptop screen.

Jesse knelt on the seat beside Eden and stacked his forearms across the top of it, watching Amber. "She hasn't slept in twenty-eight hours."

"I'll sleep when this is done," she argued without looking up.

Now that Eden looked closer, there were deep shadows beneath Amber's eyes. She looked drawn, exhausted. They were overworking her.

"Here." Chloe thrust a can of something at Amber. "Drink this."

Amber eyed the energy drink warily, then shrugged. "What the hell," she said, then popped it open and downed a large swallow. She groaned and made a face. "Gross. How the hell can you drink these things?"

"Because they're the bomb," Chloe said. "Just drink it. It'll help."

"You get four hours, and not a minute more," Jesse said to Amber, his tone making it clear he meant business. Either Amber did as he said, or he would make her. "After that, you're sleeping the rest of the way back to the UK."

"Fine," Amber said, but this time there was no annoyance or heat in her tone. "Now everybody get to work and help me out. Eden, you take this and search that second burner with Meg." She handed Eden a palm-sized electronic device from the backpack next to her, and the phone. "Plug the phone into this, and then into the laptop."

Megan already had another laptop open across the aisle. Eden plugged the burner phone into it along with the device. "Now what?" she asked Amber.

"Double click on the icon that pops up on screen. It'll download a list of calls to and from the phone. Then enter the numbers into the program Meg has open, and you'll get a location for each."

It worked. As soon as Megan opened the program, a list of numbers started showing up. "There's a list of about twenty calls or so," Megan told her sister. "Starting a couple days ago, and last one was this morning."

"Great. Send me the info when you've got a list of

locations for them."

Eden and Megan worked together to find out where the calls had come from. Most from around the D.C. area, but the one from this morning had gone to an unlisted number. They sent the info to Amber's computer, then traded spots with Jesse so they could sit next to her and go over everything.

Amber looked over at Eden. "He called Zack's old number twice last night."

"I saw that." Her gaze strayed to the closed cabin door at the end of the aisle. She'd been suspicious of Zack from the start, part of her refusing to accept that he wasn't somehow involved on some level. But the man had since taken a bullet for her and killed his own handler to protect her. She felt horrible for ever doubting him now. "Trying to get a location on us."

Amber went back to referencing the numbers, toggling between several screens she had open on her laptop. A couple minutes later she frowned, clicked back and forth between two screens. "Well, isn't that interesting," she murmured.

Eden craned her neck to see better. "What is?" Megan crowded close too. A second later Chloe popped over the back of the seat in front of them, draining the last of an energy drink, her eyes shooting to Amber's screen.

"After trying Zack the second time, he placed a call to a phone in the same vicinity as the final call from Bennett's phone," Amber said.

"Where?" Eden asked, looking at the map Amber pulled up.

"Here." She touched a finger to the screen.

Atlanta? "You think they're connected?"

"Can't be coincidence. Bennett's last call was to a burner there. It lasted thirty-four seconds, and he winds up dead ten hours later with his tongue cut out. Then Zack's handler makes a call to the same area and ends up shooting at you guys in that alley four hours later."

"Can you get a better lock on the location?" Megan asked.

"No, the signal was scrambled. But—"

A sharp ding sounded, and an alert came up on screen. Eden looked at Amber. "What's it mean?"

The hacker's face was somber. "It means I need to talk to Kiyomi, asap."

****

Seated on a sofa in the library at Laidlaw Hall, Kiyomi was in the middle of compiling data on the list of remaining suspects they needed to look into when her cell rang. Seeing the number on the display, relief hit her. "Hi, Amber. You guys on your way here now?" The team had had one hell of a scare. Well, several of them, but thank God everyone was okay.

"Just landed at the Cotswold Airport."

"How's Zack?"

"He's hanging in there. Just wanted to let you know we're all still alive. See you in a bit."

"You bet."

"They're back?"

Kiyomi's heart skipped a beat when she looked up to find Marcus standing in the doorway. His powerful frame all but filled the opening. "Yes, and coming straight back here with Zack. He's apparently doing okay."

"I'll get his room ready."

"I'll help." She followed him up the stairs, turned the covers down on Zack's bed and started gathering towels and other things they might need for him. Marcus came in a minute later carrying an Army-issue med kit and set out various instruments and dressings.

When the others arrived fifteen minutes later, Eden and Heath immediately brought Zack up to check his wound while everyone else gathered in the library to talk with her and Marcus about what had happened.

As soon as they finished the debrief, Amber pulled her aside. "I need to talk to you about something."

A thread of unease wound its way up Kiyomi's spine at the other Valkyrie's somber expression. "All right." She followed Amber over to the teal velvet sofa and sank down on it. "What is it?"

"We can talk alone if you prefer."

The unease intensified. Everyone was watching her, as if they knew something she didn't. "No, if everyone else already knows, they can stay."

Amber nodded and opened her laptop. The guys began to file out of the room, leaving the women behind. Marcus turned to leave with them but she shot a hand out to grab his forearm on the way past.

He stopped instantly, his gaze darting to hers.

"Please stay," she said quietly. Whatever Amber was about to say, Kiyomi wanted him here. He was part of this and deserved to know what was happening.

He nodded once and walked to the other side of the room, moving toward the fireplace. The fire he'd lit just before everyone arrived snapped in the grate behind him as he sat on the upholstered leather fender bench bracketing the hearth.

Unable to take the suspense any longer, Kiyomi sat next to Amber on the tufted, teal velvet couch. "What did you need to talk to me about?"

"I'll show you." Amber turned Lady Ada around so Kiyomi could see the screen. "I found something on the flight back," she said, opening several files.

Kiyomi scanned everything. A list of names, phone numbers and geographical coordinates. "What does it mean?"

"Both Bennett and Zack's handler placed a call to a number in the Atlanta area prior to dying. And I found someone else who's been calling that area periodically as well." The gravity in her gaze made Kiyomi's heart beat faster, then Amber hit a button and brought up another screen.

More numbers and coordinates. Some painfully familiar to her. "Damascus?"

"Yes." Amber hit another button, and a picture popped up on screen.

Kiyomi's stomach clenched, all her blood vessels constricting as she looked at the man's face.

Fayez Rahman. The man from her nightmares.

Her skin prickled, a chill washing over her. "You're sure it's Rahman?"

Amber nodded. "I told you I've been keeping tabs on him. He's hard to track, but every now and again I get a lock on him. And I've been able to record bits of calls over the past few weeks."

The other Valkyries moved closer. Almost like they were closing ranks around her to protect her.

Pushing aside her visceral reaction to Rahman, Kiyomi focused on the words on screen. Transcribed phone conversations between him and others. A few emails.

"Is there anything you can think of, anything at all that will help me figure out what his connection to the others might be?" Amber asked.

Kiyomi started to shake her head, then froze as her eyes caught on a particular line of an email. A title.

The Architect.

"What? Do you recognize something?" Amber asked.

Kiyomi sensed Marcus watching her from across the room as the others waited for her to answer.

She took a steadying breath, struggled to sift through her hazy memories. The pain and drugs had dulled her mind, but she was sure what she'd heard. "That name. The Architect. I heard him talking to someone about it once.

I…"

A chilling laugh. Black eyes filled with hatred and lust as he stood over her, bullwhip in hand.

Then that evil, cold voice saying something that hadn't made sense until right this minute.

Ice speared her gut, the blood draining from her face.

"Kiyomi? Hey." Eden was beside her. Her hand was on Kiyomi's shoulder, the touch pulling her out of the dark memory.

"No, I'm fine."

But who was the Architect?

Instinctively she sought Marcus's gaze across the room. He maintained eye contact with her, concern written in every line of his scarred face. And in that moment, more than anything she wished she could feel those strong arms around her. To feel, just for a moment, that she was safe. Even though she knew it was an illusion.

"The Architect," she said, her voice slightly unsteady.

"What about it?" Amber asked.

"I think I might be able draw him out."

The room went deathly silent, and her insides twisted as she thought of what might have to happen for this to end. She was convinced that Rahman knew who the Architect was, had intended to sell Kiyomi to him. That made her the perfect bait, the only person who could make the Architect materialize—through Rahman.

"What?" Trinity said. "How?"

"The Architect might be the key to all of this. Rahman knows who it is." She explained what she'd heard, what Rahman had told her moments before unleashing the bullwhip on her bare back. "He's obsessed with me, so much that he's got a three-million-dollar bounty for my capture. If we can't find the Architect on our own, we can find him from Rahman. He'd do anything to get me back—"

"*No.*"

Startled by the deep voice across the room, she and the others looked over at Marcus. He'd shot to his feet, his expression dark as a thundercloud as he glared at them all. "That's not happening." His gaze bored into Kiyomi's, almost daring her to argue.

"Kiyomi, how do you know this?" Trinity pressed, bringing her attention back to the others.

She licked her lips. "He told me he had a buyer lined up. A top-end buyer he was saving me for. And he said... He said 'I know what you are. I'm going to send you back to your maker.'" She paused, glancing at the others. "All this time I thought it meant he was going to kill me, send me to face my maker. But now I think he meant something else entirely."

Resounding silence greeted her words as everyone connected the dots.

Her skin crawled at the memory of being that helpless. Unable to defend herself or go on the offensive. Caged like an animal, beaten and starved, too weak to move. "Their deal was, he had to keep me alive and unharmed until the sale happened. But he lost control and broke his end of the bargain. And he was afraid he would die because of it. Afraid of the buyer. My creator."

The Architect. That had to be it. It was the only thing that made sense, even if she didn't understand why he wanted her specifically.

She met Amber's gaze, fighting to ignore the way her insides twisted at the thought of putting herself at that animal's mercy again. "What if the Architect is the one behind all of this?"

Chapter Twenty-One

M arcus was ready to explode as Kiyomi's words faded into silence, looking at the other women as his pounding heart threatened to come through his ribcage. These were her sisters. Her fellow Valkyries, and they should be telling her—

"You're not doing that," Trinity announced curtly to Kiyomi, and Marcus released a ragged exhale in relief.

"Yeah, let me add to that," Chloe said, arms folded and a pissed-off expression on her face. "No way in *hell*."

Megan nodded. "Yep, what they said, forget it. Wash the idea of you going to Rahman right out of that pretty head, because it ain't happening."

"Only over our dead bodies," Eden finished, staring hard at Kiyomi.

Marcus eased his death grip on the top of his cane, his heart rate slowing. This was what he'd needed to see. Since voicing his opposition to Kiyomi's suggestion he might have been another ornament on the fucking mantelpiece for all the attention the women had paid him so far...except Kiyomi had kept glancing over every so often, as if seeking his reassurance.

Hearing her say what she'd been subjected to at Rahman's hands made it feel like someone was driving nails into the pit of his stomach. He'd seen her when she'd first come here. He'd seen the state she'd been in, bleeding and broken as they'd placed her in bed. Hearing her imply that she was willing to consider offering herself up to the brutal son of a bitch who had abused her so badly, all in an effort to try and draw out this "Architect"?

No. Just fucking *no*.

"We'll find another way," Amber told Kiyomi, reaching out to squeeze her shoulder. "Together. We'll get him together, just like I promised."

Marcus didn't know what promises Amber had made to her, but he didn't like the look in Kiyomi's eyes. That quiet determination and resolve that said she hadn't let her idea go at all.

The meeting broke up, and the women all headed for the door. Jesse walked in, caught Amber two steps from the door and took her laptop away.

She reached for it. "Hey—"

"Hey nothing," he told her. "Bed. Now."

She opened her mouth to argue but he merely bent and hoisted her over one shoulder, carrying her out of the room and ignoring the heated string of arguments she unleashed on him.

Too right, Marcus thought in approval. He sought out Megan and stopped her from leaving while everyone else filed out. "What's wrong?" she asked when she saw his face.

What's *wrong*? "I'll tell you what's bloody wrong. *That*." He thrust a finger at Kiyomi's retreating back, barely keeping his voice down. "She just told you she's willing to offer herself up as bait to the man who tortured and violated her. You need to go talk to her, alone, and make sure she drops that whole bloody line of thinking," he shot back, outraged and heartsick at the thought of Kiyomi offering herself up to that sadistic bastard like a sacrificial lamb. "She's one of you. You've all been through enough, especially her."

Megan frowned. "I know that. We all do. We'd never let her do something so reckless."

"So you'll go talk to her until she drops it," he challenged, unwilling to let this go. "That none of you would ever let her sacrifice herself for the rest of you—because that's what she's bloody well thinking."

Megan's eyes widened. "Marcus. We'll handle it, I promise you."

"So then handle it *now*—"

"Is everything okay?"

He whipped his head around to find Kiyomi watching them from the doorway. Her expression was composed, her voice calm, but he didn't believe she was calm at all inside, and it sliced him up to think of what she was prepared to do to help the others.

"Yes, fine," Megan answered with a smile. "Marcus just wanted to talk to me for a second but we're done now." She gave him a pointed look, then started for the door. On the way by, Megan set a hand on her shoulder. "It's been a long day. Let's all get some sleep and then we'll talk again in the morning, okay?"

Kiyomi nodded. "Sure. Sleep well." As Megan stepped past her into the hallway, Kiyomi turned back to Marcus. "Thank you for staying."

She might as well have reached into his chest and crushed his heart in her fist. "Of course." If she needed him, he'd be there.

She gave him a little smile that belied the shadows lurking in her eyes. "Think I'll go up too, maybe read for a bit." She turned to leave.

"Wait." He caught her forearm. She stopped, her eyes snapping to his, and he felt the connection between them crackling like a live wire, sizzling from his hand up his arm. He released her. "What you said…"

She waited, watching him.

"You'll all find another way to get what you need."

"We'll all do whatever it takes to end this, me included." Her brave smile and surprised expression damn near broke his battle-scarred heart, as if she couldn't fathom him worrying about her. "It's all right, Marcus. I'm well aware of the risks and what my role is in all of this. I'm not afraid."

Yes, she was, she just would never admit it to anyone, maybe even herself. But it was also the first time she'd said his name, and hearing it wrapped in her soft voice made his chest hitch.

He took hold of her upper arms, determined to get through to her. He was afraid for her. For what she might do to see this thing through. What she was prepared to sacrifice. "You'll find another way," he repeated, sure of it. "Whatever happens, the team will handle it together." And dammit, he wanted to be part of whatever shape that took. He was sick of sitting idly by while all this shite was playing out in front of him.

Pain flared in the depths of her eyes for an instant, then was gone. "None of us are safe, including you. Not even here. And we won't be until this is all over."

Her words resonated inside him. From day one he'd known that bringing Megan here, then the others, was only a temporary reprieve. That sooner or later, his home would no longer be a safe haven for them. That the day would come when it posed more of a threat than safety.

And, selfish bastard though he was, he wanted to delay it as long as possible. Because when that day arrived, Megan and the others would leave, scattering to the wind once more, and Kiyomi with them. He'd thought losing Megan would be the hardest part. But now the idea of losing Kiyomi hurt just as much.

"I want to show you something," he said. Only Megan and Trinity knew about it, but he needed Kiyomi to see it now.

She nodded slowly, searching his eyes. "All right."

He released her, grabbed his hated cane from where he'd hastily leaned it against the wall, and turned right down the hall. The familiar, comforting scent of wood smoke and leather beckoned as he neared his study, but it was far more than just his place of refuge.

Flipping on the overhead light, he shut the door behind her. "This way." He crossed to the section of built-in bookshelves to the right of the fireplace. "Here," he said, bringing her to stand next to him.

Her feet were silent on the Persian rug covering the cold, hard stone beneath. "What am I looking for?" she asked, perusing the leather-bound volumes before them.

"This one." He took her hand, placed it on the spine of The Secret Garden, and watched her face. "Press it."

She did, her expression fascinated as a quiet snick sounded in the still room, revealing a tiny gap in the wood between that row of the bookshelf and the one above. She looked up at him, so close he could drink in her warm vanilla scent and see the various colors of brown flecks in her eyes. "A secret passage?"

Rather than answer, he pushed the panel inward to reveal a short corridor carved into the stone wall. Taking the battery-powered torch from its holder on the inside wall, he shone it down the corridor, illuminating the space beyond the corridor. "Go inside."

She went without hesitation, him right behind her, and stopped at the trap door in the floor. "Do you have a dungeon?" she asked.

"No." Setting aside his cane, he eased into a crouch, covering a grimace of pain as his hip and thigh muscles spasmed, and reached for the old iron loop on the trap door. The old hinges were almost soundless as he pulled it open, thanks to the oil he'd recently put on them.

Easing back, he aimed the beam of the torch downward so she could see inside. "It's a priest hole."

She frowned. "A what?"

"They date back to the Reformation, during the Tudor age. Religious upheaval was the order of the day back then, and Catholic priests were persecuted for maintaining the old faith. Some of them sought refuge in houses like this one, where they would stay out of sight until the people looking for them were gone."

"What's inside it now?" she asked, peering down the ladder he'd built inside it.

Reaching past her, he slid a hand into the opening and found the switch he'd put on the wall. With the flick of his fingers, the lighting system came to life.

A soft gasp escaped her, her face full of wonder as she took everything in. "An armory."

"Aye." Dozens of pistols and rifles were mounted in neat rows along the stone walls at the base of the ladder, along with knives, ammo, food, emergency cash and medical supplies. "Megan and I started working on it when she moved in. There's a tunnel on the far side that leads to another trapdoor on the south side of the house, just outside the garden wall."

Kiyomi gazed around the space for a moment longer, then looked at him. "Why are you showing me this now?"

"Because I want you to know you're safe here." *With me.* He bit the last words back before they could escape. But shit, yeah, if it came down to it he would defend her and the others here to the last bullet.

Kiyomi's expression softened. Easing back on her haunches, she lifted a hand to cup the unscarred side of his face. Marcus stopped breathing, the warmth of her touch seeping through his beard. "We're safe here for now," she murmured, her eyes holding him captive. "But that's a promise you can't keep. None of us can."

Before he could argue she dropped her hand and stood to leave.

He quickly turned off the light, closed the trapdoor and followed her back into his study. Karas was sitting at the tunnel opening, and greeted them with a thump of her tail on the rug.

"Hi, sweet girl," Kiyomi said to her, reaching down to stroke the dog's head. Karas nudged into Kiyomi's hand, asking for more, and it surprised Marcus. Karas was aloof with everyone except for him and sometimes Megan. But she obviously liked Kiyomi, and that in itself was meaningful.

Kiyomi turned to Marcus. "Thank you for showing me. See you in the morning."

It took all his strength not to reach for her. To pull her close and crush her to him. Take that lovely face between his hands and wipe away every trace of fear and pain from her eyes with his touch, his lips. "Aye. Sleep well."

The door closed behind her and the room suddenly felt colder, her earlier words haunting him. He'd once failed to protect the men under his charge. They'd all paid the ultimate price for it, while for whatever reason he'd survived.

Never again. He would protect Kiyomi and the other Valkyries while they were here, by whatever means necessary. He was prepared to do whatever it took to keep them safe.

Full of restless energy, unsure what the hell to do about his escalating feelings for Kiyomi, he roamed the lower floor of the house, finally stopping in the kitchen. While the kettle heated he leaned over the counter to peer through the window into the growing gloom outside, unable to shake the unease growing inside him.

The October sky was gray and leaden, heavy clouds looming to the west. A storm was coming, and not just of Mother Nature's making.

They'd all best be ready when it hit.

*****

Wow. That meeting had been one hell of an eye opener, and Eden wasn't sure what would happen now.

She crept into Zack's room and gingerly shut the door behind her. He was asleep on his right side, facing away from her, and the sight of him like that with his torso bared and the bandages wrapped around his waist turned her heart over.

The meds she'd finally forced him to take a few hours before they landed should be wearing off now. She stripped, snuck around the other side of the bed and carefully crawled up beside him. The blinds on the windows were open, allowing just enough light from the twilit sky in for her to see his face. He needed a shave, though she liked the rugged look on him.

He stirred and opened sleepy eyes to focus on her. "Hi."

"Hi." She smoothed his hair back from his forehead. "You've got a bit of a fever."

"Yeah, feels like it." He winced as he shifted to slide an arm around her. "What'd I miss?"

She told him about the meeting, about what Kiyomi had said.

Zack's brows drew together. "Is she okay?"

"I don't know. And whoever the Architect is, sounds like they've been after us for a while now."

"Would she really do it? Hand herself over to Rahman?" he asked, frowning.

"She's prepared to do it, but it'll never happen because we'd never allow it." Sending Kiyomi back into the hands of her captor just on the chance that they might be able to find out who the Architect was? No way. "Between you and Amber working your magic together, hopefully we can get a lock on Rahman and an identity for the Architect so we can come up with some plans and go after them as a team."

He hummed thoughtfully, his thumb sweeping across the skin between her shoulder blades. "And if we can't?"

"Then we'll figure out something else." She wasn't sure what exactly had happened to Kiyomi, but she could imagine easily enough. No way would they subject her to more of it.

"Glad to hear it," he agreed, tugging her close to brush a kiss on her lips.

"Amber found evidence that Bennett ordered the hit on Chris and me, and your friend John. Bennett wanted to be thorough in covering his tracks."

"Fucking bastard."

Yep. At least he'd died a traumatic death, though they still didn't know who the killer was. "Oh, and Megan and Ty are engaged."

"Huh? When the hell did that happen?"

"I guess it's been coming for a while now, but she finally said yes just before we boarded the plane."

"The one that caught on fire, or the other one?" he said dryly.

Eden grinned, thankful everything had turned out. "The first one."

Setting a hand on his chest, she eased back to look into his eyes. Today had been a massive wakeup call. She'd come so close to losing this man, and hearing about Megan and Ty had given her the added strength to go after what she wanted. To believe that kind of happiness could be possible for her with Zack.

"I couldn't stand for anything else to happen to you," she began. "For you to get hurt again. You…" She swallowed, gathered her courage. "You mean too much to me." She'd tried everything to get over him and put him behind her, but she never had, and now he'd cracked open something inside her that can't be sealed up again.

His gaze intensified. "Yeah? How much do I mean

to you?"

"A lot," she whispered back, suddenly feeling shy and vulnerable. "So much that I think you should go home to visit your dad for a while, and—"

"No way in hell." He caught her chin between his thumb and fingers, lifted it until she met his gaze. "I love you."

Her heart clenched, part of her unable to believe he'd just said that, but before she could respond he continued. "I've been in love with you for almost a year, and I'll be damned if I let you go now. So I'm not walking away, from you *or* this."

The sudden sting of tears made her blink and pull in an unsteady breath. "You sure you love *me*? The real me?"

His fierce expression softened. "Sweetness, I'm lying here with a bullet hole from trying to protect you, and I'd take a hundred more bullets to keep you that way. What the hell else do I have to do to prove it to you?"

She gave him a watery smile. "I don't know. Maybe I need to be knocked over the head with it."

He gently bopped her on the top of her head with the bottom of his fist. "There. Now you believe me?"

Teetering on the verge of dissolving into tears, Eden wound her arms around his back, careful of his wound as she melted against him. "I'm sorry. And I'm sorry for being suspicious of you, for ever thinking you might sell me and the others out."

He gave a dramatic sigh and hugged her to him. "This whole trust issue thing got old a long time ago."

She nodded, not trusting her voice.

He nuzzled the side of her face, then went dead still, his body tensing. "Are you crying?"

"No."

"Pretty sure you're crying."

"Am not."

He eased her head back to look into her face, wiped the tears from her cheeks. "No more hiding from me. No more lies, even little ones."

That was fair. It wasn't going to be an overnight change, though. "Okay."

"Thank you." He kissed the bridge of her nose.

He hadn't pressed her to say the words back to him, but she could feel him waiting for them. Though it wasn't bright enough in the room for him to see it, she flushed, squirming under his scrutiny and the acute vulnerability. She couldn't say it back to him. Wouldn't let herself. Not yet. Not until this was all over and she no longer posed a threat to him.

He grinned. "I can't really tell, but are you *blushing* right now?"

She laughed softly and kissed him, glad for the reprieve. "You're such an idiot."

"I know," he murmured against her lips. "But I'm *your* idiot."

Her heart felt swollen to twice its normal size, like it might split her ribcage open. As incredible as it seemed, Zack loved her. He'd almost died today because of her, yet they finally had a chance at a future together.

If she wanted it, she was going to have to put her most secret fears aside and take it.

"True," she agreed. "But if you were smart, you'd still walk away."

"If I was smart, I'd have locked you down months ago and never let you out of my sight."

Eden smiled in the dimness, wanting to pinch herself. "I wasn't ready." *But maybe now I might be.*

Chapter Twenty-Two

"**Y**ou were *what?*"

Zack winced at his father's shout and pulled the phone away from his ear. "Dad, easy with the volume there. I'm fine, really."

"Calm down? You tell me you were fucking *shot* and then expect me to stay *calm?*"

"It's a flesh wound." Hurt like a mother, but every day was getting a bit better. "Barely slowed me down." Okay, that was a lie, but he wanted to put his father's mind at ease. "A few stitches and some downtime, and I'll be good as new."

"Where are you?" his father demanded, voice taut.

"In the UK."

"The UK," he repeated, his frustration palpable. "That's all I get?"

"Sorry, but yeah." He wouldn't even be having this conversation at all if it weren't for the heavily encrypted phone Amber had given him. With the kinds of enemies hunting them now, they had all doubled up on precautions.

"I'm sorry about John. He was a good man."

"Yeah, he was. Did you send the card to his parents like I asked?"

"Put it in the mail yesterday. I hope they get some closure eventually."

"They will." He couldn't say more, but they'd since found evidence that Glenn Bennett had also sent a hitter after Penny.

As for Bennett's death, the attacks on the way to the airport the other day and Rod's involvement, it was looking more and more like it had to do with the Architect.

"Can I talk to Paula for a minute?"

"Sure. Hang on."

A rattle sounded in the background, then Paula's voice came on the line, soothing and calm. He assured her he was fine, talked for a minute and then got serious.

"By the way, I've met someone. I want to bring her home to meet you guys soon."

He could just picture her reaction. Ears perking, eyes sparkling with excitement. "Really? That sounds serious."

"Yep." He was deadly serious where Eden was concerned. He loved her. She hadn't said it back to him yet, but he hoped that was only a matter of time.

In the background he could hear his dad trying to pump his wife for intel, but then the bedroom door opened and Eden walked in. Zack smiled. "Gotta go, Paula, but I just wanted to let you both know I'm okay and I promise to visit soon. Good luck with Dad."

"I'm gonna need it. We love you—stay safe, and if you need anything at all, let us know."

"I will, and love you too."

Eden drew the sheet back as he ended the call. Zack dropped the phone on the bedside table as her soft hands and even softer mouth began roaming over his naked chest. He groaned, didn't even wince as he rolled to his back. His wound was sore but the stitches were coming out any day now, and he'd been dying to make love to

Eden again.

Having her hands on him now was exquisite torture. He was hard as a rock beneath the sheets as she kissed her way down his abs, pausing to nip and lick at the sensitive spot where his hip and groin met.

He slid a hand into her curls, squeezed them in his fist and let out a low growl of arousal. It had been way too damn long since they'd been able to enjoy each other. "I'm liking this wakeup call," he murmured, pulse racing with anticipation as that mouth hovered oh-so-near to where he needed it.

"Hmm," she replied, her fingers stroking feather-light patterns on the insides of his thighs. "I came up to see if you wanted me to bring you a tray. You hungry?"

The scent of coffee and something sweet clung to her, but the sweet was probably Eden herself. "Not for food." He tightened his hold on her hair, dying for the moment those sexy lips closed around his aching cock.

"Ah. Maybe this, then?" She closed her fingers around his erection, gave him a long, slow stroke that had him seeing stars.

Zack arched up off the bed, ignoring the pain in his side. "Yes."

He was a little afraid she intended to tease him to death, so he shuddered and sighed in pleasure and relief when the heat of her mouth surrounded the sensitive crown. "Oh, God, Eden..."

She hummed and ran her tongue around him, then took him deeper, sucking, enjoying it damn near as much as him. She loved turning him on, or maybe it was that she loved reducing him to a quivering mass of need. Either way, he loved it too.

He closed his eyes, let himself sink into the bliss she lavished on him with every sexy pull of her talented mouth. It was so damn good.

Forcing his eyes open, he looked down at her. She

was watching him as she took him deep, making his breath stutter in his throat. He wanted it to last forever but he was too on edge, it had been too long and he needed to come. Needed *her*.

"I'm getting close," he finally rasped out, unsure if he wanted to beg for mercy or beg her to finish him off then and there.

She gave him two more slow, torturous sucks before releasing him and shimmying up to straddle his thighs. And she was naked. Utterly, gloriously naked, the morning sunlight coming through the windows gilding her light brown skin with brushstrokes of gold.

He slid one hand around her back and cupped one perfect breast with the other. She leaned forward, settling her core directly over his aching cock as he took a pert nipple into his mouth.

Moaning softly, she rocked her hips, sliding her wetness along his rigid length. A crinkle registered at the back of his mind, then a quiet tearing sound. He released her nipple just long enough to look down as she stood him up to roll a condom down his length.

Eden shifted, planting one hand beside his head while she settled him against her core, her gaze locked with his. Zack stared back at her, utterly lost in this gorgeous woman as she sank down on him, her teeth sinking into her plump lower lip.

"Fuck, yes, ride me," he groaned, gripping one curvy hip while he reached up to squeeze and roll her nipple.

Eden gasped and shifted once more, changing the angle slightly. Her eyes slid closed and her head fell back, her free hand sliding down to touch the swollen nub at the top of her sex.

It was so fucking sexy to watch her take control like this, to take her pleasure from his body while he watched. Every slow, slick stroke of her core pushed the pleasure higher. It raced across his skin, up his spine, making his heart slam and his breathing turn rough.

"You're so hard," she breathed, her face awash in ec-stasy as she rocked herself toward release, her fingers stroking her clit in gentle circles he wished he could be giving her with his tongue. "So *thick*."

Christ, the way she said it in that pleasure-roughened voice, the way her breath caught and her inner muscles squeezed him, had him breaking out in a sweat. He firmed his grip on her hip, watched her face as he lifted his hips, following the pace and rhythm she set. Soon she was breathing fast, her face tightening.

So close. So close he could almost taste it.

He wrapped his hand in her curls. Squeezed tight. He needed to see her eyes. Craved that most intimate connec-tion with her. "Look at me."

She opened pleasure-drenched, heavy-lidded amber eyes. Held his gaze and moved faster. Harder. Then her eyes squeezed shut, her face contorting with pleasure as orgasm took her. She moaned and threw her head back, that gorgeous body undulating in the throes of ecstasy.

Breathing hard, Zack gripped her hips and pulled her down on him as he thrust up, burying himself deep inside her, and let go. The pleasure ripped through him, powerful and sweet. He groaned and tugged her down on top of him, gathering her close against his chest. "Good morn-ing."

She chuckled drowsily. "Morning. You okay?" Her hand drifted down to brush the edge of the bandage cov-ering his stitches.

"Fantastic. Feeling no pain whatsoever at the mo-ment."

"I thought we'd fixed our trust issues because we agreed no more lies," she said in a pointed tone.

A chuckle escaped him. "Okay, I'm still in pain. But that was worth it." She was worth any amount of pain.

Her arms slid beneath him, her head tucked beneath

his jaw. "I tried to be gentle with you."

"You were." He smoothed a hand down her satin-smooth back. "What time is it?"

"Seven."

"Why were you up so early? Did I miss something?"

"I was just talking with Kiyomi."

"About?"

"Various things. She's been trying to remember things she heard when she was in captivity. She's convinced Rahman intended to sell her to the Architect."

It turned his stomach to think about it. "Has Amber got a lock on him yet?"

"No, but she's getting close."

"I'll help her work on it this afternoon. I've still got some connections I might be able to use to help us find him." Zack wanted to find Rahman so they could solve the final piece of this puzzle, but he also dreaded it. Because once they had a location nailed down, Eden and the others would go after him.

Not wanting to spoil the peacefulness of the moment, Zack set his worry aside and stroked a hand through her curls. Eden was going to be in danger again at some point, and he had to deal with that. He wanted to shield her from everything, protect her from any threat, but that would never work with her. All he could do was stand beside her and face whatever came together. "Is everybody else up?"

"Yes. They're getting set up in the conservatory right now."

"What time's the wedding?" Megan and Ty had decided waiting was pointless, so they'd somehow managed to get a wedding license and were getting married today here at the manor.

"Ten. Reception's right after, then they're taking a two-night honeymoon in York. Megan and Amber are headed into town shortly. Amber bribed the wedding dress shop owner into giving them private access to the

shop before it opens. I should get back down and help."
She sighed. "Except I'm too comfy to move."

"Me too. Best wakeup call *ever*." Her chuckle
warmed his heart.

She was quiet a moment. "I've never been to a wedding before."

"Really?"

She shook her head. "I'm kinda excited about being
there today."

Ah, so she had a romantic side after all, much as she
tried to hide it. So many layers to this woman. But now he
was curious about something else. "What about you? Did
you ever imagine getting married one day?" He hadn't
brought it up yet, wary of pushing too far too soon. He
could definitely imagine marrying her, however.

She lifted her head to raise her eyebrows at him.
"With *my* life? What do you think?"

"I think probably never."

"Exactly."

"And what about now?"

She stared at him for a second, surprise and something else moving in those pretty eyes, then laid her head
back on his chest. "I think I might start letting myself imagine it."

Zack smiled and kissed the top of her head, savoring
the victory. That couldn't have been easy for her to say,
let alone admit to herself. "I'm glad to hear it," he murmured.

Because one day, when she was ready, he was making this incredible woman his forever.

But his smile faded as he thought of what stood between now and then. The obstacles that loomed like a giant cliff in front of them, creeping closer every day.

He tightened his arms around her, a fierce protectiveness roaring to life inside him. Eden was his and no one
was taking her from him.

Not even the so-called Architect, whoever the bastard was.

****

Outside the window, the trees quivered in the cool evening breeze. Fall in Atlanta was still warm compared to most of the country, but the shorter amount of daylight was reflected in the brilliant vermillion and amber leaves scattered across the mansion's grounds.

After an almost unbearable wait, the time was finally near.

The groundwork was laid, the most threatening enemies neutralized, including that fucker Bennett with his impotent threats and big mouth. Killing him in such a messy way had come with significant risks—and had been worth every one of them. Few kills had ever been so satisfying.

Unfortunately, the attack on the Valkyrie team in Virginia had failed. Now another CIA handler was dead, along with other members of the hit squad, while all the Valkyrie team had walked away.

It wasn't supposed to happen so publicly. The story had been splashed all over the news, making things more difficult. One of them had been wounded, but no one knew how badly. All reports said they'd gone back to the UK. But where?

The Architect's gaze strayed to the initial design laid on the drafting table set near the large picture window at the back of the house. The latest rendition of the secret facility about to be built, with all the treasured tools laid out beside it.

Everything on the desk was lined up in neat, exact lines. Rulers, pencils and pens, protractors and other measuring devices. Technology was a wonderful thing, but rudimentary tools were still superior for some things.

There was something satisfying and tangible about putting pencils to paper to create something that couldn't be replicated by—in fact was ruined by—automated computer programs. Although technology was a necessary evil.

One of three computer monitors was on, positioned on the table to the left. Headshots of the remaining Valkyries filled the screen. Eight of them. The Architect knew every one of them, knew all about their personal histories...some more intimately than others.

Trinity. Megan. Amber. Chloe. Eden. Briar. Georgia. And Kiyomi. The most perfect of them all.

A soft ding pierced the silence. An email from a source in the UK.

Wounded member was Zack Maguire. Non life-threatening gunshot wound, treated and released, visit and tests paid for in cash. Maguire identified via security cam footage outside the private medical clinic in Cheltenham. Unidentified female with him.

Eden Foster.

No other information at this time.

It was the first solid lead as to their possible whereabouts. Cheltenham was in the countryside, on the edge of the Cotswolds. They wouldn't have taken Maguire to a clinic near their base. But they wouldn't have transported him too far away. That narrowed the geographical area down considerably.

Now it was time to finish this.

Above the table on the windowsill sat three framed portraits. Pictures of certain Valkyries when they were younger.

Two were links to the past. The other, to the future.

Planning all this out, waiting for just the right moment to enact the plan, had taken years of meticulous work. Now Bennett was dead, one of the more serious threats removed.

The eight women on screen were the only obstacle now. They were working together now, having teamed up in the face of their annihilation, as predicted. Now it was just a matter of finding where they were based.

The images on screen and in the frames beckoned, echoing with memories, triggering a bittersweet pain. They were a reminder of all the sacrifices and accomplishments paid for in blood, sweat and tears. Of anguish and death.

Unfortunately, all of them but one would die. There was no other way.

A necessary sacrifice to ensure a world made safer and more perfect by the most gifted of all her creations.

Chapter Twenty-Three

Her first wedding.

Eden couldn't stem the excitement buzzing inside her as she made her way around the conservatory with the garden shears. The chairs had been set up in neat rows in front of the arbor the guys had set up, and Eden and Kiyomi had covered it with garlands of ivy and brilliant crimson Virginia creeper from the property.

She took the cuttings she'd gathered into the breakfast room, where Kiyomi helped her trim, arrange and tie them into two bouquets with lavender ribbon. When they were done, Eden held one up and smiled in satisfaction. "Perfect."

"Yes, they are," Kiyomi said, her smile momentarily dispelling the shadows in her dark eyes. Since telling them about the connection between Rahman and the Architect the other day, she'd withdrawn from everyone.

They would do their best to prevent it, but it seemed the team was on a collision course with Rahman, and one day, Kiyomi would likely have to face him again. "I love that they're doing this here in front of all of us," Eden said.

"Me too."

"Is one of those for me?"

They both turned as Megan swept into the room, stunning in her gorgeous gown of pale cream, the bodice made of delicate lace and the skirt a soft chiffon that flowed as she moved. "Yes, the big one," Eden said, handing the large purple and white bouquet to her.

"Oh, it's gorgeous."

It really was. "The irises are for valor, faith and hope. Lavender for devotion. And the arborvitae and ivy are for unchanging friendship." As deserving of a Valkyrie sister.

Megan gave her a big smile and pulled her into a hug. "I love that you put so much meaning into this, thank you."

"You're welcome. Now go hide so Ty doesn't see you by accident. Kiyomi, take her out of here, quick."

Kiyomi grinned and led Megan from the room. Alone, Eden gathered up the special boutonnière she'd made for an even more special man.

"Thought I might find you here."

She turned to smile at Zack, looking ridiculously handsome in the suit Amber had brought back from town for him. "You caught me." Perfect timing.

He crossed to her, his movements a little stiff, then wrapped his arms around her waist and kissed her soundly on the lips. "Dare I ask what you're doing?"

"I just finished making the bouquets."

He eyed the plant clippings on the table. "Any of those poisonous?"

She grinned. "You don't think I'd risk poisoning the bride on her wedding day, do you?"

"No," he answered, though he still looked a little wary. "But could you? Kill someone with that stuff?"

Eden looked down at the specimens she'd gathered, some from a florist in town, but most from Marcus's gardens. The mop head-shaped hydrangeas had long since faded into a rusty purple color from their former bright blue, but the foliage was beautiful with tinges of red and purple amongst the green. In high enough concentrations, its cyanogenic glycoside could be lethal. "Technically? Yes."

"Well that's…terrifying. Which ones are poisonous?"

"Most of them. And there are a lot more toxic plants out in the garden, too." Yew, hemlock, nightshade, holly. Rhododendron, hydrangea and lily of the valley.

He focused back on her. "Did you get a chance to talk to Marcus about the garden thing?"

"Yes. If we're still here next spring, he said I can create my own poison garden, as long as it doesn't put Karas or the horses at risk."

He nodded. "Smart of him to stipulate that."

Eden poked him in the shoulder with her forefinger. "I'm quirky, not careless. I'll make sure it's still safe for all the people and animals living here. But it'll be great to make a garden in honor of my grandma. I'm going to clear the plot Marcus showed me and plant a whack of narcissus bulbs later this week, if you want to help."

"What are those?"

She laughed at his worried expression. "Daffodils."

His eyes widened. "They're poisonous too?"

"In the right concentration. You're so funny," she said with a grin.

"And you're kinda scary. But I love you anyway."

"Good. Because I have something for you." First she picked up the single bloom she'd cut from the garden earlier, and handed it to him. "Look familiar?"

"Looks like the one you left floating in the glass the morning you left."

She nodded. "A pink camellia symbolizes 'I'm longing for you.'"

Awareness filled his eyes. "And the dead leaves?"

247

"Sadness."

He stared at her as her message hit home. She'd been trying to tell him without words how she felt about him, even then.

"Today, I'm giving you this." She picked up the boutonnière. "Are you allergic to ragweed, by chance?"

He eyed her, a grin tugging at his lips. "No." He took it, twirled it slightly in his fingers. "So what does it mean?" he asked, watching her.

"It's also known as ambrosia." Nerves tingled in the pit of her belly, but it was time. She had to give the words back to him. "It symbolizes love returned."

His expression changed and he curved a hand around her nape. "Eden…"

Her heart thudded against her ribs, wanting to burst free. "I love you, Zack."

His forceful exhalation gusted against her hair, and then he was crushing her to him, his arms strong around her. "God, I love you too. So much."

Eden smiled against his shoulder and closed her eyes, memorizing everything about the perfection of the moment. Finally saying the words was liberating, helping her shed some of the chains from her past. Zack was her future, she was done with holding back.

After a moment he eased back to study her, mischief twinkling in his eyes. "I'm gonna go out on a limb here and guess ambrosia's toxic too?"

"Yes, but you'll be safe, I promise."

"Okay then, pin it on me so we can get this show on the road. Sooner it's done, sooner I can get you all to myself again."

She couldn't help the stupid, sappy smile on her face as she pinned it to his lapel. "I'm going to plant a lot of this in my garden." She had big plans for it. Oleander, foxgloves and wisteria were a necessity to honor her grandma.

Only she wasn't sure if she and the others would still be here in spring. So much could happen between now and then. As soon as they got a solid lock on Rahman and an ID on the Architect, they could start planning an end game.

"Hey." He cupped her cheek in his hand, brought her gaze up to his. "Whether we're still here in the spring or not, it doesn't matter. I'll help you plant a poison garden wherever we wind up."

That probably wasn't romantic to most people, but to her it was, and underscored just why she'd fallen in love with him. "Thank you."

"You're welcome." He leaned in for another kiss, then swatted her butt. "Let's get in there before all the good seats are gone."

She laced her fingers through his, filled with joy and excitement about the event she was about to witness. As incredible as it seemed, she was finally part of a family, unconventional though it may be.

Chloe came rushing in, her hair swept up in a sophisticated twist, wearing a skin-tight purple dress that made Heath's eyes pop out. "You like?" she asked him with a smile, twirling so he could see everything.

"Hell yeah, I like, firecracker," he growled, and Eden shared a secret smile with Zack.

Jesse arrived. Trinity came in next, leading Karas. The dog had a big bow made of the same lavender ribbon Eden had used on the bouquets tied around her neck. "Ring bearer's here," Trinity said, giving Karas a pat.

The minister stepped inside a moment later, ushered to the arbor at the front by Trinity. "I think we're ready."

Music started playing from speakers around the conservatory, a classical piece Eden couldn't name but recognized. Jesse pulled out his phone to start recording just as Ty appeared in the doorway in his tux, the lavender rose in his boutonnière symbolizing love and adoration.

He smiled at them all as he walked up to meet the minister, followed by Heath, who was acting as best man.

Amber came next, dressed in a lavender gown, her long brown hair swept up and Eden's bouquet in her hands. She came down the aisle slowly, matching her pace to the music. She aimed a wink at Jesse on the way by, and stopped opposite Heath at the arbor.

The music paused and everyone turned as the bride stepped inside. Eden put a hand to her chest, overwhelmed by the sight of her fellow Valkyrie standing beside Marcus, handsome as hell in his tux, his cane in his right hand.

A different piece of music began. Smiling down at Megan, Marcus offered her his arm.

"Aww," Eden and Kiyomi whispered together.

Eden leaned closer to Zack, a lump in her throat. "I didn't know he was giving her away. Aww."

Zack grinned and wrapped an arm around her shoulders. "Such a romantic under that tough exterior. You're not gonna cry, right?"

"Not unless you want me to punch you in front of everyone."

Marcus gave Karas a quiet command. The dog immediately jumped up and padded down the aisle, mouth open in a doggy grin. Marcus escorted Megan up the aisle, stopping in front of Ty. After lifting Megan's veil he turned to shake Ty's hand, a solemn, unspoken vow passing between the two of them.

Hurt her and you'll deal with me, Marcus's expression said, and no one in their right mind would take on the former SAS member.

The lump in Eden's throat grew bigger, threatened to choke her when Ty took Megan's hand, the smile on their faces so beautiful it almost hurt to look at them.

The minster began the ceremony and said a prayer. Megan and Ty exchanged vows next, then Heath bent and untied the rings from Karas's ribbon collar.

The bride and groom exchanged rings. Eden's heart beat faster, squeezing Zack's fingers tighter and tighter without realizing it.

"I now pronounce you man and wife," the minister declared. "You may kiss the bride."

Eden sucked in a shaky breath as Ty took Megan's face in his hands and bent to kiss her. Zack squeezed her tighter to his side and suddenly a tissue was thrust in front of her face.

"Thank you," she choked out to Kiyomi, dabbing at her eyes and sniffing.

The moment Ty and Megan broke apart and turned to face them, everyone shot to their feet. Applause and cheers filled the conservatory, amplified in the small space. Hugs and handshakes were doled out, then Chloe grabbed all the women and dragged them into a knot in the center of the room.

"Bitchilantes ride or die!" she cried.

"Ride or die!" they all chorused back, and Eden found herself laughing.

Trinity wrapped an arm around Eden's shoulders and gave her a squeeze, her deep blue eyes sincere. "We've all got your back, lady. Forever."

"Fuck yeah," Chloe answered, looking juiced, as though she was itching to find a target to blow up.

A quivering sensation hit Eden deep in her chest. "And I've got your backs too." These incredible women were her family now. They'd all faced insurmountable odds and survived. They would stand together, take on hell itself to protect each other, along with the exceptional men in this room.

It was the best feeling in the world.

"That sounds like trouble," Zack said to Ty from behind her.

"Brother, you know it," Ty said.

Everyone filed outside to head back into the manor

for the reception. Eden and Zack were the last to leave.

At the door he stopped her, gazing down at her with an expression full of tenderness. "So what did you think of your first wedding, my little romantic?"

"Loved it." Ty and Megan looked so happy. So perfect for each other.

"That's gonna be us someday, sweetness," he said, the conviction in his voice turning her heart inside out.

Eden flushed and lowered her gaze, secretly thrilled that he was already thinking along those lines even with all the uncertainty that lay ahead. While she might never have allowed herself to dream of anything like that before … Now it was different.

Because she had Zack, and he would stand with her always.

—The End—

Dear reader,

Thank you for reading *Toxic Vengeance*. I hope you enjoyed it. If you'd like to stay in touch with me and be the first to learn about new releases you can:

- Join my newsletter at: http://kayleacross.com/v2/newsletter/
- Find me on Facebook: https://www.facebook.com/KayleaCrossAuthor/
- Follow me on Twitter: https://twitter.com/kayleacross
- Follow me on Instagram: https://www.instagram.com/kaylea_cross_author/

Also, please consider leaving a review at your favorite online book retailer. It helps other readers discover new books.

Happy reading,
Kaylea

Beautiful Vengeance

Prologue

*H**e's coming.*

At the sound of the footsteps moving overhead, Kiyomi struggled to open her eyes. The lids were so swollen her field of vision was reduced to a single tiny strip on the left side. Fear crawled through her, foreign and terrifying.

Chains rattled as she gingerly turned onto her belly, the manacles around her wrists and ankles biting into her skin as she faced the front of her iron cage. A shadowed staircase stood mere feet away in the dim room. In moments he would appear in the doorway at the top and advance down those stairs.

Her entire body ached from the deep bruises he'd already inflicted all over her. The shimmering gold lamé dress she'd worn to the private party a few nights ago was now torn and filthy. She shivered, pushed up a bit on her right arm, struggling to overcome the weakness that hung over her like a fog. Through the gloom she was able to make out the shape of the woman lying in the cage next to hers.

She was still curled into a ball, appearing not to have changed position since Kiyomi had passed out.

"Hannah," she whispered, blood trickling over her tongue as the cut in her lip broke open. The other Valkyrie didn't move or respond in any way. She was probably dead by now.

The unexpected pang of empathy caught Kiyomi off guard. She had come here to kill Hannah because Hannah had killed Kiyomi's best friend, and had wound up Rahman's personal captive instead. Now he and his men appeared to have taken care of Hannah for her. The other Valkyrie's suffering was over, while Kiyomi's was only just beginning. She'd betrayed Rahman, made him fall in love with her, and he would make her hurt for it.

The footsteps upstairs drew closer to the door.

Kiyomi's flesh crawled at the knowledge of what was coming. He wanted to break her. Not just physically. Mentally and emotionally too. He wanted to watch her break, hear her beg him for mercy.

She'd die before she gave him the satisfaction of either.

The door opened. She stayed completely still, gathering her remaining strength to endure what was coming.

His silhouette appeared in the doorway. She squinted when he switched on the lights, the sudden brightness piercing her sore eyes. The door shut and he started down the steps in slow, measured steps as her eyes adjusted.

He was dressed as he always was. Immaculate in his custom-made suit, his white dress shirt open at the neck and startlingly bright against his bronze skin. He was clean-shaven, his dark hair perfect, swept off his forehead and without a trace of gray in it yet, though he was in his mid-thirties. "You're awake. Good." Satisfaction and anticipation dripped from every word.

He had something in his hand.

She stared at it as he drew nearer, stepping out of the shadows and into the light. Something round.

Then he reached the bottom of the stairs and turned toward her. Rage and helplessness exploded inside her when she saw what he held.

A coiled bullwhip.

He glanced briefly at Hannah, dismissed her a heart-beat later and turned to stare down at Kiyomi, a half-smile on his handsome face. Shrugging out of his jacket with slow deliberation, he let her see the whip.

"I know what you are," he said as he came to stand in front of her cage.

Cold rippled through her. He'd seen the brand on her hip. Did he now know what it meant? Or did he just think he did?

He stood there staring down at her for a long moment, his chilling gaze filled with rage and lust as he let the silence drag out. Underscoring the lopsided power dynamic between them. His control pitted against her helplessness.

Revulsion slid through her as she recalled what had passed between them. Him touching her intimately, her pleasuring him all those times, taking him inside, acting the ecstatic lover while she made her mind go elsewhere. Lying next to him in his bed night after night, waiting for him to reach for her. Playing the role of worshipful syco-phant she'd chosen to gain entry into his world in order to get within striking distance of Hannah. All the while, waiting. Waiting.

He'd fallen for it completely, believing she revered him and his body, that she couldn't get enough of him. That she was falling in love with him.

Then everything had gone horribly, irrevocably wrong.

The terrible memories of her capture four nights ago flashed through her mind as he unlocked the cage door and swung it open.

She forced herself to lie still and not react as he came to stand above her, filled with hatred as she stared up at him through her slitted eye. Only a pathetic coward would chain a woman down so he could beat her. And that's exactly what Fayez Rahman was, even if he wasn't stupid. Because he knew if she hadn't been chained, she would kill him.

He was more afraid of her even than he was obsessed with her. And his fear was the only comfort she had in this terrible, desolate moment.

"I'm going to send you back to your maker." An evil smirk split his face, the outline of an erection pressing against the front of his pants. "The one who created you."

She braced for the pain and stared defiantly up into those dark, cruel eyes, refusing to cower or let him think he'd won. His taunting words were an empty threat. He wouldn't kill her. He was too afraid of the wealthy buyer he had lined up for her to do that, the one he'd taunted her with for the past three days. But anything short of death was fair game...

Anything short of death, she could handle. She had no other choice.

Her training kicked in. The only thing stopping her from cowering now.

You can take this, Valkyrie. Separate your mind and body. Don't give him the satisfaction of reacting, no matter what he does.

Rahman relaxed his fist, allowing the long tail of the bullwhip to touch the concrete floor. He gave a deliberate flick of his wrist, making the leather slither back and forth over the concrete like a snake ready to strike. Then he raised his arm, lifting the braided handle high.

Kiyomi bit down hard to keep from crying out as it snapped across the skin between her shoulder blades. Fire raced along her nerve endings. She sucked in a breath and tensed, clenching her teeth and fists as she awaited the next blow. She fought to stay above the pain, to let her mind float free. But as she did, she made a vow to herself.

You will not break me. But one day, I'll kill you for

this.

Someday, she would stare down into those evil, dark eyes. She would watch his triumph turn to shock and then abject terror just before she snuffed the life from him.

End Excerpt

About the Author

NY Times and USA Today Bestselling author Kaylea Cross writes edge-of-your-seat military romantic suspense. Her work has won many awards, including the Daphne du Maurier Award of Excellence, and has been nominated multiple times for the National Readers' Choice Awards. A Registered Massage Therapist by trade, Kaylea is also an avid gardener, artist, Civil War buff, Special Ops aficionado, belly dance enthusiast and former nationally-carded softball pitcher. She lives in Vancouver, BC with her husband and family.

You can visit Kaylea at www.kayleacross.com. If you would like to be notified of future releases, please join her newsletter: http://kayleacross.com/v2/newsletter/

Complete Booklist

Vengeance Series
Stealing Vengeance
Covert Vengeance
Explosive Vengeance
Toxic Vengeance
Beautiful Vengeance

Crimson Point Series
Fractured Honor
Buried Lies
Shattered Vows
Rocky Ground

DEA FAST Series
Falling Fast
Fast Kill
Stand Fast
Strike Fast
Fast Fury
Fast Justice
Fast Vengeance

Colebrook Siblings Trilogy
Brody's Vow
Wyatt's Stand
Easton's Claim

Hostage Rescue Team Series
Marked
Targeted
Hunted
Disavowed

Avenged
Exposed
Seized
Wanted
Betrayed
Reclaimed
Shattered
Guarded

Titanium Security Series
Ignited
Singed
Burned
Extinguished
Rekindled
Blindsided: A Titanium Christmas novella

Bagram Special Ops Series
Deadly Descent
Tactical Strike
Lethal Pursuit
Danger Close
Collateral Damage
Never Surrender (a MacKenzie Family novella)

Suspense Series
Out of Her League
Cover of Darkness
No Turning Back
Relentless
Absolution

PARANORMAL ROMANCE
Empowered Series
Darkest Caress

HISTORICAL ROMANCE
The Vacant Chair

EROTIC ROMANCE (writing as *Callie Croix*)
Deacon's Touch
Dillon's Claim
No Holds Barred
Touch Me
Let Me In
Covert Seduction